SQUEEZE
PLAYS

SQUEEZE PLAYS

JEFFREY MARSHALL

atmosphere press

CHAPTER 1

The traffic heading south on Park Avenue stranded the Mercedes like a raft in the Sargasso Sea. Taxis jockeyed and edged in during their endless game of chicken; pedestrians crossed against the lights, a time-honored Manhattan tradition, like cockroaches skittering across a kitchen floor. It was hard for the car to make more than two lights at a time, and Corbin van Sloot looked at his watch in annoyance.

"Bad morning, hey, Pieter?"

His driver and sometime bodyguard, Pieter Stroganov, gave a slight backward glance. "Worse than usual today, boss. I think there's some construction south of Grand Central." Corbin had learned to understand Pieter most of the time, but his accent sometimes seemed thicker than borscht in February.

"Ay yi yi." Corbin deemed himself no more impatient than most men, but being stuck in traffic always got his goat. Each day was a crapshoot, and he wasn't the one rolling the dice. At least he had copies of the *Times* and the *Journal* to go through during the ride. The commute home was always faster—well, almost always.

In his more reflective moments, Corbin knew he had a lot

to be thankful for. His position as CEO of Whitehall Banking Group, one of the world's twenty largest commercial banks, put him in the catbird seat. He had a mansion in a blue-chip suburb, a lovely wife, three good kids, and all the creature comforts a man could hope for.

Of course, the downside was that for Corbin, as for any top chief executive, the seat of power was almost always hot, often uncomfortably so. Restive investors, competitors battling for market share, consumer watchdogs, his own board and executive team, there was no telling where the next crisis would come from. Sometimes it felt like being holed up in a wagon train in an old Western with a band of circling Indians pumping arrows at you.

Corbin had the requisite résumé for the job—undergrad from Dartmouth, MBA from Harvard, twenty years at J.P. Morgan Chase—which had persuaded the Whitehall directors to hire him three years ago when their CEO had retired. Though based in London, they sensed that the US market was going to be key to their future, and so two senior executive vice presidents at headquarters were summarily passed over to bring Corbin in. Both left within two months of his arrival; nothing stings more than ambition unrequited. Meanwhile, the company chairman, Sir Reginald Downing, mockingly referred to by many in the company as "Regicide," remained in London.

Having major seats of power on opposite sides of the pond can be daunting, Corbin soon discovered; the time difference alone was vexing as hell. Major discussions and decisions often had to be postponed so that all the parties could be present. Worse, in Corbin's mind, was the habit of Sir Reginald, now in his early seventies, to take afternoon naps on a leather recliner in his office. Corbin was almost twenty years younger, and he swore he would never work at an age when naps were a necessary evil.

Corbin looked out again. The car was just passing Fifty-Sixth Street on its odyssey south, and the traffic seemed as knotted as ever. He sighed and opened the *Times* to the Arts & Leisure page. He flipped back to the crossword. It was a Wednesday, and the degree of difficulty was medium. He decided he'd at least start it. He was reasonably accomplished, and he could usually finish a Wednesday puzzle, but the latter days of the week were another story; Friday puzzles, he'd concluded, were simply a bitch.

He took out his mechanical pencil from his briefcase and started on the top grid. He'd just filled in 3-down when he heard the sirens. The light, which had been green, went to red as the two hook-and-ladder fire trucks crawled cautiously through the intersection. *Christ, what's next?* he thought. *A water main break? No, no, don't go there—it could happen.* Everybody knew that the mains in Manhattan had been put in before women's suffrage and were slowly rotting away. One or another gave way several times a year. It was just the way things were, like knees going out on football running backs. It was gonna happen.

Twenty minutes later, he rode the elevator up to the forty-third floor and stepped out into the cool gray carpet of the executive suite. Corbin gave his executive secretary, Angela D'Alessio, a broad smile; he'd already called her and told her of the delay.

"It was pretty bad out there, Angie. You're lucky you get to take the subway."

She smiled, showing long canine teeth. "I suppose you're right, Mr. van Sloot," she said evenly. "Traffic jams won't ever reach down to the subway." Angela was a stout middle-aged woman who wore a bit too much makeup and was given to long print dresses and cardigans in the winter. Angela had worked for his predecessor and was good-hearted and more than efficient; she was a repository of knowledge about the office and who did what. She was indispensable, and Corbin saw no reason whatsoever to bring in someone younger and prettier.

"Is that merchant banking call on for this morning?" Corbin asked.

Angela looked at her notes. "Yes. It's a video conference call at ten." She kept a strict calendar for him, and he relied on her more than he was willing to admit.

Corbin suppressed a frown. "Okay, let me know when it's five till." He had been sent a memo two days earlier that suggested that one loan in particular, to Star Enterprises, a newspaper chain, wasn't doing well—in fact, it was like a carton of milk that was going from sour to rancid.

"I will." She looked at him and nodded. Corbin had a smooth, unlined face; a firm jaw; and dark hair going to gray at the temples. With deep-set blue eyes, he was just over six feet tall and reasonably slim; he could have been a model for showing aliens what a CEO looks like.

Corbin walked into his corner office, large enough for a small luncheonette, took off his suit jacket, and hung it on the wooden coat tree in the corner. He gazed out the floor-to-ceiling windows, which afforded a spectacular view of the East River and the glistening tower of the United Nations. It was May, and the trees below were clad in the light green of spring, shimmering from this distance like a Monet canvas. High up in the clear sky, a passenger plane was a silvery beetle making its way east to LaGuardia Airport.

He turned his mind back to the present. Merchant banking? It was a troubled business that was being run out of London, as it always had been. Too many merchant bankers thought they were top bananas, rubbing shoulders with the rich and powerful in places like Monte Carlo or Gstaad. Hell, he'd never been to Gstaad. The Whitehall unit was like an old boys' club for graduates of Oxford or Cambridge, and it was barely breaking even. Corbin wanted to hear the latest, but if things weren't turning around, changes would be in the wind. And he'd probably have to be the one to make them.

CHAPTER 2

It was 10:00 a.m. New York time, a common hour for a conference call involving London. Corbin walked into the walnut-paneled conference room and took his seat in a black leather chair at the head of the table. The rest of the seats were already occupied; these things were run punctually.

"We're all here, it seems," Corbin said cheerfully. "Jason, make sure the video is good," he said as a younger man, tieless, adjusted a panel on the far side of the room, where a large video screen dominated the wall.

About a minute later, the screen came to life with a picture of another wood-paneled boardroom, this one in London. The picture was clear and sharp considering the size of the screen, and it showed five men, mostly middle-aged, and one woman around an oval wooden table.

Timothy Eggersby, the head of the merchant banking unit, looked at the camera and spoke. "Thank you for being here for this call," he said. "What we intend to do, quite simply, is brief you on the state of the business. You know my colleagues here—wait, we do have a new member since the last call. Robin, please introduce yourself in a few words."

Robin, seated next to Timothy, stood up, and Corbin

snorted. *What's with these Brits?* Robin was lanky and ecto-morphic, with rolled-up shoulders and what seemed to be something of a sunken chest that his tie had retreated into. Corbin suppressed a frown. As a former college soccer player and a fine weekend tennis player, he appreciated men with an outward degree of athleticism. Robin looked like he would barely be able to swing a cricket bat without flopping over.

"Well, hello," Robin said a bit sheepishly. "I'm Robin Piggot-Townsend. I joined the group two months ago after ten years at Standard Chartered." To Corbin, his accent was plummy and clearly upper-class. "Tim has been kind enough to take me under his wing, and I'm delighted to be part of the team."

"Okay, well, thanks, Robin," Tim said a bit too loudly. "You all should have a summary of the latest quarter's business in front of you. I'll walk you through it, and each of my colleagues can elaborate on any points or questions you may have."

"Sounds good, Tim," Corbin said. "We all have the sum-maries, so feel free to plunge ahead."

"Will do," Tim replied. The camera, fixed on the wall in London, displayed the same scene whoever was speaking; there were no close-ups, and the static nature of the picture made it hard for the people in New York to concentrate.

For the next half hour, Tim and another colleague, Rupert Granger, led the discussion through the various accounts. The group in New York was able to see highlights, but the London-ers supplied the details. For anyone not in the business, the recitation would have been stupefyingly boring: names of the accounts, the payment history, assorted and sundry details about the principals holding the loans, and the likelihood, if any, of the loans going sour.

Virtually all of the accounts were in Europe; most were in the UK. A lot of the loans were for working capital, which meant closer supervision than what would have been expected for a regular-term loan. Indeed, the working capital structure often meant that the borrowers would come periodically asking for new money as the business required. In keeping with Whitehall's history as a lender to the top tier, very few of the borrowers were new businesses, and a few were clearly firms whose fortunes hadn't fared that well in the new century — they underlined the *why?* in Y2K.

On the screen, Tim stopped for a moment to run his hand through his hair and clear his throat. "And now we come to one on your side of the pond," he said. "Star Enterprises."

"Oh, right," Corbin said, reminding himself not to over-react. He paused. "Who is handling this? Someone in New York, I hope."

"Indeed, yes," Tim replied. "Cary Clothier. She reports to Ashleigh here," he said, gesturing to the one woman at the table.

"Okay, well, what are the issues with Star?" Corbin had a pretty good idea, but he wanted to hear it from the source.

Ashleigh, a blonde with a white pinpoint blouse and a stylish pair of blue-framed glasses, leaned forward. "The company has been in a bit of executive turmoil, with a series of top executives coming and going in the past few years. As you know, the media business is in a bit of bother these days, and it's been affecting them."

Corbin looked at the payment history on his summaries. "I see that they've swung into being in arrears by close to $15 million in the past quarter. Obviously, that's not good. What seems to be going on?" He tried to speak matter-of-factly, and not intimidate Ashleigh, whom he'd never met.

Ashleigh spread her hands on the table. "Well, there seem to be a few issues. One, they've spent a lot on digital, both people and technology, but there is very little revenue to date. Two, they needed to upgrade their printing presses, which were aging badly. Three, the local newspapers they own are hurting. Many are limping along these days, and some have even shuttered." She paused. "I'd have to say they are a bit under the cosh."

Corbin frowned in puzzlement. "I'm sorry—under the what?"

He could almost see Ashleigh blush on the screen. "I'm so sorry. It's an idiom we use a lot over here. It means they're in a difficult situation."

"Oh, okay," Corbin said, and he grinned as he looked around the table. Surely, he wasn't the only one puzzled by the term.

The banker sitting next to Corbin, an executive vice president named Richard Jacks, spoke up. "We all know the media business is having a rough go these days. Is this really an important relationship for us?"

"You could say so." Tim sounded a bit sheepish. "Sir Reginald personally brought in the business five years ago, and I think he regards it as a personal coup."

Coup? Christ, Corbin thought, *Sir Reginald would probably get in bed with anyone who would splash his photo around or otherwise kiss the knighted ring.* Courting the publisher of a New York tabloid didn't strike Corbin as a good risk/reward proposition. If there was an upside, it was hard to decipher.

"Is Winston Crumm a factor in any of these issues?" Corbin asked, referring to Star's chief executive.

"I think you could say that," Ashleigh said slowly. "It's a private company—really something of a family company—and as the CEO, he has a lot of latitude. The board is relatively weak and unlikely to try to rein him in if he wants something."

Winston Crumm, the horse's ass, Corbin thought. *He'd probably entertained Sir Reginald on his yacht in Florida, swilling gin and tonics in the winter sun. That would certainly be the basis for a "relationship."*

"Can we increase the margin on our loan?" Corbin asked.

"We could, I suppose, with your permission," Tim said. "But I think, in light of everything, we should try to scale back our relationship. As it is, we're the only bank bidding for their business, that I'm aware of. Nobody else wanted in."

"And if we did that? Would they squeak?"

Tim sighed. "I'm afraid Winston Crumm might well run to Sir Reginald. We'd have to be very careful. I don't think we could drop them altogether."

"So, we just need to get more blood out of the stone?" Corbin said.

"I'm afraid so," Tim said softly.

Corbin blew out a breath. Being Crumm's only major lender was more than a little troubling, he mused, like being the only liquor distributor at a teetotalers' convention. Having other lenders at the table was always helpful if trouble was afoot. Moreover, Sir Reginald's stake in all this was disturbing. Was this any way to run a railroad?

CHAPTER 3

Riding down the elevator from his penthouse apartment on a splendid Manhattan morning, Winston Crumm ignored some lint he noticed on his jacket sleeve. He glanced at his watch, a Patek Philippe his wife had given him a couple of years earlier. Eight-thirty. He'd be in the office at nine, give or take; he was never one to race to work to impress others in the office.

Who had he to impress other than himself? Supremely self-confident and equally insecure, Winston controlled his world so that he would always be top dog. As the publisher of the *New York Star*, a feisty tabloid he'd inherited from his father, Winston was one of the top media figures in the world's top media town. With the help of some talented subordinates and his bounteous inheritance, he'd built the company into Star Enterprises, with newspaper holdings around the Northeast, mostly in smaller markets in New York State, Pennsylvania, and Massachusetts.

The Town Car sat at the curb, as always, and Winston eased into the back seat like a saddle-sore cowboy mounting his horse. As the car made its tortuous way to Midtown, Winston stared out the window and fiddled with his tie, a staid number with diagonal red and black stripes. He was a publisher, but unlike book publishers—learned and worldly—Winston wasn't a reader. Any memo longer than two pages bored him; he hadn't read a book since college. Board meetings bored him unless they offered snappy PowerPoint presentations and brightly colored flowcharts that he could take in quickly. Detailed presentations, however meaningful, were likely to cause ennui.

Some of his power was belied by his physical presence. He was only of average height, about five-foot-ten, and had a generally skinny frame with a middle-aged belly that had been swelling for years. His head, however, was uncommonly large, with a square face and gray eyes that could freeze an underling like a fly immobilized in a web. His sandy hair, worn a little longer than was currently fashionable, was parted in the middle—an old-fashioned style—and starting to show gray at the edges.

Winston could praise and cajole when it suited him, but his default setting was smugness, delivered with a variety of expressions, from a blank look with his arms folded to a smirk, a sneer, or a dismissive wave. If something really bothered him, a short, profanity-laced tirade was likely, like a burst from a flamethrower. Apologies for such outbursts were rare but did happen; for a man so poorly self-aware, he did realize on occasion that he'd gone too far.

None of this might be surprising considering his background. He was an only child, and his father had lavished attention and dollars on his offspring despite Winston's generally mediocre talent at just about anything. He'd barely made it through prep school and had a degree from C. W. Post on Long Island—in that day, a party school that had a lot of rich and footloose kids like him. In baseball terms, it's often said that the privileged were born on third base; Winston surpassed that. He was born on the third baseline, halfway to home.

Other media moguls in town sensed—oh hell, they *knew*—that Winston was basically a figurehead, a carved dragon on the front of a ship plowing haltingly through the urban waves. He wasn't actually running the company; those duties were filled by smart people hired from elite colleges who spent long hours massaging numbers and running spreadsheets. But those jobs had been run through a revolving door in recent years as the executives came to understand that the newspaper business was in the midst of a four-alarm blaze and their boss was no more a fireman than Mickey Mouse holding a hose in an old one-reeler.

The most frequent defections had come from the financial side, charged with keeping the company in the black. At best, it was a smoky gray, as the newspaper business bled jobs and money like a hemophiliac tossed into a thorn bush. That wasn't just in New York, of course; it was everywhere. But wages in New York were among the highest, and to stave off the red ink, there had been several staff purges at the *Star* that snipped the ranks of reporters and editors—with the longest-serving and the highest-paid the most vulnerable.

These purges came despite the several advantages Star Enterprises had, not the least of which being that it was a private company, so there were no unhappy shareholders watching a tumbling stock price or analysts issuing sell recommendations. The flip side, however, was Winston, who used the company like his private piggy bank to finance his lifestyle, which included the penthouse off Fifth Avenue, a huge waterfront mansion in Boca Raton, and memberships in a half-dozen yacht clubs, some of which he didn't visit in any given year. He didn't even keep track of the membership dues—an accountant working from a general expense account made sure those were paid.

It was this tension between trying to keep the company profitable and Winston's extravagance that had sent several recent chief financial officers around the bend. Star Enterprises was currently on its third CFO in twenty-seven months; this one, a forty-five-year-old woman with impeccable credentials, was only in her fourth month. She was brisk and attractive, and it was this latter quality that Winston appreciated. He considered himself a connoisseur of good-looking women.

This CFO had been given the daunting task of trying to shore up the finances of the other papers in the company, both dailies and weeklies. There wasn't much hope on the revenue side; advertising dollars had fled to the web long ago, and malls—once a reliable cash cow for advertising big sales—were shrinking as their anchor retailers did what anchors do: sink. That left costly items such as staff, rents, and printing expenses, and each property needed individual attention.

All of which was of little interest to Winston. If it wasn't in New York City, he acted as if it might as well be in Kansas. He hadn't been to more than three of the outside newspapers in the past two years, and those visits were like ceremonial occasions, in which the publishers had to treat Winston and his small entourage like royalty. Winston wanted people in the outlying publications to know that New York exacted certain standards. That wasn't easy when the king was used to dining at Manhattan landmarks like Nobu or Per Se and was allergic to a lot of small talk; going to the local brewhouse for lunch was out of the question.

Winston did like to be seen at society events in Manhattan, where the famous, the almost famous, and the wannabees mingled, envied, and gossiped. His second wife, the designer Adrienne Rogers, was a fixture on the social scene, and Winston went along, at first grudgingly then with less resistance when he found that, A, he and Adrienne got a lot of attention, much of it fawning, and B, the buffet spreads at many events were glorious. Winston loved things such as raw oysters and imported cheeses, and the more time he spent grazing at the buffet table, the less he had to spend socializing.

One such black-tie affair was coming up tonight, he remembered as the Town Car pulled up to the curb outside the *Star* building. He leaned over toward the front seat as he grabbed the door handle.

"Pick me up at five sharp, will you, George?" Winston said in his gravelly voice. "The missus and I have one of those things tonight."

"Will do, Mr. Crumm." George was in his sixties, with curly gray hair and a boxer's patched-up face; his neck was a mere ribbon of flesh between his head and his massive shoulders. He was a cigar smoker, and his halitosis could knock over a badger at ten paces. But George had driven for Winston's father, and loyalty mattered a lot to Winston—far more than competence. He could be generous and pleasant to his extended "family." To the rest of the world, he could be very different.

CHAPTER 4

Winston smiled broadly and slung his arm around Adrienne as the *Star* photographer circled closer and snapped a series of shots. The man accepted Winston's brief thanks and almost bowed as he turned away. Winston couldn't suppress a grin; a big photo of him and the wife would be splashed on Page Four of the *Star* the next day. That was literally standing orders when the boss went to a fancy charity soirée and could be perceived as giving something for a good cause that might redound to his reputation.

Adrienne smiled, and Winston caught himself staring at her. To the rest of the world, she was still the lovely brunette whose creativity had generated a line of classic clothes that populated colorful displays in the toniest department stores. But in her glance, Winston caught just a hint of insecurity, evidence of her nightly regimen of face creams and emulsions that had merely slowed the inevitable decay of age. The skin around her eyes furrowed when she smiled.

He looked back at the photographer. Fifteen years ago, there had been other cameras, scores of them at his and Adrienne's wedding. What a beautiful bride she'd been. He sucked in his stomach and sighed; fifteen years already? That's when her business had just been taking off, and he'd showed his affection by throwing a few million at it. She'd done well, but he knew he had no real understanding of the business. He had come to understand Adrienne was no supernova, but she was a star. That was plenty.

Like most rich men of a certain age, Winston had gently insisted on a prenup before taking a second trip to the altar. Adrienne had gone along without a peep, and no issues had arisen in the intervening years to bring it into play. Winston had a son and a daughter from his first marriage, now in their early thirties; Adrienne had a daughter who had just started at Swarthmore.

His children had distanced themselves from the family business as if it gave off a lingering and unseemly odor. His son was an executive at Google who was doing very well. His daughter worked for a nonprofit in Boston that promoted women's rights in Third World countries. Since the editorial stance at the *Star* gave such issues short shrift—if they mentioned them at all—she seemed to take pride in having left the family business far in her rearview mirror. Plus, she had taken her husband's name, O'Shaughnessy, which made the family connection even more tenuous.

Winston was just making his second run to the buffet table when he heard a voice almost in his ear.

"Winston, how's business?"

He glanced over his shoulder and saw Martin Hargreaves, someone he never chose to encounter. Hargreaves was another scion of a publishing empire, but his holdings were in magazines, mostly the glossy, high-end variety that Winston sensed wouldn't mention him except to needle him. Liberal, intellectual content was splashed all over their pages—everything the *Star* snubbed its nose at. Hargreaves was tall and notably thin in a town where wealthy men tended to be portly in a tradition dating back to the Gilded Age. He had a long neck, a receding forehead, and a casual comb-over that he frequently adjusted with the sweep of a hand as he was talking.

"Oh, hi, Martin," Winston said without much enthusiasm. "Things well with you?"

"Just peachy. Nice to see you here—this is one of my favorite charities."

"Yeah, well, Adrienne really likes it too. So, we're dropping a few dimes on it every year." He smiled.

Hargreaves smiled broadly, showing a gleaming row of regular teeth that Winston assumed were dentures. "That's great. Adrienne seems to support a lot of good causes." He looked down for a moment, then up. "How is her business going?"

"Really well," Winston said, though the truth was that he seldom asked and didn't especially care. "She's looking at bringing out another line in the fall." He hadn't the faintest idea if that were true, but it came to him in a flash of inspiration and sounded authoritative.

"Wonderful. And I hope the *Star* is flourishing?" The question seemed innocent enough, but Winston thought he picked up a note of sarcasm, like a fly buzzing insistently in the distance.

"Oh, things are good. But it's dog-eat-dog out there, as you know. And you never wanna be the Chihuahua." He chuckled loudly at his own joke.

Hargreaves laughed. "No, you don't. Good to see you. Best to Adrienne." He nodded and walked away.

Smug bastard, Winston thought to himself. *He always seems to look down on me—must be how they teach you to act at Harvard.* Winston would never let on that the newspaper was in a bit of a bind; never show weakness, especially to those capable of exposing it.

Indeed, Winston was consumed with not showing frailty— at least, nothing that anyone could call him on. At the back of his mind was the notion that he would be pushed aside by the board, that his shortcomings would be actionable. The past few years had been hard ones for the business, and Winston knew he had no rabbits to pull out of any hat. His younger cousin Robert Graves, known to everyone as Rob, was, in Winston's mind, cleverly angling for the top job and was probably seen by most as a stronger leader. Being put out to pasture like an aging bull too tired to battle was a nightmare that Winston was determined to avoid, even if he wasn't sure *how*.

He filled up his plate like a river guide loading a raft for a weeklong trip and sauntered back to the round table, where five couples were seated. Adrienne was busy talking to Betsy Talbott, the wife of the man who ran the local CBS affiliate. Sitting down, Winston waved at the husband, Charlie. He knew him as a fellow Yankees fan and a guy who didn't seem to put on airs. *Damn*, he thought, *I'd like to be next to him.* He picked up his fork and ate in silence but not before lifting one cheek and surreptitiously ripping off a soft fart, mostly inaudible. Flatulence was a curse of the Crumms.

CHAPTER 5

Agatha Higginbotham tapped three times on the thick wooden door before she walked in. Sir Reginald was in his customary position in his office recliner, a piece clad in deep burgundy leather to which he retreated every working day in the mid-afternoon. Naps refreshed him, got him through the usual late afternoon mental lull. Agatha, his secretary, was under standing orders to wake him after half an hour.

To Agatha, this ritual was hardly a bother. She'd been his personal secretary for more than ten years, and these naps had begun five years ago. Sir Reginald was unfailingly polite, if a bit paternalistic, about his slumber time and had told her in no uncertain terms that she needed to make sure he was awake before leaving the room.

"It's time," she said from the doorway with a brief smile.

"Ah, good. Thank you, Agatha." As a dog-fancier, Sir Reginald often made mental notes comparing others in the office to various breeds. Agatha, he had decided long ago, was like a collie—long and lean, with a narrow face and fluffy light-brown hair that fell in a somewhat-unruly tangle to her shoulders. His former secretary, short and effusive, was more like a beagle.

"You have a call at four from Mr. Mortimer," she said.

"Oh, yes. Put him through, of course."

"Will do." She smiled and closed the door gently.

Nigel Mortimer was his solicitor, and the subject had nothing to do with Whitehall. It was about Sir Reginald's country house in Essex, which he'd had for twenty-five years and now wanted to expand through the acquisition of a neighboring property of five acres that had come on the market three months ago. He'd snapped it up, paying slightly above the listed price, but there turned out to be a snag: the property abutted a county wildlife sanctuary, and a local nonprofit had asked him in a polite but no-nonsense letter not to build on the property, which was still in its natural state. The group said it hoped to acquire the property to expand the boundaries of the park and suggested it was willing to buy it from him.

That request didn't sit well with Sir Reginald. He wanted to build a house for his daughter, son-in-law, and their two children, who were coming back to England like homing pigeons after a decade abroad, mostly in the Middle East. Having an adjacent property now was pure serendipity, like a bingo card that quickly filled out for a win. Mortimer had recently been in talks with the group, so this would be an update. Sir Reginald expected to prevail; he was keen on wildlife, especially birds, but private property rights in Britain had roots as strong as an ancient oak and probably as old as Stonehenge.

Sir Reginald's Tory sympathies rose up like an Arabian kicking up its front legs. He often expressed to his wife that he had no regard for the young, sometimes-unwashed protesters who made signs and sat outside proposed housing projects. But Mortimer had warned him that this group was more than likely made up of middle-aged or older professionals, empty nesters who had made nature, not their families, their top priority. They were likely to dig in.

Mortimer also advised him that if the group failed to get

what it wanted, it could sue. That would be calamitous, headlines taking a knighted banker to task for presumptuously opposing a wildlife sanctuary. In the court of public opinion, he would be in the dock, unfrocked. Maybe there could be some kind of compromise before then—this kind of publicity would be as welcome as a gaggle of leeches.

Sighing, Sir Reginald eased the recliner back to its upright position, rose, and stretched. His enormous desk was cluttered with family photos and memorabilia, including some items from his brief service in the Royal Navy: a nautical clock, a replica ship's wheel, a penholder in the shape of an anchor, a nameplate that read "Lt. Reginald Downing." A casual visitor might have assumed he was a naval lifer, not a man who'd put in just four years for God and country.

He sat down and pulled over the papers he'd been looking at earlier. *Budgets*, he thought grimly, *why must I deal with budgets?* Corbin van Sloot had the final word, but they'd agreed long ago that Sir Reginald had the right to question anything he saw and to argue for something he didn't. The budget each year ran to ten pages of spreadsheets, and Sir Reginald wasn't willing to examine every line item. Still, it was a bit like being a line inspector at an assembly plant; if he didn't speak up about something, it might seem as if he wasn't doing his job. For appearance's sake alone, that was unsupportable.

For a Friday evening, it was an unusually domestic scene. Sir Reginald and Pamela, his wife of forty-three years, often went out to a local restaurant—they had three or four they rotated among regularly—and had a fine, relaxing dinner with a bottle of wine. But Pamela had a mild cough with a touch of a head cold, and they had elected to stay in and make do with leftovers.

Sir Reginald was unambiguously fond of his home, which

he and Pamela repaired to every weekend after a workweek spent at their flat in London. It was a sturdy, fieldstone house flanked by towering copper beeches—baronial to some, perhaps, but nothing resembling the monstrous country homes handed down over generations to the aristocracy, the Downton Abbeys of the world. The spiraling upkeep on those homes, however, had forced many of the gentry to give them up, turning them into a host of new lives as museums, municipal offices, or members of the National Trust, where anyone with an inkling and a few pounds could come and tramp all over the hallowed grounds that had once been reserved for fox hunts, country picnics, and other pursuits of the idle rich.

His knighthood was honorary, meaning Sir Reginald wasn't a member of the landed aristocracy who had ruled British society for so many years. He and Pamela had no full-time staff of any kind, just a caretaker and a periodic cleaning service. But Pamela was a good cook, albeit mostly stuck in the age-old, unimaginative British tradition of Yorkshire pudding and bangers and mash, who branched out now and then into French or Italian dishes.

In the spacious kitchen, Sir Reginald peered over his reading glasses from his seat at the large marble island. "What sounds good for dinner, dear?"

Pamela smiled at him from across the island. She was nursing a glass of French Burgundy.

"We have some veal scallopine from last weekend. It's been in the freezer," she said, holding the glass near her face.

"Well, that should be fine." He studied her face, round and soft with a small nose and a few wrinkles, like crosshatching, around her mouth. Her gray hair was cut in a short pageboy that curved up at the ends like a smile.

As she busied herself reheating the veal, Sir Reginald reflected on the contretemps over the wildlife sanctuary. Bad publicity, he knew, could be a slow-acting poison, one he'd strenuously managed to avoid. His standing, his good name, was everything, and he took every opportunity to burnish it. Some might not have accepted a knighthood, which many saw as an anachronism, but he delighted in the acclaim. He was quick to assent to invitations to speak or accept awards, and he eagerly sought out the company of those he felt could spread the good repute of Sir Reginald Downing.

That included people in Europe and America, though those opportunities were relatively rare. Invitations to rub shoulders with peers or those he deemed to be such were quickly accepted. Indeed, Winston Crumm's invitation to Florida a few years ago remained a memory as bright as a shiny new automobile. He and Pamela had been treated to a weekend with an American plutocrat, who, while too ostentatious for their British sensibilities, had wealth and power that Sir Reginald could only admire. Doing business with Winston had been a quid pro quo that Sir Reginald had been only too happy to extend.

CHAPTER 6

Skyler van Sloot trotted across the kitchen floor and toward the vast living room with its high tray ceilings. She stopped at the entrance to the room when she saw her father on one of the couches reading the paper.

"Hi, Daddy."

Corbin glanced over and saw that she was still in her jodhpurs and riding boots. "Take off your boots before you come in here, please, young lady."

Skyler screwed up her face. "Okay, sure." She bent over and pulled the boots off one at a time and set them on the pale kitchen tile.

"How was the riding?" Corbin asked. He was happy to indulge her favorite pastime, but he bridled now and again at the cost of keeping a horse stabled and fed throughout the year. He could afford it, of course, but it stuck in his craw a bit to pay so much for something that was used so little, no more than a few hours a week. But Skyler was twelve, and he knew a lot of girls her age were mad about horses. Hopefully, she'd outgrow it.

She walked over in her stocking feet and plopped down on the aqua-blue padded armchair next to him.

"How did it go?" he asked.

"Oh, fine. Angelo took us to the main bridle trail, and we went around. We did a little trotting too. I'm learning how to handle Rocky in different situations."

"That's good," Corbin said, smiling. Rocky was the horse they'd bought for her two years earlier. The nickname was short for Rocket Man—Skyler loved Elton John—but the name was a bit ironic since Rocky was a gelding.

"Where's your mom?" Corbin asked. "She picked you up, didn't she?"

"I dunno," Skyler said flatly, studying her nails in a "how should I know?" fashion. "Maybe she went into the garden."

"Alright." He set the paper down and stood, then walked to the French doors and looked out. He saw his wife bending over with what appeared to be a set of pruners. "Yeah, she's out there," he said, half-turning to his daughter. "I'm going out too."

"Okay," she said as listlessly as if he'd asked her to wash the dishes.

Walking out into the semiformal garden, Corbin was struck by how accurately he could tell the time of year by the foliage, what was blooming, and what had passed. The azaleas had blazed magenta a couple of weeks ago but were fading; the rhododendrons and the laurels were almost at their peak. That put it at mid-May, more or less, and it was the sixteenth. Right on schedule. Meanwhile, the lower-growing flowers, the peonies and the irises, were busy budding.

He strolled across the rectangle of trimmed lawn, now emerald-green with the blessing of spring, and past the first rock wall, toward where his wife, Patricia, was working, deadheading some of the azaleas and dropping the debris into a straw basket. Gardening was one of her favorite pastimes from early spring into the cool mornings of November.

"How go the labors?" he asked with a grin.

She looked up with only a trace of a smile. "Just fine. I'm trying to stay up with all the stuff that's gone past. You know, the usual." She stood up. "You could deign to help me one of these days."

He chuckled. It was a standing joke of sorts between them: he did no gardening. It was her thing, and he'd made it clear he didn't want to get involved. But there was an edge to her reply that lingered in the air, and he *knew* she would like his help.

Corbin, however, held his ground. He found gardening laborious and boring, and he didn't like dealing with the dirt he found on his hands and shoes. It was odd, in a way; as fond as he was of the floral display, he couldn't bring himself to help nurture it. As a sort of compensation, he did other lesser chores, such as cleaning the windows and trimming the bushes. He went at the latter with gusto, wielding a battery-powered trimmer and taking genuine pride in the results.

"Justin had a great game today—three goals and an assist," he told her. Their son, sixteen, was a first-string midfielder for the local country day school. "Too bad you missed it."

"Good for him," she said with what sounded to him like a lack of genuine enthusiasm. "Maybe all those damn lacrosse camps are paying off."

"Too soon to know that for sure. But he's playing well."

She looked at him and cocked her head slightly. "No tennis today?" Her honey-brown hair was pulled back in a loose ponytail, and she had a blue denim work shirt on over a white t-shirt.

He shook his head. "Roger twisted his knee or something the other day and couldn't find a sub. So, we scratched."

"Too bad," she said. "And tomorrow?"

"We'll see. The forecast is for showers, so I'm dubious."

"Okay. Well, I'll be in in a while."

Turning back to the house, Corbin took in the graceful

symmetry, the white clapboard siding and the dark green shutters looming above the flagstone terrace. He loved this view almost as much as he did the front, with the long gravel drive and the arching spray of wisteria above the front portico. It was a large home, even in New Canaan, with fifteen rooms and a four-car garage; it was his ideal home, and by God, it was something to be proud of.

A smiling group of vacationers beckoned to Corbin from a family photo on the end table. It had been just over a year ago, and he sensed how the kids had grown since then. Patricia, her face half-hidden by dark glasses, stood at the left in a one-piece suit on the beach in St. John, her hand on her hip. Her hair was tied back in a ponytail, and she looked great, the epitome of casual elegance. It wasn't the first time that notion had rolled through his brain.

And why not? Patricia DuMoullin was the product of first-rate genes dating back to the 1700s, when some great-something had arrived in Montreal as a colonel in the French Army. The family had moved to New York State a century later, and Patricia's father, a Harvard grad, had started a packaging company that had become one of the country's largest. Patricia—facetiously, Corbin always wanted to put an *n* after her name, even though he usually called her Trish—had the best of everything, and being tall and lovely never exactly counted against her.

They had met at Skidmore when he and two of his Dartmouth buddies had piled into a car one sophomore weekend and driven to Saratoga Springs. Patricia had actually been set up with one of his friends, Tom, but she and Corbin immediately connected. She had other men after her, but Corbin had the inside track, and two years after they graduated, they married in a precious little chapel one beautiful June day in Katonah, New York, not far from her family home.

Their relationship had evolved from love to something

more like domestic companionship, the predictable arc in so many marriages, but there were still sparks between them. For all her genteel upbringing, Patricia had a salty tongue, and while she worked hard to suppress it around the children, she could cuss like a sailor around him. If anything, it turned him on.

His reverie was broken when his middle child, Morgan, sidled into the family room and sat down next to him on the leather couch. She had on jeans and a sweatshirt, but her feet were bare, as they often were. Her blonde hair fell straight past her shoulders.

"What's for dinner?" she asked.

He shrugged. "No idea. Ask your mother. I don't plan to grill anything."

"Oh, okay." She tucked her legs under her and turned to the TV, where the weekend news anchor in New York had gone to a live report of a subway fire in Manhattan.

"Ooh, that's kinda scary," she said, staring. "But you never take the subway, do you?"

"Not anymore," he said simply. "I did for years, but I always go by car now."

"Oh, right."

A few minutes later, a familiar face came up over the anchor's shoulder, and the anchor began reading:

"And here's an item that will probably be a good one for the gossip pages. Winston Crumm, the owner of the Star *and one of the city's richest men, is being sued by a tenant in his building who lives just below his penthouse. The tenant is claiming that a leak from Mr. Crumm's unit did substantial damage to the tenant's unit.*

"Normally, such matters would be settled by the co-op board. But it seems that Mr. Crumm has refused to ante up and has essentially forced the matter to go to court. There is no word on just how much money is at stake ..."

Corbin's forehead furrowed in a frown. If Crumm, with all

his millions, wasn't willing to make good on such a minor issue, that showed a troubling level of—what, obstinacy? Or was it arrogance? Whatever it was, it certainly wasn't a happy signal about a client with a troubled loan.

He glanced out the window and gazed at the pink crabapple tree, now a mass of blooms, and felt himself relax. There was something about nature that could take one's mind off virtually anything.

CHAPTER 7

"This isn't good, Winston." Adrienne turned to him from her perch on the other side of the couch. "I don't believe that old saying that any publicity is good publicity."

Winston shook his head slightly. "I'm on top of this, honey. We'll win this thing; don't worry." He wore a pink-striped Oxford shirt and khakis, typical weekend attire, though it was just Friday night. Jeans, he'd decided long ago, were for the hoi polloi.

She stared at him. "Well, I do worry sometimes. This will be all over the papers; it's already all over TV." They had just seen a report on the suit against Winston for the water damage.

"This will blow over in a day or two," he said. "And you know me. I'm not going to roll over for anyone. If I settle with this guy, who knows who'll come after me next?" He jutted out his chin in a Churchill-type pose.

She sighed, and her brown eyes narrowed slightly. "I wish you wouldn't get your back up over little things. It's as if your ego is at stake. We could have settled this long ago, and no one would have been any the wiser."

"I think you're wrong there," he said, his voice rising

slightly. "Someone would make it public, and suddenly I look weak. It would be like there's a target on my back." In the back of his mind, Winston knew he was wrong to do battle over minor issues, but he couldn't help himself; by forever projecting strength, he was sure, he could deter people from going after him.

Adrienne went silent for a few moments, as if sensing that further argument was as futile as beating her fists on a heavy door. "Maybe you're right and things will just blow over. Meanwhile, this thing will be headed for court. How soon might that happen?"

"Beats me," he said with a shrug. "I'll call Mitch on Monday and see where we are." Winston admired Mitchell McCloskey, his primary attorney, a no-nonsense bulldog who'd worked for him for over a decade and was just the kind of legal eagle Winston wanted in his corner. He was among the most hated lawyers in New York, people assured him, but Winston liked that; he paid McCloskey a hefty retainer to have his undivided attention whenever anything controversial arose.

"Alright."

He turned to her. "You know, I ran into Martin Hargreaves at the dinner the other night. He's just the kind of guy who would tell his people to skewer me for this."

"I like Martin," she said quietly. "He's a generous man, and he's clever."

"Clever?"

"Well, I mean that he's witty and makes good conversation."

"Oh." He decided not to show any irritation. "You know, he asked me how you were doing, and I said great. Then I told him you were coming out with a new line for the fall."

"You did what?" There was noticeable heat in her voice.

"It was funny, dear," he said, sounding a bit sheepish. His eyes went to the floor for a moment. "It just came into my head, and I said it. I don't think he cares a bit. Just idle chitchat."

"I hope so. There's nothing in the works right now, so I'd be pretty embarrassed if that got out and there were expectations ..."

"Oh, I don't think so," Winston said, smiling and reaching over to pat her hand. "Like I said, just chatter. And his magazines don't exactly cover fashion."

Adrienne forced her lips into a smile and turned back to the TV, which was reporting on a new community center in the Bronx. She stood and walked toward the kitchen, where their cook, Carmelita, was busy preparing dinner; the aroma washed over the kitchen with notes of garlic and rosemary.

It was two hours before sunset thanks to daylight saving time, and the seagulls squawked and darted around the harbor like restless spirits. Since it was May, Sag Harbor hadn't yet experienced the summer invasion of polo-clad lemmings, and a lot of the moorings were vacant—all of which made Winston's yacht, the *Northern Star*, stand out a little bit more.

Winston and Adrienne had arrived a few hours earlier from the nearby helipad, where a driver had dutifully picked them up and deposited them on the pier. It was a nice spring day in the high sixties, though the southwest wind, carried across the tip of Long Island, had the bracing feel of the ocean. Here they were wearing sweaters to ward off the breeze, sitting on the main deck of the ninety-five-foot powerboat, and entertaining a couple who felt delighted to be there.

Not surprisingly, they were Adrienne's friends—a designer blogger Adrienne had befriended and the blogger's husband, a financial analyst. Winston had made few friends in adulthood; friendship to him was a transactional relationship based more than anything on admiration for him and what the person could do to advance Winston's interests. Apart from those on his payroll, it wasn't a null set, but it was the kind of circle you could put in a broom closet.

The two women were chatting amiably about other designers and the general world of fashion in New York, which visibly bored Winston. He nursed his gin and tonic and stared vacantly, occasionally turning to give Adrienne a closed-mouth grin that announced he was indulging her. The woman's husband was more engaged in the conversation, with an occasional contribution that showed at least that he was paying attention.

"He's one to watch, Adrienne," the blogger, Ruth, was saying.

"I really don't like the boxy silhouettes he's pushing," Adrienne said, swirling the drink in her glass. "But maybe that's just me. Do you think it's going to be big?"

Ruth leaned back in the deck chair. "Oh, I think so. Maybe not here in the fall, but I wouldn't be surprised if it shows up in Paris." Her voice was high, almost childlike; it reminded Winston of Dolly Parton but without her accent.

"Okay, well, I'll have to keep my ears to the ground." Adrienne smiled at her conspiratorially.

Winston had had enough and stood up. "I think they're getting some hors d'oeuvres ready. Let me go see if they're done." He smiled and stood up a little gingerly—getting out of a deck chair was getting harder; it might require a derrick in a few years.

"Thanks, dear." Adrienne smiled up at him. She was clearly enjoying the company.

Winston sidled across the teak decking and into the main cabin, going past the red-carpeted parlor area and into the galley, where two caterers had been busy for the past hour creating the dainty items that Adrienne had ordered up.

"Hi, hi," Winston said as he walked up. "How we doin'?"

"Just fine, Mr. Crumm. We're just finishing the last of the crab cakes. The rest of the platters are ready to go, and Jorge will bring them out." The woman who spoke was a pretty, young brunette, fashionably thin; she wore a white smock embroidered with the firm's name, Divine Delectables, over what appeared to be jeans. Her male colleague, tall and equally thin, smiled at Winston with a flash of white teeth. *I bet they're both vegans*, Winston thought to himself. He equated the woman's thinness with giving up on meat or sweets or almost anything worth eating.

Winston bent over and peered at one of the oval silver platters, which had a raft of small rectangular items, perfectly spaced apart. "What are these?" he asked.

"Tuna tartare with cream cheese and dill on focaccia," she said with a decided touch of what sounded like pride. "Jorge will bring them right out."

"Well, they look great." Winston was a little dubious but decided it was a good thing at this moment to humor the help. He turned to leave. "We have a table out there on the deck where you can set these."

"Thank you. Again, they'll be right out." She smiled winsomely; Jorge said nothing but did the same.

Jorge? Winston thought to himself. *I wonder if he speaks English—or if he's here legally.* He decided he didn't want to know; he gave the pair a quick smile and walked back toward the deck.

He sighed inwardly. All this chatter about design was starting to give him a mild headache, a slight throbbing in the temples. But any talk involving his favorite subjects, sports and business, wouldn't happen tonight. He walked to his chair, sat down, and smiled perfunctorily. "Things will be right out, they tell me."

The next morning, back in the city, the day stretched before him like an arid plain—there just wasn't much for Winston to think about. It was a Sunday, and he and Adrienne rarely went out. They weren't churchgoers, and while Winston might be amenable to a nice restaurant brunch now and again, Adrienne was opposed to big meals on principle.

That left sports. It was spring and the major leagues were in full throttle, but Winston had soured on baseball, especially after an attempt several years ago to wrest the New York Mets from their owners—a plan he had put together with two other rich investors—went nowhere. As a result, he couldn't watch the Mets, and the Yankees were only slightly better, despite all their championships. Winston liked winners, but baseball had become, well, boring.

The NBA was still going, but as a Knicks fan, Winston had gone through a lot of lean years and had sworn off watching them; their ineptitude gave him heartburn. The rest of the league was as interesting to him as watching curling. That left sports such as tennis and golf, both of which he had played little as an adult. He preferred watching golf, which almost always had interesting and scenic venues with emerald-green grass and tall trees throwing ornate shadows over parts of the course.

Adrienne walked into the kitchen to pour herself more coffee. She wore a light-blue cashmere sweater and khaki slacks, and her hair was pinned up the back, a look he liked.

"Last night was nice, dear," she said. "I like them, and I'd like to have them back sometime."

"Sure," he said, half turning to her. "They seem like good people." His lack of enthusiasm was as telling as it was predictable, but she appeared to ignore it. They'd parted with the couple after a good dinner at a local restaurant that Winston was particularly fond of since it served great steaks with loaded mashed potatoes—plus the owner, no dummy, always tried to give Winston the best available table, usually one near one of the windows looking out onto the harbor.

"I'm going into the office for a bit," he announced, and he smiled at her. As he walked out, his mind went suddenly to the *Northern Star*, his pride and joy. Star Enterprises paid for the ship's upkeep and the crew, and the company's slumping finances didn't bode well for maintaining such largesse. The last quarter had been ominously bad, and the immediate future held as much promise as a field going fallow. He shuddered to think what would happen if the board elected to trim some of his perks. It was frightening.

In front of his computer, he blew out a breath and turned on the machine. He waited for his email to load, rubbing his hands. He didn't get a lot of personal email, but he did get a lot of promotional stuff, much of it dross but some that interested him.

And so, he clicked on an item from the city parks preservation society. It was a good cause, he knew; New York had enough concrete, stone, and glass, and the hard surfaces that had transformed it into one of the business capitals of the world. The city's parks—especially Central Park—were its jewels, islands of grass and trees that softened the landscape and offered a window on its seasons.

He'd been giving goodly sums for years, and he did it without seeking to emblazon the family name on anything. He liked the idea of being something of a stealth benefactor, someone who wouldn't ordinarily be lumped in a group promoting preservation. It was a rare display of altruism, albeit one that was very much in the public interest. He clicked to "star" the email. He'd come back to it as a reminder to see how recently he had donated and to consider another gift.

CHAPTER 8

Corbin's eyes went to the ceiling—not surprisingly because he was flat on his back. He also happened to be naked and spread-eagled, cinched securely at the wrists and ankles by brightly patterned silk scarves.

He raised his head slightly and looked at Larissa, who was sizing him up from behind the bed. It was one of the twin beds in her guest room, which allowed her to put Corbin in this position—no way could she have tied him in her king bed. Her dark eyes danced as she appraised him.

"Not too tight, are they, *cheri?*"

"I don't think so," he said, a bit nervously, and smiled.

"Well, I see you are warming to the idea," she said, chuckling, looking at his crotch. Indeed, for a man in an utterly defenseless position, Corbin had achieved a commendable erection. This was the second time in the last two weeks he had submitted to this request, and he had to admit, it was something of a turn-on. *At least she doesn't have a whip and stilettos*, he thought. *That would be a bit over the top.*

Larissa unhooked her bra and let him admire her body, which he drank in eagerly. Then she stepped out of her black lacy panties, put one knee up on the bed, swung the other over, and straddled him. She tossed her black hair back with both hands and grinned a huge grin; he grinned back.

"Now, just relax," she purred. "Remember, this will be fun."

Conflicted: that's how Corbin felt about his mistress. Larissa Thibault was the most exciting but also the most demanding woman he had ever been with. She was a handful. But he allowed himself one evening a week with her, for a few delicious hours at a time; he wanted more now and then, but he realized that he was skating on the edge, trying to keep his domestic life and his amorous id in precarious balance.

He thought of his relationship with Patricia, which had traveled through the predictable arc of so many marriages in which passion had cooled. But there were still sparks between them—just fewer and with less voltage, as the years passed. But Larissa was different: she had an exotic, mysterious air that he had never encountered before with American girls and it was something he couldn't really pin down. She was a rare butterfly, a gleaming blue morpho who flitted here and there, allowing him to net her when it suited her.

It was a calculated decision to vary the day of the week that he spent with Larissa. He told Patricia he needed to work late one night a week, and that's all he felt he could spare without raising a small red flag. But then he had to coordinate with Larissa, who had plans of her own. While she was usually able to give him first dibs on the day of his choosing, she was a bit mercurial; he could never count on her not canceling out at the last minute. All their communication was by an encrypted phone app, What's App; he was adamant that there be no voice or email trail.

Fortunately, their trysts could be very private. Larissa lived in a large two-bedroom apartment on East Seventy-Eighth Street, but the building had no doorman, no one to observe him coming in and out. He could ride the elevator or take the wide marble stairs to her third-floor flat, whatever suited his mood.

As a rule, they had a drink or two—wine for her, often gin or vodka for him—and something to snack on before they repaired to the bedroom. By eight-thirty, Corbin knew it was time for him to leave. He'd call Pieter, who would meet him at the corner of Seventy-Eighth and Lexington Avenue for the ride home. If Pieter suspected what was going on—and how could he not?—his lips were firmly sealed. Corbin always made sure he met Pieter on a corner and not outside the apartment, couldn't be too careful.

He and Larissa had met two months earlier at an art exhibit in Soho. It wasn't a neighborhood Corbin frequented often, but the gallery had garnered some big names, old and new, for a three-day exhibit, names such as Jeff Koons, Basquiat, some old de Koonings, Rauschenberg. Corbin had a Rauschenberg and a Frank Stella at the home in New Canaan, and he and Patricia were going to see if there was something else they might pick up.

It was early May, but it was damp and chilly, and Patricia came down with a hacking cough two days beforehand. She insisted he go alone, and he agreed, albeit a little reluctantly. Pieter drove him down, and Corbin said to pick him up in an hour.

So, there he was, white wine in a plastic cup in hand, admiring a Koons that he thought he'd seen before, when a woman's voice sashayed into his ear.

"Do you like Koons?"

He half-turned and took her in, tall, comely, with long dark hair and something of a lopsided smile that beguiled him. She wore a loose black blouse over ivory pants and low heels. He caught the sparkle of what seemed to be a diamond earring in the bright white gallery light, which bathed her face in an artificial glow.

"I do, I do." He nodded and smiled. "I wish I had one, but ..."

"They are very pricey," she said quickly. "I just came to admire them." She had a slight accent, vaguely British, that intrigued him.

"So, you like modern art?" he asked. "Some people say it's an acquired taste."

"Well, if it is, I've acquired it," she said, holding her red Kate Spade purse in two hands in front of her. She cocked her head slightly. "And you seem to have it as well."

"Yeah," he said, trying to sound noncommittal. "I'm lucky enough to have a couple of well-known moderns at home. I came here to see if there was anything that seemed irresistible." He took a sip of his wine.

"Ah. Who do you have?"

"A Rauschenberg and a Stella."

She was silent for a moment. "Very nice. And you—you live alone?"

"No, no. My wife caught a cold the other day or she would be here. We live in Connecticut, so there wasn't much point in her trying to make it."

"Uh-huh. You're a commuter, then?"

"I am."

"I'm sorry if I sound nosy, but what kind of work do you do?"

"I'm a banker." He looked at her quizzically, trying to read her thoughts. Did it sound too boring?

She nodded. "Well, that's where the money is, right?" She smiled again; she was flirting. *God*, he thought, *she is sexy.* And probably twenty years younger than him.

Five minutes later, she'd given him her cell phone number and agreed to try to set up a lunch date. She told him she lived on the Upper East Side but worked in Midtown, so it seemed as if it would be easy to arrange. She pressed his hand, gave him a dazzling smile, and said she had a dinner date with a girlfriend. Then she turned and walked slowly away toward the door, her hips swinging. He watched every move as intently as a fly fisherman watching a dry fly waft on the current.

Over the course of the next few weeks, he learned that she was more than just a lovely face: she had a graduate degree in applied mathematics—risk theory—from Columbia and worked as a risk management consultant for major companies. She told him that during her graduate study years, she had been recruited to do some modeling for a catalog company. She didn't need the money, she insisted, but loved the exposure and the excitement of being up on current fashions.

He was bowled over. Beautiful and brilliant—those were two Bs he found irresistible.

Her history trickled out slowly; she wasn't one of those people who opened up about herself fulsomely at the first opportunity. Her father, Henri Thibault, ran an old family winery in France with the help of her older brother, Francois. Her mother, Anne, was an American and a former actress. Larissa didn't say so, but it appeared they were very well off indeed; Corbin knew simply that she had family money which enabled her to work because she wanted to, not because she needed to.

And so the affair began, lightly at first, then with more passion, much like high school friends gradually become almost inseparable. Like many married men, Corbin found himself impaled lightly on the horns of a dilemma. He loved his wife and his kids—he would be an idiot to feel otherwise. But Larissa was intoxicating, forbidden fruit that he had denied himself so long, and he couldn't pull away. He didn't know how long it could last, but he was caught in the grip of the affair like a rabbit in a snare. And, of course, she might tire of him. So, he thought he'd just ride it a while longer while he tried to sort things out. It was a pickle, but a tasty one.

CHAPTER 9

Corbin stared at the ocean a hundred yards away over a dune speckled with long blades of grass. The water was still smooth, with just a mild hint of corrugation from a light breeze. He smiled to himself. It was a typical summer day in Nantucket, that snail-shaped bastion of WASP privilege that sits thirty miles out in the Atlantic, which served as a giant moat providing some degree of serenity from the hordes that beset Cape Cod, "the Cape" to any sentient person in New England. The fog had burned off, and the sun was getting stronger by the hour, starting to cast shadows on the expansive deck that could be accessed by a series of French doors.

Dressed in a pair of Breton-red shorts and a white polo shirt, Corbin sipped his coffee and leafed through the arts section of the weekend's *Wall Street Journal*. The two girls were inside, working on a complicated jigsaw puzzle, the kind where all the pieces seem maddeningly similar; he admired their dedication but only occasionally joined them at the table. Justin was on a long bike ride with one of his friends from New Canaan who was staying not far away. Patricia was reading in the living room, immersed in one of the thrillers she had taken to in the past few years.

Christ, he was proud of his family, but even Corbin acknowledged to himself that they looked like refugees from a Ralph Lauren ad—people of casual privilege, handsome and largely unfettered by any sense of doubt or dissatisfaction with the world at large. They glided through their days with a sense of entitlement that might someday rise up and smite them, but his children wouldn't be likely to face any crises until the dreaded—well, he dreaded it—college choice fandango.

Corbin was on a break from Larissa; not only was he far from New York, but she was on her annual summer visit with her family, two weeks back in the *terroir* in France. Corbin thought about her now and then, but not with real longing. She was an indulgence, a favorite flavor of ice cream stuffed into a waffle cone on a hot summer day. There would be plenty of time to reengage when they were back in the city.

The house was a one-month rental arranged by the bank; Corbin simply had to choose from among several suggested to him. This one, a classic white-framed number with green shutters, had a fantastic view and space galore: five bedrooms and six baths, plus a shuffleboard court and putting green off a lower deck. He knew what it cost, a few dollars short of a king's ransom, but no matter; this was a perk for the CEO. The family was used to luxury, a warm blanket that coddled them endlessly. Now and then, Corbin thought of all the privileges they'd been given, and a *frisson* of guilt tried to work its way through his brain. But he was a captive of the elevated status that they had moved into, and those thoughts would dissolve.

This stay was very different from his first trip to the island. He'd gone with a Dartmouth buddy whose family had a summer house there, a whirlwind trip that left a few lasting memories, like initials carved into the trunk of a tree. Corbin went there yearning to meet up with a girl he had a crush on, a pretty blonde who was waitressing at one of the harborside hotels.

But they'd never connected; she wasn't working there anymore, and he and his buddy had wandered the cobbled streets of downtown, getting wasted on gin and tonics as the sun was swallowed by the treetops and the mild summer night embraced them. He'd spent two fitful nights on a couch, nursing hangovers by day, as well as a sunburn he picked up from falling asleep on their deck. It was a great trip.

He heard the sliding door open as Patricia came out. She had on a light-blue cotton top over white Capris and colorful espadrilles on her feet. She moved wordlessly past him and started deadheading the pink geraniums in a large clay pot, set in a bench on the gray deck, that they had bought a week earlier.

She called out over her shoulder. "Do you have a tennis game later?"

He set down the paper. "Yep. About an hour. I'll be home for some lunch."

Patricia looked at him and stroked a wisp of hair off her forehead. "Okay. I'll probably be making a salad."

"Sounds good."

The light breeze augured well for tennis; too often, the southwest winds would whip up and make the game an adventure, like chasing a butterfly with a flimsy net. While that was more often an afternoon phenomenon, it could happen at any time; nature was fickle, and in the grand scheme of things, wind was usually no more of a nuisance than a random mosquito buzzing near one's ear.

He was there to recharge, a mechanical toy getting a new battery. It was a time-honored practice for the bank's CEOs, and Corbin didn't exactly protest. The job was plenty stressful, he reminded himself now and then, with the unpredictable London group and pesky regulators in both countries peering at their financials like strangers reading over your shoulder on the subway—highly annoying and inescapable.

Thankfully, things slowed down in midsummer, and he

could manage his affairs with a couple of conference calls a week, usually limited to the bank's top corporate officers in New York. If anything untoward happened in London, it would be routed through New York before it got to him.

But there was that damn loan to Star Enterprises. He'd fielded an email from Timothy Eggersby two days earlier reminding him of the peril the loan was in, and it took him aback. The fact that Eggersby had reached out to him and not to Sir Reginald was ominous, a sign that things had reached a serious stage. Blood was in the water. He'd replied that he would review the matter as soon as he was back in the office.

Corbin's mind returned to the challenge he had given himself: to move on his goal of gaining a seat on the board of the Museum of Modern Art. He was a collector, true, but he had a yen to be esteemed for his range of knowledge and the breadth of his interests. To him, the perfect manifestation would be a MOMA directorship. In many ways, that seemed utterly attainable—such boards are often drawn from the ranks of rich and powerful executives. He had daydreamed about it but hadn't yet acted.

This notion had asserted itself more and more in the past few years as he'd grown comfortable with his job and the shape of the challenges he faced. Now he needed a mentor, someone who could provide the necessary contacts. And he knew a likely candidate: Edward "Ned" Turner, a retired banker from Chase Manhattan who had worked with David Rockefeller, one of the great art mavens of the twentieth century. Now in his late seventies, Turner had spent years on the MOMA board. Corbin had met him at Chase and felt sanguine about the chances that Turner would help him.

So, he thought, he would try to set up a meeting, probably a lunch, with Turner after Corbin got back, assuming Turner was in town. As the owner of several prominent pieces by modern artists, Corbin sensed he was in a good position if he played his cards right, like a bridge player using the proper convention. Maybe he'd even bring photos of his own collection. They certainly could help.

His reverie was broken suddenly. He heard shouting from inside, Patricia's voice and one of the girls'. He got up quickly and walked inside, realizing they were in one of the bedrooms.

He hurried down the carpeted hall and through the doorway. Patricia stood, hands on hips, her lovely face transformed by fury. She turned as Corbin walked in. Morgan stood silent, her face flushed.

"She has some Ecstasy," Patricia told Corbin.

He clenched his jaw. "My God. How did you find out?" he asked Patricia.

"I was going through the medicine chest in their bathroom looking for some ointment, and there was a small jar that I didn't recognize. I looked in it and saw the pills. She admitted they were hers."

"How did you know what it was?" he asked. He had never seen it.

"Diane Foreman told me about it. She apparently caught Teddy with it, and she described it to me. The pills have an X marked on them."

"Morgan, this isn't good." Corbin's voice was cold, then grew more heated. "We've warned you to stay away from things like this. Nothing good can come from it, especially not at your age."

Morgan screwed up her face; she looked close to tears. "I haven't used any. One of my friends gave it to me in case I wanted to try it. That's all."

"Do you have any idea of how bad this stuff can be?" Corbin nearly shouted. "It's a serious drug. You can experience some major side effects." He turned to Patricia. "Flush it down the toilet."

Morgan's mouth worked, but she said nothing.

"What kind of punishment should we give her?" Patricia looked at him, implicitly assigning him as judge and jury.

Corbin raised his hands. "Well, we can't ground her on vacation. That will have to wait until we get home." He turned to Morgan. "Young lady, this is serious as hell. This can't happen again."

"I hear you, both of you," Morgan said in a soft and quavering voice. She averted their eyes.

"Good," Corbin heard himself say as he heard Patricia flush the toilet, a sound he now associated with something decidedly different from the usual.

He and Patricia walked into their bedroom, and she closed the door and swung toward him. She seemed livid.

"You know, this is partly your fault." Her voice simmered with anger.

"My fault? Why?"

"You're just not around enough for them. If you're home, you're playing tennis or doing something else out of the house. You're leaving most of the parenting to me, and they need a strong voice, a real role model."

"You know how time-consuming my job is, and with the commute," he said, raising his hands in protest. "I don't have a lot of energy when I get home during the week. But I understand that parenting kids, especially teenagers, takes two. Neither of us has done this before, Trish. I-I'll try to do better."

If she was mollified, it wasn't evident. Glaring at him, she said simply, "You'd better." She turned and stalked out without another word.

Standing there, Corbin had a flash of introspection. Was he really too disengaged from the kids' lives? He didn't think so, but there were no external judges to score him, just Patricia. As a boss, he considered himself available, calm, and understanding, rarely having to raise his voice. But this was different.

He didn't want to be the parent from hell. He never had been that way; he always wanted to offer more light than heat. But this was something they couldn't abide. Rich suburban kids had so many temptations, so many glittering things, and drugs were like the serpent in the Garden of Eden. He sighed. Parenting, he mused, must have been a lot easier when kids worked in the fields.

CHAPTER 10

It was August, to most New Yorkers one of the worst months of the year—outside of winter, that is. Mornings were steamy, and the word "muggy" seemed to have been coined particularly for most afternoons. Smells were enhanced, which often meant that garbage and the stale water in puddles, final resting places for much urban detritus, were that much more noticeable. The warm southwest breeze brought no relief, just the promise of thunderstorms.

It was now August 15, and Winston and Adrienne were far away, on the north shore of Boston on a regular cruise on the *Northern Star*. Winston had long ago developed an aversion, almost an allergic reaction, to being in Manhattan at this point on the calendar. So, he joined the corporate exodus for the bracing tang of the ocean and a series of ports that offered different scenery and an escape from the pressure cooker that New Yorkers often found themselves in.

In some respects, these cruises simply mirrored what was going on at the *New York Star*. He was nominally in charge of the ship, Captain Crumm, but Dirk Wilson was really running things; he maneuvered the ship from the bridge or had an able hand do it. Besides Wilson, there was a crew of five, including a chef, and they answered to Wilson. They were mostly young and footloose, and crewing on a fancy boat such as the *Northern Star* enabled them to enjoy something of a high life. Whatever they thought of Crumm—and they certainly had their opinions—it was dished out behind closed doors.

Winston looked out at the crowded harbor in Salem and its sea of sailboat masts and stroked his chin and its light layer of stubble. He shaved only occasionally on these summer cruises and liked the idea that he could let himself go somewhat, far from prying photographers. It was his equivalent of letting his hair down.

They had just finished breakfast in the dining area, with its broad mahogany table and blue upholstered banquette. It was a typical spread with eggs, toast, and thick-slabbed bacon for Winston, and fruit, granola, and yogurt for Adrienne. There was dark coffee—Adrienne insisted on fair trade beans from South America—and hand-squeezed orange juice, both of which would also be available to the crew. Winston was oblivious to this fact, but Adrienne had made sure that as little as possible would be wasted. She was a detail-oriented person, and vacations were no exception.

Winston stretched out his legs, pale under the khaki shorts, and folded his arms behind his head. "I've got one of those damned conference calls today," he said, turning to Adrienne. "It's the fifteenth."

She gave him a wan smile. "Okay. That's not really a big deal, is it?"

"No, not usually."

"When is it?" she asked.

"Ten sharp." He looked at his watch—eight-thirty. "I'll take it in the stateroom."

"Fine. I'll probably read. We can go ashore later." She was wearing a gauzy white shirt over a swimsuit as glossy and black as a raven's wing.

He smiled. He really was fond of her, and she looked

particularly fine with her summer tan, which she nursed most days on the broad front deck. "Sounds good to me."

The call, which Winston took by dialing in on his cell phone, started off in the usual way, with a parade of numbers delivered mostly by the CFO. Details flew over Winston's head like a flock of starlings, and this was nothing if not detailed: circulation, advertising revenue, the state of the website, payroll—the nuts and bolts of the business. Then the paper's editor, James Flaherty, a gruff veteran in his late fifties who had started as a reporter on the metro desk, spoke briefly about a few longer-term stories the paper would be working on, including a series on the woeful New York Knicks, the basketball franchise that had once been the toast of the town. Willis Reed, Bill Bradley, Walt Frazier, Earl Monroe, Dave DeBusschere were names for the ages. But that glory faded long ago, like a once-bright umbrella that had spent too long in the sun.

Winston's phone was on speaker, and he had been mostly staring into space. But this story idea intrigued him. "I like that," he said. "You know, when I was growing up, they were special. Now, they're crap. The owners should get some heat. Ah, what's their name?"

"The O'Connors," the editor replied.

"Oh, right. The old man is still in the picture, isn't he?"

"Yes, he is, but the sons are really running the team and running it into the ground, most people think." Flaherty paused for a moment. "We think it's an appropriate time to be asking some hard questions about where this franchise is going and if it's ever going to recover some semblance of competence."

"Well, again, I like that idea." Winston was happy to see a sports story getting such attention. "Take whatever you need."

"Yes, sir." Flaherty didn't often address Winston as "sir,"

and Winston warmed to it.

A few minutes later, the CFO, Susan Donahue, cleared her throat and said, "There's something important that I wanted to bring before the board. It involves our finances."

Silence.

"More specifically, this relates to our working capital loan with Whitehall. We've been struggling to keep up with payments, and I've just been told that they are seriously considering pulling it."

Winston sat up as if someone had kicked him in the derrière. "What? Are they serious?"

"They seem to be," she said. "And what's more distressing, there really isn't another lender out there who seems willing to work with us."

George Granger, one of the longtime board members, spoke up; Winston recognized his raspy voice immediately. "That sounds pretty dire. Are you sure no one else might step forward?"

"It seems unlikely," the CFO replied. "I've tentatively explored some kind of syndicated loan that would spread the risk, but I've gotten no takers. I'm going to keep trying."

"Wait a minute." Winston's voice had more than a touch of irritation. "If I remember right, I did this loan deal with Sir Reginald himself. He basically gave me his word that everything would be fine."

"Well, Mr. Crumm, perhaps the situation there has changed," Donahue said. "The merchant bankers have been pretty clear about where things stand. They're basically giving us forty-five days to pay up in full or they'll pull the credit."

"Forty-five days, huh?" Crumm sounded reflective. "Is that enough time to put us in a stronger position?"

"Ummm," Donahue said, "I really don't think so. All the trends are pretty negative at this point. We may be able to break even over that time, but I don't see us making up any of the difference. We're not generating that much cash."

"And how much are we short?" Crumm asked.

"More than $15 million," she replied.

Rob Graves spoke up. "Susan, I think we need to convene a special committee to look at this situation. It sounds like we're in real trouble."

"That's a good idea," the CFO replied. "Let's talk about it offline."

"And while you do that," Winston said, "let me call Sir Reginald and see if I can't use my powers of persuasion on him." He smiled to himself, but he couldn't see the eye-rolling that broke out among the people seated in the boardroom. Winston fancied himself as a great negotiator, but the truth was that he'd be hard-pressed to sell ice cream to eight-year-olds on a hot summer day. "Can someone back there text me with his office number?"

CHAPTER 11

Corbin stared out the windows in his office and pursed his lips. It was always difficult coming back after a summer vacation—hell, it had been hard when he was a student. It was the seasonality of it. *We're all conditioned*, he thought, *to treat summer as the highlight of the year, a golden balloon ride, lovely and languorous.* It was a chance to escape, physically and mentally, from issues such as routine, responsibility, and corporate rigmarole—a different set of the three *R*'s that he had grown up with, to be sure.

It was his second day back, and the summer doldrums were still in place, like a mist that hung almost invisibly in the air. Labor Day was still almost a week away and with it the "official" end of the summer season. A number of his top lieutenants were still on vacation, as were quite a few of the Brits "on holiday," and things wouldn't really ramp up until the holiday had come and gone. The situation in Britain was clearly different, however, unencumbered by a seemingly artificial holiday that had long ago ceased to celebrate the labor movement, other than to give it lip service.

He rocked forward in his chair and looked at his calendar again. There, in a corner of the square marking the date, was the letter *L*. Larissa. It was another of their nights, another romp in the hayloft—no, not quite. Larissa had only the best furniture, and the bed was no different: a king-sized Intellibed, which cost more than a month's rent, even on the Upper East Side. Definitely luxurious, the kind of bed Roger Moore would have been propped up in one of his Bond films. Not a bad analogy, Corbin thought idly; Larissa was definitely Bond girl material.

Turning back to his computer, Corbin called up his schedule and leaned forward, peering at the print. Damn, he thought, he was going to start needing reading glasses. He'd always been proud of his keen eyesight, which was a huge boon on the tennis court, but now that he'd crossed the threshold of fifty, reading, especially fine print, was becoming an issue. But he'd move into that situation slowly and only as needed.

A call to Ned Turner's office—he was still working as an investment manager—had proven fallow. Turner was in Maine for a few more weeks. Corbin jotted down in his calendar that he would call Turner in the second week of September.

Corbin turned his mind back to the present and clicked on the box for the next day, Wednesday, and saw there was an executive team meeting. Most of his group would be there; a few would call in from vacation spots in the Hamptons or Martha's Vineyard, probably cursing under their breath that they had to take an hour out of a day otherwise free of business. Corbin wasn't a fan of conference calls, but he realized they were a necessary evil, a kind of centralized armature for knitting together the disparate parts of the enterprise. But it was a rare call that was truly productive.

It was almost noon, his watch announced, and Corbin lurched out of his reverie and hit the intercom for Angela. He was going to meet Ted Parkinson, one of his executive vice presidents, for lunch in the executive dining room. It wasn't business, but it wasn't exactly pleasure either, though Ted was one of his better friends in the building. It was hard for the CEO to let down his hair, he thought to himself; the walls have ears.

"Angela, would you remind me when it's 12:25? I have a lunch upstairs."

"Certainly, Mr. van Sloot," she said.

"Thanks," he replied simply and spun his chair around to face the window. Outside, cumulus clouds dotted the sky like balls of cotton and threw parts of the river, a steely blue from this high up, into shadow. *I do love this view*, he thought to himself and let his mind drift to admire the color of the sky.

Larissa walked to the couch and handed him a gin and tonic, her fingers encircling the glass. She smiled a lascivious smile and brushed her hair back from her face as she sat down next to him, drawing her legs up beneath her. She wore a white sundress with thin straps that accentuated her shoulders. His eyes ran down the nape of her neck to the hollow above her collarbone, one of his favorite views of the female anatomy.

It was only seven, and the sun was still shining on the apartments across the street. In the Bronx, families would be out on their stoops, laughing and gossiping and enjoying the weather while it still beckoned, taking in the smells of a myriad of different cuisines. To Corbin and Larissa, however, this urban melting pot was as distant as Mumbai. They were holed up in their own little cocoon, away from prying eyes and ears. They cared nothing for stoops, only for *shtups*.

Corbin had told her a little about the vacation in Nantucket, about the way it scrubbed away the daily worries and ad hoc decisions that dominated his time in the office.

"We took a wonderful little trip to Bordeaux," she said, recounting her vacation with her family. "We don't go to vineyards very often—you know, no busman's holiday—but we did go to a great little one in Pessac that had a terrific vintage." She raised her glass to her lips and sipped.

"Sounds very restful," Corbin said. "And I imagine you can just relax, knowing that your family is handling all the business aspects and you don't have to be involved." He looked down for a moment, then back up. "How is the business doing?"

"Very well, actually. This year may be one of our best, based on the temperatures and rainfall over there. You know, grapes can be very fickle." She grinned.

"Just like a woman," he said, smiling back.

"Oh, you didn't just say that!" She pulled her head back in mock horror.

"Just kidding," he said quickly, then he was silent for a moment. "You know, I wish you and I could get out and do dinner one of these days, but I'm a little leery. I would hate to be recognized."

"Are you ashamed to be with me?" she laughingly asked.

"Of course not. It's just—just challenging. I would never be tabloid fodder, but I can't handle the notion of anything getting back to my family." He pulled hard on his drink.

She cocked her head and studied him for a moment. "Am I the first affair you've had?"

There it was in black and white: affair. He had no love for the word, which to him implied something that could last for years. This, to him, was a dalliance.

"Perhaps I shouldn't admit it, but it is," Corbin said. "It took someone like you to lead me astray."

She laughed a throaty rumble that sent a quick shiver through him. "I can't say the same. There are lots of single men in New York and a lot like you, who are married but available." She raised a hand to her cheek. "I've sampled a few."

He was momentarily taken aback, as if a firecracker had gone off in the street below. "What is a few?"

"Oh, fewer than twenty." She stared at him, assessing his reaction.

"Twenty?" His eyebrows shot up in something like shock.

"Don't be upset, *cheri*," she said, smiling. "Much less than that. I'm just teasing you."

Corbin sat back and hooded his eyes. "Well, I wasn't sure. It's pretty clear you've been with men before. You're very good at what you do, and our time together is pretty special to me. I hope you know that." The words were trite and mundane, and he knew that as they came lurching out like a sot leaving a bar; he gazed at her beseechingly, looking for affirmation.

"Oh, I do. It is to me too."

He moved over, close enough to touch her dress, and reached his right arm around her neck, drawing his head in close. Her lips swam into view. "Now, where were we?"

CHAPTER 12

It was a beautiful September morning in London, the kind of rare blue-sky day when an army of nannies was pushing prams in Regents Park, nodding in common recognition as they passed each other. The holidays were now just memories and photos stored on cell phones. Pigeons swooped in to peck at the grass, still ordered and emerald.

In his office, Sir Reginald sipped his morning tea and read through the first section of the Financial Times, pleased by what he was seeing about the state of the John Bull economy. British firms were reporting record orders, the pound was stable, and news from the Continent seemed anything but alarming. All in all, it seemed like a good time to be in banking. The Brexit imbroglio was only a bad memory, a reminder of how foolish and sclerotic the country could be, how insular, how badly it responded to rumors of new restrictions from the EU mandarins in Brussels.

It being a Monday, there was no point in checking Whitehall's stock price. Like other big banks, Standard Chartered and HSBC among them, Whitehall was a fixture on the FTSE, the principal British exchange. Their stock prices generally rose or fell more or less in tandem, depending on the vicissitudes of the day, interest rate movements, housing starts, and other things over which they appeared to have as much control as a toddler trying to fly a kite in a stiff breeze.

Yet, as Sir Reginald knew well, stock prices were the barometer investors used to judge any company and a major determinant in allotting bonuses to the company brass at year's end. He wasn't a big fan of stock buybacks, which helped goose prices, but a new generation of MBAs and red-suspendered money managers had made the practice almost obligatory, and his board had gone along, as complacent as lemmings. His mild protestations—there were no raised voices at bank board meetings—went acknowledged but unheeded.

He rang Agatha, who answered on the first ring as usual. "Agatha, isn't there a meeting this morning?"

"Yes, sir. Mr. Eggersby and some others from merchant banking have asked to see you."

"Aha. When is this? Now? Ten?"

"Yes."

"Please show them in. I'll be ready." *Eggersby is a smart young chap*, he thought to himself. *He must be here on good cause.*

Half an hour later, Agatha knocked at the door and ushered in three men, led by Timothy Eggersby, who smiled and, holding a slim folder in front of him, made the introductions. He seemed at ease, confident but not overly so in front of the chairman.

"Sir Reginald, thanks for seeing us," he began. Eggersby wore a pin-striped suit with a light-chalk stripe, with a cream-colored shirt and striped tie. His attire said "banker" but not a slave to rigid dress codes. "This is Rupert Granger, whom I believe you've met"—motioning to the portly fellow to his left—"and this is Robin Piggot-Townsend, who is new to our group in the past few months."

Sir Reginald sat back in his tall chair and smiled. "Very well, Timothy, gentlemen; let me ask Agatha to bring in another chair." There were only two velvet-cushioned chairs in front of his desk.

"That's alright, Sir Reginald. I can stand," Eggersby said.

"Nonsense," the chairman said firmly as Agatha appeared at the door. "Please bring in another chair if you would, Agatha."

"Very good, Sir." The three merchant bankers stood, as awkwardly as unfavored boys at a school dance, while the chair was brought in, then they all sat down facing Sir Reginald.

"Very well, then," said Sir Reginald with a smile intended to put them at ease. "What brings you here?"

Eggersby cleared his throat briefly. "We've been monitoring some of our loans that seem to be underperforming, and there is one that stands out that we'd like to discuss with you."

"Which one is that?" This was unusual; Sir Reginald wasn't often asked to look at individual loans.

Eggersby looked at him a bit sheepishly. "The working capital loan to Star Enterprises in New York, Winston Crumm's firm."

The chairman's face clouded over. "Really? Ahhh ... how bad is it?"

"Well, they are almost $20 million in arrears," Eggersby said. "And we really don't see how they have the wherewithal to make that up."

"We've alerted them to the situation," Granger pitched in. "We think their CFO is very competent, but the newspaper industry is facing huge headwinds, as you know. They've assured us they are trying to find an answer, but the signals we're getting are not good."

Sir Reginald folded and rubbed his hands. "I see. I'm sure you're aware that I facilitated that business after I met personally with Mr. Crumm."

"Yes, Sir. That's why we asked to see you," Eggersby said, shifting in his chair.

"And you want what from me, permission to call the loan?" He looked at each of them in turn.

"Essentially, yes," Eggersby said. "We don't feel we could do that without your say-so."

Sir Reginald leaned his head back and stared briefly at the ceiling before pulling his head back down. This was troubling, but he knew there was only one way to proceed. "Well, this is a banking business we're running, and as much as it might pain me personally, we have to treat our clients equally as best we can." He drummed his fingers on his desk. "You have my permission to pull back, on the condition that if things do change materially in a year or so, we might renew the loan, albeit on terms more favorable to us."

"Absolutely, Sir. That seems like the right course of action." Eggersby smiled, visibly relieved. The British were known for bad teeth, but his almost gleamed. If he'd been asked, he would have said the chances of the loan's renewal were remote; the *Star*'s finances were as buoyant as a lead weight.

"Tell me, Eggersby, would you be doing this forthwith?" Sir Reginald asked.

"Yes, I think so. There's no point in waiting for things to worsen."

"Very well. Please, do go ahead, then. And thank you for bringing this to my attention."

"Certainly, Sir. And thank you." He stood, and the others did as well, offering perfunctory smiles as they walked back out.

Sir Reginald leaned back and stared at the ceiling for at least a minute, thinking about Crumm and the trip to Florida he and Pamela had made those short years ago. Crumm probably wasn't going to take this sitting down, he thought glumly; the man was used to getting his way, and Americans could be so unpleasant if they wanted to.

Less than two miles away, in a plush new office complex with a view of the placid Thames, Maxim Ripovsky was reading the *Financial Times* and drinking black coffee from a china cup. Very tall and slim, the Russian financier turned the page to the stock price tables and scanned them quickly; he had few investments in conventional British securities that would be listed. But his eyes drifted down to Whitehall Banking Group, and he noted the closing price and yearly highs and lows. The stock was at the low end of its range and was down slightly for the day. He leaned back in his chair and rubbed his hands lightly before reaching for his intercom.

CHAPTER 13

"No, I don't think that's the look we're going for. It looks a little, I don't know, retro. Does anyone disagree?"

Adrienne looked about the glass table in her conference room, a white-walled room decorated with large, bright posters showing swirling drawings of models in various fashions over the years. This was the latest of the weekly gatherings she called to help knit together her little band of designers, women she had hired over the years to bring out her vision, to translate scribbled lines and proportions into skirts and dresses and jackets that women, her customers, would embrace.

Here, she was responding to a drawing by Roxanne, one of her youngest designers. Adrienne didn't dictate. She wasn't a Coco Chanel, frosty and unbending, a picture of Gallic imperiousness. She sought consensus, the kind she could achieve by speaking softly and coolly, making it clear that while she made the final decisions, this was a team effort.

Nicole, a woman in her forties who specialized in dress design, peered over her round-framed glasses. "I think you're right, Adrienne. Jackets are trending short this season. But I think going this short could be a mistake. We don't want to look like we're reviving the Jackie Kennedy era."

Adrienne chuckled. "No, we certainly wouldn't."

"I'm with you and Nicole," said Terri, a tall blonde in a blue chenille sweater. "I like what Roxanne has done, but I just don't think the overall direction is right for the fall, not with what we're hearing from Milan."

"Okay," Adrienne said. "Roxanne, try lengthening it a little and experiment with a different treatment on the collar."

Roxanne nodded. "I'll do that."

Adrienne turned to her left. "Marianne, let's talk about your sketch."

Twenty minutes later, the meeting broke up quietly and the designers filed out, holding their sketch pads under their arms like schoolgirls toting textbooks. Adrienne walked alone to her office and sat down behind her desk. It had been a good meeting, collegial as usual. She didn't tolerate prima donnas, something the fashion industry had too many of in her view, women and men so certain of their talents that any criticism was met with barks of indignation. Adrienne hired carefully, but over the years she'd had to let go a few women whose egos had made them stand out like brats in a grade school class.

Her mind went to Amanda, her daughter, who had just started school at Swarthmore. Adrienne strove mightily not to be a helicopter parent, the kind who needed to constantly keep tabs on her only child. But having her daughter a couple of hours away, living independently, was going to be an adjustment. It had been easy when Amanda was home in the apartment; there were rules and expectations that had been set, and Adrienne's daughter was a smart girl who understood such arrangements. She'd excelled in school and had run the gauntlet to get admitted to an elite college.

So, Adrienne thought she would wait a couple of more days to call her. She wanted to show Amanda that she was affording her daughter space, letting her break free like a novice skater letting go of a protective hand. Adrienne remembered that her own mother had allowed her that first heady sense of independence when she had gone to Sarah Lawrence and how thankful she'd been in hindsight for that.

Adrienne pulled a lock of hair behind her ear and looked down at her calendar. There was another charity dinner the next night, supporting a charter school in Harlem. This was a new group for her and Winston, and she knew it was her cause and that he'd go on her account. Deep down, Adrienne knew she was privileged in ways that rich, well-educated women in New York often seemed to take for granted. That wouldn't be her; she was eager to involve herself—and her husband—in good causes that could possibly better society. At least she told herself that.

Winston had changed since their marriage, though not in ways obvious to most of those they knew. He could still be loud and boastful, but she sensed that the *Star*'s recent troubles and his role in the company were gnawing at him. He kept much of this to himself; she often felt like a bridge player trying to guess what was in his, her partner's, hand, and to play accordingly. Now and then, he let some details slip, and she knew that Rob Graves and the chairmanship weighed heavily on his mind.

Back when they were courting, when they both were dressing the wounds of divorce, she felt he often tried too hard, overplayed his efforts at charm. She wondered at times if he saw her as a life raft, a way to keep his head above the waves. His children had gone with their mother, and it was an ugly split, with bitter words that Adrienne picked up now and then on phone calls when she and Winston were together. She had issues of her own, but her divorce was much more amicable. Her ex-husband had no lust for combat. The notion that Winston was rich enough to support her business was hardly unimportant, even if she had a tough time admitting to herself that it inexorably helped move her toward him.

Fortunately, she had Amanda, and she'd found a kindred

soul in Winston's mother, who loved fashion and seemed delighted that her new daughter-in-law was making a name for herself in the industry. Winston's father had died some years earlier, and Adrienne saw that Caroline was lonely and enjoyed the time spent with another woman, particularly one who, age-wise, could have been her daughter.

Adrienne rolled back her hands and looked at her nails. *They need attention*, she thought to herself; the pale pink, her color, was starting to fade. Not for her a regular shift to different colors, the kind she saw on others on her staff: navy; magenta; dark red; even, to her horror, black. She looked down at the pad again and remembered she had jotted down the number for the linen wholesaler in Queens. She picked up the phone and punched in the numbers, sat back in the chair, and waited for it to ring.

CHAPTER 14

Winston strolled into the boardroom as if he hadn't a care in the world. He was vaguely aware that his insouciance rankled many other board members far more aware of the company's situation. But he didn't care, certainly not enough to change. He approached his customary seat at the head of the long table and said simply, "Nice to see everyone. So, let's get this show on the road." He offered a vacuous smile and sat down.

This was a regularly scheduled board meeting for Star Enterprises, ten days before the books would close for the third quarter on September 30. Virtually all the board members were there, with notepads and pens arranged in front of them, though a few younger ones had brought their laptops. The overhead lights were on; it was a gloomy day, with the remnants of a small, fast-moving hurricane lashing the tall windows with rain.

"If we're ready to begin, let's start with the state of the *Star* itself, then move on to the outside properties," said Lawrence Ahearn, known around the table as Larry, who, as chief operating officer, was the de facto publisher given Winston's slender skillset and his generally poor handle on details. Unfortunately for the company, Winston's CEO chair gave him decision power, occasionally even veto power, on most projects. If he had been a mechanic, a car he was working on would barely run—if it started at all.

The group proceeded to work through the agenda. Months ago, Winston might have yawned at times or stared off into space, but the still-vague threat to his chairmanship had changed things. He felt he needed to be more attentive even though this meeting, focused on the operating business, was almost certain to bring on ennui.

Not that the board would likely notice any real change. Winston offered a less-than-meaningful comment now and then: "That sounds good," "You guys are on top of this," or "Can we get more information on that?" Like too many boards forced to suffer fools, very often from a founding family, the Star board was very accustomed to Winston's inability to "add value." They tried hard to stick with the task in front of them and treat Winston and his musings as a minor distraction.

About halfway through the agenda, the CFO took over, drilling down into cash flows and various financings. The general tenor, Susan Donahue said frankly, was troubling. Her attempt to line up other lenders in a syndication had fallen flat, and it was hard to see any big bump in revenue on the horizon. The most likely scenario, she said, would be a cost-cutting effort that would involve layoffs and a slimmed-down purchasing program. The *Star*, she said, would be almost on a "wartime footing."

This analogy stirred Winston. "Whoa, war? Just how bad is it?"

"Pretty bad, in a few words," she replied, her reading glasses perched firmly on her nose. "What we need is more money, and it's hard to see where that could come from."

Winston made a point of pouring water from the pitcher in front of him into his glass. "You say our lenders don't want to deal?"

"That's right," she said. "We showed them our financials, which we have to do, and they balked."

"What about that loan from Whitehall—you know, Sir Reginald?" He had never followed up with the phone number he'd been given from the August call; it had slipped his mind as quickly as a bird fleeing a cage.

"They have told us that they are pulling it, though it could be reinstated if we can show them how the loan could be repaid," she said. "But that doesn't seem possible, not in the near term. The numbers just aren't there." She paused. "But there may be another source out there. Larry and I have recently had emails from Primo Capital, an investment manager here in New York. You may have heard of them. They are buying up newspapers around the country, and they want to sit down with us."

Winston felt something like shock course through him. "What? They're looking to buy us?"

Donahue looked at him and nodded. "Yes."

"Over my dead body," Winston shouted. "The Crumms aren't selling. This is our legacy." He looked over at Rob. "Don't you agree, Rob?"

Rob, tall and carefully groomed, looked at him and then around the table. "Well, we don't know what the future holds and where the industry will be in a few years. Things aren't looking good, that's for sure," he said, pursing his lips. His glasses glinted in the light from the fluorescents in the ceiling. "But I don't like what people like Primo are doing. They come in and start shredding the staff and paring costs wherever they can. They don't care about the product, just the bottom line."

Winston spread his arms. "Can we just tell them to go to hell?"

"I think we can tell them we're not ready to entertain any offer," Larry said. "I assume that's the consensus of the board?" Heads nodded around the table, and there were murmurs of assent.

Donahue spoke up. "Since we're a private company, they can't buy stock and pressure us. That gives us a lot of protection. But if what I've read about it is any indication, they won't give up easily. All of which makes it more important to try to see if we can get funding from traditional sources."

Winston crossed his arms. "I didn't call Sir Reginald the last time, but I'm gonna call him now. Adrienne and I showed him and the missus a very good time in Florida. I think he owes us."

Rob Graves stared at him for a moment. "Winston, you said you would call him after our last call during the summer. I think the situation is urgent." Winston froze for a long moment. He realized he couldn't put this off any longer, sweep it under the rug like a pile of unruly dust. He had to act, show that he could come through for the team when it counted.

Failing to deliver on this loan, he sensed, would put him in Rob's crosshairs. Losing the chairmanship was almost inconceivable in his mind, like a king being deposed by a mutinous band of courtiers.

"Can someone give me that number again? I'll call him today." Winston had assumed his take-charge mode, much of which he had to force on himself. Fundamentally, he knew he was lazy, a lifelong defect he had a hard time concealing from those around him.

A half-hour later, as the meeting broke up, one of the finance team gave Winston the number. He smiled, slid the slip of paper in his jacket pocket, and walked out the glass door toward the elevator as if he owned the place.

Winston dialed the number, which went directly to Agatha in London. It was 11:00 a.m. in New York—and 4:00 p.m. on the other side of the pond. It rang four times before a distinctly British voice, a woman's, answered.

"Hello, this is Sir Reginald's office."

"Hi, I'd like to speak to Sir Reginald. This is Winston Crumm calling from New York."

There was at least a five-second pause on the other end. "I'm sorry, Mr. Crumm, but Sir Reginald is indisposed."

"Well, can I leave a number for him to call me back? It's important." Winston looked reflexively at his watch.

Another pause. "Mr. Crumm, Sir Reginald suffered a massive stroke two days ago. He's in hospital, and things look grave."

This news came like a blow to the solar plexus. Winston gasped. "Ah—a stroke? I'm so sorry." He fumbled for words. "And you say it looks very serious?"

"Unfortunately, yes. He's been unconscious and is being fed intravenously. I know very little beyond that."

"My God," Winston said. "And—and who is taking his place?"

"We haven't determined that," Agatha said. "Our American CEO, Corbin van Sloot, was given the additional title of interim chairman."

"I see," Winston said. "And you say this just happened?"

"Two days ago. Sir Reginald had just eaten dinner at home when he collapsed."

"Oh my, my." Winston picked at his lower lip and thought hard. "If I leave you a number, would you call my secretary and give her the details about the hospital? We would certainly like to send flowers. And—and if you would be so kind as to also give her a number for Mr.—what, Sloot? And is he in New York?"

"Van Sloot. Yes, he is in New York. Thank you for your concern."

"Again, I'm so sorry. Terrible news, terrible. I wish you and the bank the best." He dutifully recited the number for her to call.

"Thank you, Mr. Crumm. I will call your secretary with that information. Goodbye."

Winston put down the phone and stared at his hands as his mind worked. He'd never met this Sloot fellow, and he had a bad feeling about the loan. Sir Reginald had been his benefactor, and without him, he feared his leverage had evaporated like a puddle in an Arizona summer. But he'd call the American and see if he could use Sir Reginald's name. Surely, that was worth something, wasn't it?

CHAPTER 15

The clock had just struck two, and Corbin was reading an economic forecast generated by the bank's economists. It was something he generally didn't spend much time with, but the forecasts always had a few tidbits of useful information, a handful of golden threads among the dross. Not without reason, he mused, was economics called "the dismal science."

Angela called him. "There's a call for you from Winston Crumm. He's the publisher, isn't he?"

Corbin sighed—this wasn't good. "He is. Go ahead and put him through ... Hello, this is Corbin van Sloot."

"Mr. van Sloot, this is Winston Crumm. I'm the CEO of Star Enterprises here."

The gravelly voice was something of a surprise; he realized he'd never actually heard Crumm speak.

"Hello to you, Mr. Crumm. I certainly know who you are. What can I do for you?"

"Well, it's a little complicated. I was so sorry to learn about Sir Reginald's stroke. They tell me you are taking his place."

"Not exactly, no, but I do have an interim title as chairman."

"I did hear that. Now, Sir Reginald was kind enough to

approve a loan to us several years ago. I understand that the bank wants to cancel that loan. I'd like to see if there is a way it can be reinstated."

Corbin blew out a breath; he hadn't seen this call coming, especially from Crumm, but he knew he couldn't waver. "We've had some meetings on this loan, Mr. Crumm, and I'm in full support of the team in London that decided to pull it. I'm sorry, but that's where it stands. I do realize that Sir Reginald was helpful in securing that credit, but given the circumstances, he is no longer involved."

Silence. "So, you're saying there is no way to give us more funding?"

"Not at this point, no. Of course, things could change in the future."

"And that's your final word? No negotiating?" It sounded as if Winston was trying to keep the teakettle of his temper from whistling.

"It is. Perhaps the answer might be different at other banks in New York." Corbin felt obliged to say that, though he knew it was as unlikely as a cold day in July or a taxi driver who never used his horn.

Silence. From what Corbin understood of the man, Winston was summoning up one last dig.

"I'm sorry you guys are refusing to play ball. We have a few problems now, yeah, but they won't last, and when we come roaring back, we'll find another bank who will be happy to work with us."

Fat chance, Corbin thought to himself. "I hope you do, Mr. Crumm."

"Oh, we will. Goodbye."

Corbin could practically hear the phone slam down. He sat back and put his arms over his head. Thank God, he thought, the Crumm empire would no longer be a drain on the bank's books. As for earning any enmity from Crumm himself, he couldn't care less. He was a paper dragon that the winds would quickly blow away.

CHAPTER 16

The cell phone rang, and Maxim Ripovsky picked it up on the third ring after seeing it was from Ivan, one of his chief lieutenants.

"Yes, Ivan?" he asked in Russian. He knew Ivan's English was suspect.

"We may have a good opportunity in Marseilles," Ivan told him. "There is a ten-story commercial building that has been put up for bid. It's in downtown, and the opening price is attractive, 8 million euros."

Maxim grimaced slightly. "I don't know anything about Marseilles, Ivan. I think we agreed you would look chiefly at Paris and the surrounding suburbs."

"Yes," Ivan said, "but I thought this could be an exception ..."

"I don't know," Maxim replied firmly. "This really would be a leap for us. But I trust you to scout out some worthwhile properties. So go ahead and send me the particulars."

"Will do, boss," Ivan replied. "Expect the details tomorrow."

"When is the auction?" Maxim asked.

"Next Tuesday."

"Alright, we'll talk after I get a chance to look it over."

"Thanks, boss."

"Talk to you later."

Maxim laid the phone back on the desk, sighed, and looked out the window, which afforded him a drone's-eye view of Tower Bridge and the giant Millennium Wheel, the icon of the new London, looming over the Thames. London had been his home for more than a decade, and it had proved a far better base of operations than chilly Moscow. There, the phone service was sporadic, a soul-crushing bureaucracy ruled people's lives, and everything decent needed to be bought on the black market.

He was proud of what he had accomplished without any rigorous business training. He'd been an athlete, a basketball player, shortly after the Soviet Union had disbanded. Playing in a Russian professional league had afforded him a princely living by Russian standards—but the money given to even individual American basketball stars would have run a small city in Russia. Maxim realized, however, that even if he had been willing to defect, he probably wasn't good enough for the National Basketball Association.

He had been approaching his last season when he was taken under the wing of the team's owner, an older man, very wealthy, with major interests in oil, timber, mining, and other raw materials. Maxim started working for him, and in a few years, Maxim was number three in the company. He was a quick study, and he had a kind of roguish charm, coupled with great height that had others looking up to him.

After a time, Maxim had grown impatient. The company was doing well, but Maxim was savvy enough to realize that the days of draining raw materials profitably were finite: timber was often inaccessible or threatened by fire or pests, mining was intensely competitive and hobbled by government strictures, and oil was subject to intense price fluctuations and ever more expensive to extract.

His boss, a fireplug of a man with a scruff of gray hair on his head, was obstinate and declined to consider Maxim's suggestion to turn more toward finance and real estate. When the old man said "*nyet*" once more, his brown eyes flashing in defiance, Maxim decided to resign and strike off on his own. He never looked back.

Soon afterward, he moved to London, where the Russian worked hard to ingratiate himself with major business and cultural groups. With his investments booming, he gave generously to local charities and to the arts, most often orchestras and the ballet. He did interviews and cultivated an image as a new arrival who was eager and ready to support the finer things in his adopted country. Some writers labeled him an oligarch, but he protested the term, which carried a kind of stain in his mind.

But the charities that he gave so generously to and the patrons he rubbed shoulders with never saw the other side of Maxim, the cruel, sometimes almost sadistic side. Just as he paid his people well, he expected—no, demanded—loyalty and obedience to his rules.

He remembered that he had summoned Anton Cherbinsky to his office later that afternoon. Cherbinsky had extorted a sizable sum from a developer of a new building in the London suburbs, something a member of Maxim's security group had uncovered a few days ago. Extortion might have been tolerated by some in Moscow but not in London.

Anton Cherbinsky walked into the office and glanced about. He gave off a hint of menace, almost like a cheap cologne; there was something in his eyes that hinted of danger, of latent brutishness. His suit bulged at the chest and the thighs.

"Good afternoon, Maxim," he said in heavily accented English. Maxim had made English the primary language of the company in Britain; it was different in Russia, where he had a few holdings.

"Welcome, Anton. Let's take a seat at the table," Maxim said, gesturing to a lovely mahogany conference table, polished to a high sheen, with a number of office chairs around it. The two sat down, and Cherbinsky looked at Maxim a bit nervously. It was clear Cherbinsky had no idea what this meeting was about.

"It's come to my attention," Maxim said slowly, "that you have taken money from a developer in Islington. Is this true?"

Cherbinsky's eyes went wild with fright, like a rabbit staring at a lynx with no means of escape. "I, I ... wanted to make sure they would recognize us as the high bidder. This—this is how we often had to do it in Moscow." His expression appealed for mercy.

"This is London, and what you did is unacceptable. And I think you know it. Moreover, it appears you kept the money for yourself."

Cherbinsky licked his lips, which had suddenly gone dry. "I will give it back," he said, his voice quavering.

"Oh, you will," Maxim said with a sneer. "But first you need to be taught a lesson." He motioned toward the other side of the room, where two burly men had entered quietly and were waiting for his command.

They sprang forward. One grabbed Cherbinsky from behind, wrapping his arms around Cherbinsky, who uttered a squeal of fright. The man's grip was immobilizing.

Maxim nodded, and the other man stood next to Cherbinsky and produced a rubber mallet.

"Anton, are you right-handed?" Maxim asked.

Cherbinsky squirmed to no avail.

"I'll ask you again—are you right-handed? I need an answer."

Cherbinsky snorted with fear. "Y-yes."

"Put his right hand on the table," Maxim said, as calmly as if he were ordering lunch.

The man with the mallet pulled Cherbinsky's right arm to the table as the other man adjusted his grip. Cherbinsky fought to pull the arm back, but it was no use.

Maxim nodded, and the mallet came down hard on the back of Cherbinsky's hand. The bones were surely shattered. The victim shrieked, an animal squeal of pain, and his head fell forward on the table with an audible thunk.

"Anton, this was regrettable, but you brought it on yourself," Maxim said. He glanced at the two lieutenants. "Take him out, wrap his hand, and put him back in his office. Then come back here. I may have another job for you."

Maxim turned back to the papers on his desk, more contracts to analyze. He liked to think of himself as simply a disciplinarian, no different from a nun in a black habit wielding a ruler to whack a mischievous schoolboy who threatened the order in the classroom. Object lessons had their place. Spread by word of mouth, by whispered asides and furtive emails, they kept the organization on the straight and narrow as much as it was possible in a world of possibilities where too many felt rules were meant to be bent.

CHAPTER 17

Once the jet reached cruising altitude, Corbin reclined his seat slightly in the first-class cabin and sighed. Sleep never came easily on a red-eye flight, and the travel pillow around his neck helped only slightly. The flight had left JFK, headed for London, at 10:45 p.m. Corbin had stayed in the city, having dinner with one from his executive team before the company car picked him up and ferried him to the airport.

A flight attendant, a young brunette with a warm smile, got to his row. "Can I get you a beverage?" she asked, meeting his eyes with trained friendliness.

"Yes, I'll have a whiskey and soda, Jack Daniel's if you have it."

"Certainly, sir. And would you care for a snack?"

He'd looked at the list of available food earlier and knew he wanted to keep it light. "I think I'll just have a package of the biscuits," he said.

"Very good. I'll have those to you shortly."

Corbin bit his lip softly. A call to Ned Turner earlier that day had brought bad news: Turner had just been diagnosed with stage four renal cancer and was being treated near his home in Westchester. There would be no meeting about the

MOMA board, perhaps ever. Corbin had no plan B at this point; he'd have to work on one.

He managed a few hours of restless sleep on the remainder of the flight, ragged stretches of somnolence interrupted regularly by twitching in his legs, which caused him to shift positions. The seat, now fully reclined, was comfortable enough, and the cabin was in semidarkness—all to the good— but Corbin had never fully slept on these flights, and he assumed this would be no exception. And he was right.

The plane taxied into the gate at Heathrow as gingerly as an old woman using a walker. Dawn had come but with no rosy fanfare; it was a gloomy day, and he saw the tarmac was wet. He deplaned quickly, one huge benefit of first class, and followed the signs for customs. A car would be waiting for him; he checked his messages and saw one describing the car he should look for. With his coat under his arm, he rolled the overnight bag behind him and tried to imagine what the day at Whitehall would bring.

The lobby at the Savoy looked as it always did, and Corbin had to smile. The hotel was so veddy British, top hat and tails and high tea with crumpets, and had been for what seemed like millennia. Corbin loved to soak in the atmosphere and recall all the royalty and the celebrities who had walked these carpets over the years. Staying here was yet another of his perks, and it appealed to him more than the Intercontinental, a brand he often used, and was relatively close to the bank's headquarters.

As a favored guest, he was able to check in early and make his way to his room on the fifth floor. It was a small suite, his usual, and he made for the bed. He'd try to get a couple of hours' sleep before he was due to be picked up and taken to Whitehall. Corbin suddenly felt his eyes droop, and after stripping down to his underwear, he pulled back the covers and climbed in. He set the alarm on his phone and, yawning hard, fell back into a deep sleep.

The chauffeur tipped his cap to Corbin and opened the car door for him. Corbin had made it down to the lobby promptly at ten-thirty and walked outside to see the car and driver waiting, always a good sign. *The British might not be much at cuisine,* he thought to himself, *but they know how to be punctual.*

Young and sandy-haired, the driver leaned down as Corbin got in and asked, "Going to headquarters, sir?" He wore a black suit and a matching cap, and his hair flared out from under the cap like the hem of a skirt.

"Yes, I am."

"Very good. It shouldn't be much more than ten minutes. Please just sit back and relax."

Traffic wasn't heavy, but the driver had to negotiate a series of turns that slowed their progress. Corbin's mind went to the daily crawl he faced going down Park Avenue; compared to that, this was a picnic. After about ten minutes, the car pulled up outside the glass tower, and the driver opened the rear door for Corbin.

"Many thanks," Corbin said as he stepped onto the sidewalk.

"Happy to be of service, sir." The driver smiled and walked back to his door.

Corbin walked in through the revolving doors and across the marbled lobby to the main desk, a mahogany edifice that would have left a hole in a rain forest somewhere. A pert young woman, a brunette, held court. She smiled as he walked up. "Good morning. What can I do for you, sir?"

"Good morning. I'm Corbin van Sloot. I'm expected on the twenty-eighth floor."

She looked down briefly at something on the desk. "Oh,

certainly, sir. The elevators are—"

She was pointing when Corbin gently interrupted her. "I know where they are. Thank you."

The elevators were staggered, with floors one to nine in one elevator, ten to twenty-five in another, and twenty-six to thirty, the main executive floors, in a third. He walked into the third elevator alone, admiring the polished brass accents on the wall, and pushed the button for floor twenty-eight.

When he arrived at the boardroom, large and well-appointed with Chinese ginger jars in each corner, a dozen executives, all in suits except two women, were grouped around the table. Corbin took a seat in the middle of the table, facing the windows, where the Thames appeared outside as a ribbon of gray between two tall office buildings. There were only a few smiles and no obvious bonhomie; this would be a somber meeting to discuss the succession plan for Sir Reginald, who, if he survived, was in a position to resume his duties.

In general, the tenor of the meeting was soft-spoken, ordered, and on point; there were none of the distractions, the showboating, the circular discussion of topics he might have expected in his own boardroom in New York. The British lived up to their reputation for decorum.

Much of the proceeding seemed interminable to Corbin. A piece of paper was handed to each person around the table, with a grid for ranking each candidate on a five-point scale as well as a space for ample comments. Corbin was excused from the exercise, though he had the sheet in front of him, which prompted him to doodle a bit on the blank side as the others entered their rankings.

When all the sheets were in, Thomas Ransom, the deputy director, second-in-command in London to Sir Reginald, led a discussion about each of two of the three leading candidates; he was the third and excused himself for that discussion. He was particularly interested, he said, in any negative experiences anyone had had with the other pair, David Robertson, the chief loan officer, and Frederick Frost, the chief financial officer.

"Thank you all," Ransom said a bit loudly when the meeting was ending. "I've asked Diana here"—he gestured toward one of the two women in the room—"to head the evaluation process, and she has told me she has selected three of you to assist. The goal is to reconvene this group tomorrow morning and review the results, then vote by secret ballot." He paused and looked at Corbin. "We certainly hope you will join us again, Corbin." Ransom looked at Corbin almost imploringly.

"Of course," Corbin said with a nod.

"Very well, then. Until 9:00 a.m. tomorrow, all." The meeting broke up quickly and quietly, and the group gathered outside the elevators, as silent as if they had secrets they didn't want to share.

The same young chap reappeared early the next afternoon to take Corbin back to the Savoy to check out. Once again, a black Vauxhall sat by the curb, with the driver leaning on the hood with an air of perfect nonchalance. Corbin strode up and smiled at the driver. "Ready?" Corbin asked.

"Yes, sir." The driver moved quickly to open the door and let Corbin in. "To the hotel, sir?"

"Yes. I just need to get my luggage, and then we'll head for Heathrow, right?"

"Certainly. There will be some traffic going out there, of course. What time is your flight, if I may ask?"

"Four-thirty."

"Well, we should be there in plenty of time, but you never know." He shrugged and went to the driver's door. "The roads can be a bit bollixed these days."

"Of course." Corbin leaned back and set his mind working.

As he expected, Robertson, the less controversial choice for chairman, had been chosen. The CFO post was clearly more important, which might have been a factor in the vote. But he was pleased; Robertson was more likely to be a partner, less likely to challenge the American side.

And there were benefits to this dual-country approach, he mused, such as the loan to Star Enterprises. It had come from London, and it had died in London. Corbin could wash his hands of it and of Winston Crumm. The *Star* would never get another loan from Whitehall as long as Corbin had any say in the matter.

CHAPTER 18

"Hello, dear." Adrienne accepted a peck on the cheek from Winston, who had just walked in from a day at the office. She was reading a paperback novel, perched on the cream-colored sofa with the floor-to-ceiling windows behind her open to a view that not a few would kill for: Central Park and the soaring towers of Gotham, to so many the epicenter of anything that was worth anything in this world.

"Whew." Winston blew out a breath. "I think I need some coffee." He sauntered to the kitchen. He was in a good mood. He had talked at length to Jackson, his principal financial advisor, and had started the ball in motion on a major charitable donation to a charter school in Harlem that Adrienne had embraced as a cause. Winston smiled; he'd be able to tell her about the gift. It was of little consequence to him, but he sensed it would be a sturdy signpost on the road to continued domestic bliss.

Adrienne heard her phone buzz and checked to see the message icon. It was from her daughter, Amanda, a freshman at Swarthmore. Amanda and one of her roommates, a fellow New Yorker named Gigi, had been arrested two weeks earlier during a climate change demonstration in Philadelphia. Adrienne had raced down there and bailed them out. Now, according to this text, a publication had gotten wind of the arrest and published a bare-bones piece about it.

Winston returned wearing khakis and a long-sleeved polo shirt; his belly bulged. "What's for dinner, sweetie?"

"I believe it's veal scallopini," she said, fixing her eyes on him. "Now, come sit down. There's something I need to tell you." She fiddled idly with the deep-blue pendant that hung around her neck.

He recoiled slightly in mock horror. "Do I need to call the lawyer?" He grinned.

She wasn't smiling. "No, but you need to hear me out."

He sensed this was important. "Okay." He sat down in the armchair nearest the sofa.

Adrienne folded her hands. "Amanda just texted me. It seems there was an item published in the *Scoop* about something that happened a couple of weeks ago in Philadelphia."

"The *Scoop*?" Winston knew it was one of Martin Hargreaves's magazines, a satirical weekly run, Winston was certain, by liberal Ivy Leaguers who loved to skewer people like him.

"Yes. They found out that she had been arrested at a climate change demonstration along with her friend Gigi."

"What?" Winston's voice went up an octave.

Adrienne bowed her head briefly. "It's true. I drove down there and bailed them out. I ... I didn't know how to tell you. I thought this would just go away, but obviously, someone there found out about it."

Winston gaped at her like a koi waiting for a morsel. "And they published something? What does it say?" His voice had only gotten louder.

"I don't know. I haven't seen it. She apparently has."

Winston leaned back in the chair. "Why ... so why didn't you tell me about this arrest?" He felt his face flush.

"Like I said, I didn't know how, and I thought you'd react

like this."

He pulled at his lip. "Well, if this is true, we can't very well deny it—or sue them for libel."

She was silent, then said, "No, no we can't."

"Well. Damn it all anyway," he said. "What was the charge when she was arrested?"

Adrienne proceeded to tell him the sequence of events as best she knew them. She emphasized that this was a fluke, almost more of a misunderstanding than anything, not an assault on a police officer. Amanda had simply tugged at his arm after he grabbed Gigi; it was an innocent reaction.

Winston seemed only slightly mollified. "We're paying for her education, not for going to demonstrations. And climate change? How did she get onto that?"

She leaned back. "It seems it was Gigi's thing, and she got Amanda to come along. Amanda told me that Gigi goes to a lot of demonstrations—"

"Probably never for capitalism," Winston interjected.

He saw the corners of Adrienne's mouth turn up slightly. "No, probably not. Young people are idealistic. I remember going to a couple when I was in college. But I was more of a bystander than anything, and I was certainly never arrested."

Winston harrumphed. The idea of taking part in a demonstration was as foreign to him as listening to a TED talk. What to do? He thought he'd reach out to McCloskey in the morning, have him on call if Winston felt he needed his pit bull to go after someone. But Hargreaves? He was an intellectual prince in the city, someone who rubbed elbows with the elite at the *Times* and the *New York Review of Books*. Suing him didn't seem like a good idea.

"Hmmm. Well, I wish we knew what the story said," Winston mused.

"I got the impression it was just a short, gossipy item," she offered.

"Okay, I guess I'll deal with it tomorrow." He put his hand

on his chin and smiled wanly at her. "Let's have dinner and try to forget about it, but I want to make it clear to her, no more demonstrations. Kaput. Are we agreed?"

"Yes, yes," she said. She nodded at him and made direct eye contact. "We agree."

Winston sat watching TV, but his mind drifted to his own family, his first family. He had only passing contact these days with Christine, his first wife. Theirs had been anything but an amicable divorce, and three years after the ink had dried, she had married a hedge fund manager and moved to Greenwich. All photos of her, a chic and pretty blonde with a radiant smile, had disappeared, as if she'd been abducted by aliens.

His children were only marginally more in his life. April, his daughter in Massachusetts, sent him a birthday card and a Christmas card every year and would call him on Father's Day, but the calls were brief, and she offered little about her life and her work. His son, Cary, was even more uncommunicative. Now and then, Winston would reach out to him, but Cary rarely fielded the calls and seldom called back.

Winston found this sad and confounding. What had he done to deserve such rejection? Hadn't he been a good and dutiful father, paying for music lessons and braces and sending them to the best schools? Both had no children—Cary was single—but Winston wondered at times if he would ever know whatever grandchildren might arrive. He felt an occasional twinge of something like jealousy, thinking of happy, smiling grandparents, the stuff of so many sappy TV ads, and their ability to dote on their grandchildren. It was something he might never know.

Amanda was different. He felt closer to her, more in her orbit. She would confide in him, seek out his advice. Thanks to Adrienne, who insisted on inclusion, they did things together as a family. Winston wasn't always eager to do so, but he went along; he had come to realize how important those bonds were. He would chide Amanda about the arrest, he thought to himself, but nothing more. He couldn't afford to push her away.

The intercom in his office buzzed again. "Mr. Crumm," Deana said. "Remember that you're meeting in an hour with the finance group in the main boardroom."

"Oh, right. Thanks for the reminder."

Winston looked forward to this meeting like a proctology exam. It had been convened to talk about cuts to staff, general expenses, and maybe even circulation. The water wasn't exactly circling the drain yet, but the signs were ominous. The Whitehall loan had disappeared, and the banks in the city were treating Star Enterprises like a leper with an open sore on its forehead. *What's next?* He thought grimly. He wasn't about to let his baby, the fruit of his family's loins, waste away, and he *certainly* wasn't going to condone a sale. There had to be an answer.

CHAPTER 19

He sat on her couch and caressed her face and stroked her hair. Larissa smiled, and he leaned in to kiss her neck and take in her perfume. Life was good.

"I love my time with you," Corbin said, and he meant it. "You're important to me. I guess that sounds corny, but it's true."

She smiled beguilingly. "And you're important to me too," she murmured.

They sipped their wine and nuzzled for a while. The TV was on, tuned into some detective drama. They paid it no more attention than the car horns occasionally blaring in the street. They had eaten in, and the dishes had been put on the kitchen island. Pieter would soon be parked on the corner, waiting, probably eating a sandwich from Subway. It always smelled like an Italian deli when Corbin got into the car for the ride home.

The predictable ballet began. Larissa took his hand, and they walked slowly to the bedroom. They each took off their clothes, down to their underwear, and laid them on the nearby chair. Then they sat on the bed and kissed. Corbin put his hand down the cleavage of her bra and stroked her right breast; she put her hand in the opening in the front of his boxers and stroked his member, which was already stiffening nicely. She reached back and unhooked her bra, and he took it in his hand and tossed it on the chair.

Four minutes later, they were going at it with gusto. Larissa was straddling him, her body arching over his. They both moaned in delight.

Fifteen feet away, almost invisible unless someone was hunting for it, was a very small button-like device mounted on the wall, just below a painting. It was aimed directly at the bed, and the field of focus was wide enough to take in everything they were doing. The resulting images would make it indelibly clear who was involved. It wasn't the first time the spy camera, linked wirelessly to a computer monitor many blocks away, had been on, and it wouldn't be the last.

CHAPTER 20

The crawler on the screen announced that a major earthquake had struck Iran and that there were hundreds dead. The news flew through Winston's mind in a brief second; it was just one of those things that happened out there in the world. There would be a brief wire service story in the *Star* the next day, the obligatory update, probably with a photo of poor villagers staring forlornly at a broken building. Such was life.

He was more interested in the main screen, which he was watching from his office desk. The Fox News anchors were talking about the upcoming election and touting the Republican talking points. Winston was a big fan of Fox, unlike the journalists in the newsroom; if they had anything on, it would be CNN.

The intercom beeped. "Mr. Crumm, you have a call from a Mr. Ridovsky, I think he said it was."

"Who?"

"He said it was about supporting the *Star*."

"Oh, really?" Winston wasn't sure what that meant. "Alright, put him through."

"Mr. Crumm?"

"Speaking."

"My name is Maxim Ripovsky. You don't know me, but I have a proposition for you and the *Star*." The accent was clearly European. If Winston had been savvier, he would have pegged it as Russian.

"A proposition?"

"Yes, that's what I would call it." There was a pause. "I hear it on good authority that Star Enterprises is in serious need of cash."

"Why would you think that?" Winston immediately started playing defense, like a tennis player trying to conceal a weak backhand.

"I have my sources, Mr. Crumm. I am in a position to advance the company a goodly sum of money if we can come to an understanding." His accent was a bit hard to decipher at times, but his command of English was excellent.

"An understanding, you say?" Winston had his antennae up. What was this all about?

"Yes. I understand that a loan from Whitehall was called and that Star has a serious cash crunch. I'm prepared to make a considerable investment, but, of course, with some conditions. Perhaps we could meet for lunch and we could discuss it."

Winston quickly went into hardball mode, ready to call his bluff. "I have no idea who you are, Mr. Ripovsky, was it? This sounds like some kind of hoax to me." He harrumphed for emphasis.

"I assure you it isn't," Ripovsky said firmly. "I'm a Russian with a very large fortune who is making investments in the United States: Miami, Los Angeles, and, of course, New York. I have bought a number of companies and buildings. I currently have five homes around the world. I assure you this is—how you say?—on the level."

Winston gasped. Could this be a savior? How could it hurt to do lunch? He chewed briefly on his lip. "What kinds of conditions are we talking about?"

"That would be part of our conversation. I suggest lunch at the Four Seasons when it's suitable for you. Please have your secretary call mine, and we can arrange something. Do you have a pen? Let me give you a number."

Winston reached for a pen from the black ceramic mug on his desk. "Okay, shoot."

Winston, who usually went on his gut, wasn't sure what to make of this overture, but he put the phone number under a paperweight where he kept important memos. This could be the Hail Mary he'd been hoping for.

The maître d' led Winston along the flagstone floor toward a table for four against the far wall. The lights from the high ceiling, with its architectural scaffolding of metal rods, lit the interior brightly on a gray and windy day. Winston looked around as they walked; he saw Martin Hargreaves at a far table, deep in conversation with someone he didn't recognize. Hargreaves didn't see him, which was just fine with Winston.

They approached a table with two people seated facing them; one appeared to be a tall man with dark hair combed back from a high forehead, and the other was a blonde woman, seeming equally tall, in a cream-colored sheath dress.

The two stood up as he approached and was ushered to one of the Four Seasons' plush dining chairs. The man extended his hand and said, "Mr. Crumm? Delighted to meet you. I'm Maxim Ripovsky, and this is my associate, Natasha."

Winston was taken aback. He wasn't a small man, but both towered over him like third-graders over a kindergartner. "Hi, I'm Winston. Nice to meet you both," he said, extending his hand in turn. Ripovsky's hand was slim with very long fingers—and hers felt very similar. He was intimidated.

"What I propose," Ripovsky said, "is that we enjoy our lunch and not rush into the business end of things right away. After all"—he swept his arm toward the rest of the room—"if we can't enjoy the surroundings, what is the point of coming here?"

"Not much, I guess," Winston replied, forcing a grin. "I haven't been here in a while, but it doesn't change much."

"No, indeed not." Ripovsky smiled. "And of course, this lunch is on me—"

Winston remonstrated, "I can certainly pay my share, but if you truly insist—"

"I do. So, I suggest we study the menu and order. Then we can talk shop, as you Americans say."

"Sounds good to me."

Winston spread the menu in front of him and found his eyes moving between it and the pair in front of him. Ripovsky wore what seemed to be an elegant gray suit with subtle pinstriping, with a light-blue shirt and a dark tie flecked with a red pattern. And Natasha—he'd have to keep reminding himself not to stare. She wasn't classically beautiful, but she had a round, almost sculpted face, a blonde pageboy cut evenly across her forehead, and piercing gray eyes over a wide, unsmiling mouth. He found her, well, imposing. Was she wearing high heels, or was she really that damned tall?

They murmured to each other in what appeared to be Russian as they studied the menu. This put Winston even more at unease, and Ripovsky seemed to sense that. He smiled and said, "I'm sorry, Mr. Crumm. We're so used to talking in our native language."

"Of course." Winston smiled back. "And please, call me Winston."

"Certainly," Ripovsky said and smiled widely. He had a long, aquiline nose and small ears set close to his head, and his deep-set eyes were dark, almost as dark as his hair. It was a face that proclaimed watchfulness, not friendliness. "And you can call me Max."

Winston suddenly felt a pang of renewed inferiority. Not only did this Russian speak excellent English, but he wore what seemed to be an impeccably tailored suit. Winston, on the other hand, had on one of the half-dozen suits he had bought years ago from Moshe Tannenbaum in the Garment District at a hell of a discount. Its boxy shoulders said "nineties."

Ten minutes later, after the waiter had taken their order, Ripovsky folded his long arms and set his hands on the table. "I'm sure you're very curious about what I'm prepared to offer," he said, fixing Winston with an unwavering gaze.

Winston nodded. "I sure am."

Ripovsky put a hand to his chin. "Do you know who I am? I mean—were you curious enough to do some research?"

"No; no, I didn't," Winston said softly. "I didn't know how to spell your name—"

"Oh, of course." Ripovsky grinned and bent his head slightly to one side. "Well, let me give you a very short history so that you understand what I could do for you." He proceeded to tell him about his joining the team owner's company and rising to number three before he struck out on his own. He paused frequently as he spoke, fixing his eyes on Winston; he talked, uninterrupted, for close to fifteen minutes. Winston was caught up in the tale like a child hearing a bedtime story.

"Very impressive," Winston said when Ripovsky seemed to be done, feeling he had to say something complimentary.

Ripovsky waved his hand. "I'm not boasting, merely giving you—"

Just then the waiter, an older man in a tight-fitting white jacket, rolled up the cart with their meals. He expertly set each dish in front of them, then asked, "Is there anything else you might like?" He looked at Ripovsky.

"No, no. Thank you very much." The waiter nodded quickly, spun on his heels, and strode away.

"Now, Winston, I suggest we enjoy this lunch. I'll pick up after we are finished." He looked expectantly at his Dover sole. Natasha had ordered a salad, a tuna niçoise, while Winston had ordered a lunch-portion ribeye, rare, with garlic mashed potatoes.

"Bon appétit," Ripovsky said with a smile. Winston grinned gamely and picked up his fork.

After the plates were cleared and Ripovsky had ordered an espresso—Winston had declined coffee—Ripovsky resumed his narrative. He had urged his benefactor to branch out, he said, into real estate and technology and away from raw materials, which the Chinese were ruthlessly scouring for around the world. The older man had rejected Ripovsky's advice, so he formed a new company and reached out for other, younger Russians who shared his vision. That was ten years ago.

Now and then, Winston's eyes went to Natasha. She leaned gracefully in her chair to look at Ripovksy as he talked. Her straight blonde hair fell to her shoulders. Every now and then, she swept her hair past her ears with her long arms in what seemed like a practiced move.

Since that time, Ripovsky said, he had moved from Moscow to London and made it his new base of operations. He had named his company Rubicon Investments and expanded its reach into Southeast Asia, Australia, and the US. He was a major investor, he said, in several large technology companies and had bought a number of commercial and residential properties, "trophy properties," he said with a thin smile, on each continent.

"If I can interrupt, what do you have here in New York?" Winston asked.

Ripovsky mentioned three different addresses, two on Fifth Avenue and one on Sixth, none of which Winston recognized. But he should have realized that Ripovsky was an oligarch, the new breed of Russian power player, men who enjoyed the trappings of power and wealth and moved about the world as easily as a bird flits from tree to tree, albeit on private jets. While most tried to stay out of the limelight, others flaunted their influence and their connections to the highest levels of the Russian government.

"And so," Ripovsky said, "now that you know more about me, let's talk business. I've probably talked too much here, but I wanted to make it clear that I have a lot of resources at my disposal." He paused and looked intently at Winston. "And I'm prepared to help you—or, better put, your company—out."

So now the cards would be laid on the table. "Well, I'm certainly willing to listen," Winston said, trying to sound noncommittal.

"This is what I propose. I will advance Star Enterprises $10 million this week, with an additional $10 million in sixty days if my conditions are met. I think you'll find this will essentially compensate for the loan that was withdrawn by Whitehall. And there will be no interest charged; this is an investment, not a loan."

Winston was stunned, both by the offer and the knowledge Ripovsky seemed to have of the company's financial hole.

"Very generous," Winston managed to say. "But—but how did you know about the Whitehall loan?"

"As I said, I live in London most of the time," Ripovsky said, smiling. "And my people are very thorough and very professional in what they do."

"I guess they are," Winston murmured and smiled weakly at Natasha, who looked at him impassively. "So, what are these conditions?"

"Well, first of all, this must not come back to me. I have a number of shell companies, one of which will be making this investment by wire transfer. I'm told that you're not really running the day-to-day operations, which may make things easier. If your financial people are curious about where this came from, you can tell them you don't know. But in any case, they need to accept it. Given your financial situation, that shouldn't be that difficult."

"I see." Cloak and dagger, something Winston had a hard time getting his ample head around.

"Secondly, I'd like to place some full-page ads in the *Star* for my real estate holdings, especially the residential ones. Nice photos, elegant. I want to expand my—what?—beachhead here. Advertisements in your newspaper would help. And, for all I would be doing, I would expect those ads would be free."

"I—I don't run the advertising area ..."

Ripovsky's smile took on a more sinister cast. "No, but I'm sure you can exert your influence. Remember, this is one of my conditions."

"Right, right," Winston murmured, swirling the water in his glass.

"And the last condition may be the easiest one. I'd like you to arrange a charity function for me and my company to get introduced to important people here."

Again, Winston demurred. "I—I don't do those kinds of things ..."

"No, I'm sure not. But I think your wife does." Ripovsky sat back. "She's a famous designer, and I'm sure she can put together a list of people."

Winston bobbed his head. "I'm sure she could," he said slowly.

"I'd like to do something next month, before your Thanksgiving holiday," Ripovsky said. "There should be enough time to arrange that, I think."

Winston shrugged. "Yeah, I guess so. I can talk to Adrienne, but I don't want to tell her about the money."

"No, certainly not. Tell her you've met me, and I'm a friend of the arts who wants to make a major contribution. Let her choose the charity she wants this directed to." He leaned forward with his arms on the table.

"Okay."

Ripovsky sipped his espresso. "Well, then, I think we can do business, Winston. You have my secretary's number if you have any questions." He extended his hand. "Thank you for meeting with me. I'll pick up the check, of course."

Winston shook his hand and nodded at Natasha, who nodded back. He realized this was his cue to leave. He gave a quick wave as he walked away and realized that Natasha, who hadn't said a word to him the entire time, had left quite an impression as exotic, almost, as an alien with green scales and a set of ferocious-looking teeth.

CHAPTER 21

"It would be a huge favor for me, sweetie. This guy's company is going to make a major investment in the *Star* at a time when we really need it." He leaned forward imploringly and saw confusion in Adrienne's eyes.

"I don't know, Winston. These things aren't that easy to arrange." She looked at him with puzzlement. "And you say he's Russian?"

"Yes."

"What's his name?"

"Maxim Ripovsky."

She snorted. "Ripovksy? Is that some kind of joke?"

"No, no, not at all. He's legit, owns companies and properties around the world."

"But Ripovsky, like 'rip-off'? That's rich." Her brown eyes flashed.

Winston scratched his cheek. "I hadn't looked at it that way. But—but he's the real deal. I had lunch with him today. He's new to New York and wants to get his name around, though he doesn't want his name tied to this money he's giving us."

"Well, if it's that important, I can make a call to the Cosmopolitan Club and see what they have available in November. Then I can enlist some of my friends to help me get the ball rolling." She paused. "And you say I can designate any charity or charities?"

"Absolutely. That was our deal." He tried to rein in his enthusiasm. "And we can play up his companies and his properties more than his name."

She chuckled. "That makes sense."

"Great, just great. I'm leaving it in your hands. You know how to make these things work." He beamed.

She smiled slightly, a bud getting ready to flower. "Just know that this will take a while. And—and I assume Star will take care of the costs, the room rental, invitations, food, help, flowers, and all that?"

"Of course, of course. I'll write the checks myself." He tilted his head and frowned. "How much do these things cost, anyway?"

"I'm honestly not sure," she said with a shrug. "I guess we'll find out."

It was at eight-thirty the next morning, as Winston strolled out to the car, when he saw a figure, dressed in a black overcoat and a dark-blue baseball cap, leaning down. The figure, which seemed to be a man, was looking at something on the ground in front of him. He thought immediately about an incident the week before when an investment banker for Goldman Sachs had been shot as he was leaving his apartment building. He'd survived but the gunman had escaped, and the motive was a complete mystery to the police.

Winston's heart went to his throat. With his eyes darting between the figure and the car, he shuffled quickly to the car door and jumped in.

"What's wrong, boss?" George asked, puzzled, as Winston cowered in the back seat.

"See that guy in the black coat by the building? What is he doing?" Winston asked. There was a note of near-panic in his voice.

George craned his head to look. "He's opening his backpack or something like that. Looks like a homeless guy."

"Is that all?" Winston sat up slightly and looked out the window.

"Yeah, seems harmless enough," George said. "Poor guy. Gotta be hard on the streets with winter coming."

"Yeah, you're right," Winston said. He looked more closely, and the figure was taking some kind of food wrapper out of his pack and sitting against the building. "Hard to be on the streets." He sighed with obvious relief, but then he realized with genuine annoyance that he had gotten jumpy, lost his cool. The world now had an element of danger that was both new and troubling.

Three days later, on a Friday, Winston was in his office reading the *Star*, though he rarely read it with much real interest, apart from the sports pages. He took a sip of his coffee, sweetened with milk and two packets of sugar.

The phone rang, and Winston saw it was Larry Ahearn, the chief operating officer. "What's up, Larry?"

"Winston, this is incredible. We just had $10 million wired into our main Chase account." His rich baritone seemed to have gone up a notch.

"What?" Winston feigned incredulity and thought he had done it well. "For real?"

"Oh, for real. We're trying to determine the source, but it seems to be from an offshore account, tied to something called Tyne Investments."

"Never heard of it."

"Neither have I, but it appears to be legitimate. This is amazing; we need to verify it, of course, but it would be a tremendous windfall at a time when we really, really need it."

"What d'you think? Is this some investment group willing to back us?"

"I don't know, Winston; I don't know." He sounded perplexed. "We should know more later in the day. But as I say, this seems to be real money, and it would allow us to stave off some of our layoffs and do some important capital investments. I've asked Susan to run some numbers on just what it could do for us."

"This is great, Larry, just great. Keep me posted."

"Oh, I will."

Winston hung up and leaned back in his chair with a smile that would have put the Cheshire cat to shame. Ripovsky had come through, just as he said he would, Winston thought. Things were definitely looking up. He pressed the intercom.

"Deana, I'd like you to book a table for two at Le Midi for lunch today. Any time they have."

"I'm on it," she replied.

Winston dialed Adrienne's office. "Sweetie," he said when she answered, "I want to take you to lunch. As soon as I have a time, I'll let you know, and we'll swing by and pick you up."

"Fine, Winston. This isn't a particularly busy day. What— can I ask what the occasion is?"

"I'll tell you over lunch. But I need to call you back with a time when I know."

"Okay. Where are we going?"

"It's a surprise."

"Well, then, I'll be prepared to be surprised."

Back at his desk, the captivating flavor of the steak *au poivre* from lunch was still in Winston's mouth. He was reading through the sports section of the *Star* when the phone rang again, and he saw it was Ahearn.

"Hi, Larry. Any news?"

"Well, it's pretty mysterious; we really don't know who

our secret benefactor is. We did ascertain that the account is registered in Guernsey, which is a big tax haven and a place for a lot of offshore accounts. But Tyne Investments is an enigma—a Google search goes nowhere."

"Huh. Well, as you say, the money is real, right?

"Yes, it is. We ... we'd love to know more. If this is a vehicle for a big investor or investment group, we'd like to announce it in the press. It gives Star more legitimacy, a vote of confidence. But we don't want to invite questions we can't answer."

"Sure, I guess not." Winston knew he couldn't reveal anything about Ripovsky; that was one of the conditions.

"We'll try to find out more next week. But for the meantime, we have to consider this an unexpected gift. I ... I really don't know what else to call it."

"Gift is right," Winston said. "A big, beautiful one."

"Seems that way." Larry paused. "But wonderful news. Enjoy your weekend, Winston. Too late in the year for the boat?"

Winston couldn't recall Ahearn ever asking him a personal question. "Actually, it is, by a couple of weeks. The captain has taken it down to Boca."

"Of course."

"Enjoy your weekend too, Larry. I know I'm gonna sleep better tonight."

"I think we all will."

CHAPTER 22

Bob Mandell was in a mild funk, and he'd been marinating in it for some time. He'd been chided for a silly mistake, something he had simply not fact-checked thoroughly, which he'd made a few days ago that had required his newspaper, the *Financial Times*, to run a correction.

But that was Bob, thinking of himself first and foremost. At best, that manifested itself in self-confidence, even bonhomie, when things were good and he saw himself atop the anthill. The flip side of the coin were cafards, sullen stretches of despair when the world seemed stacked against him, when stories didn't pan out, sources dried up, or others in the newsroom seemed to be pulling ahead of him in the endless horse race that defines big-time journalism.

But the race had turned in his favor. As a veteran financial reporter seasoned in the New York trenches, Bob had been able to pull off something of a professional coup. Less than four months earlier, he'd been a stalwart at the *Wall Street Journal*, reporting on major banks and investment banks—and not on the quotidian dross of earnings reports and tedious presentations from preening analysts that were dumped on lesser reporters. Nope. He did longer company profiles and interviews with CEOs and other top executives, and now and then was sprung for investigative pieces that smacked of fraud or skullduggery.

Now he'd been recruited by the *Financial Times* as a star for their American market. They'd given him a lot of latitude to set his own agenda, though not exactly *carte blanche*, truth be told. He'd be able to work on longer stories at his own pace, reporting to a deputy editor with considerable clout. The Midtown office was considerably smaller than that of the *Journal* but was well-appointed and less hectic, and it suited him. He was in a cubicle, sure, but it was a large one, larger than most, which assuaged his ego.

Not that Bob Mandell had any outsized cause for vanity. He was a small man, no more than five-foot-five, with the boyish frame of a twelve-year-old. He had a pinched, birdlike face with large, dark eyes and a beaky nose that he was often blowing into a silk handkerchief. His hair, now turning white, had been retreating for years like the ice sheets in Greenland. His voice was high-pitched and nasal; some said it reminded them of the old cartoon magpies Heckle and Jeckle. Colleagues joked behind his back that he was a cross between Richard Dreyfuss and a stork.

Bob had earned an economics degree from NYU, which had proved a great springboard into the churning pool of financial journalism; his first job had been at *Newsday*, covering general business on Long Island, until the *Journal* snatched him away. But few outside his immediate circle knew that he was first-generation, that his father and family had fled Germany a hastily arranged step ahead of the Gestapo.

High blood pressure was a curse of the Mandells, and Bob had it in spades; he'd been on medication for many years. It didn't help that he was notoriously quick to anger. Many who'd worked with him had witnessed his outbursts, seen his veins bulge and his face turn purplish with rage. "He has the lowest boiling point of any human I've ever met," one former editor had said. But his temper hadn't cratered his career; in many journalistic circles, fits of rage, as long as they were only occasional, were often viewed as merely a mild downside to genius.

Genius? Bob loved the word, aspired to hear it resounding in his ears. He was fundamentally a big game hunter, pursuing the big story, the award-winning foray into subjects and people that made a difference in the way his readers saw the world. Then he was an illustrator of sorts, connecting the dots and showing people a canvas they'd never seen before.

He did almost all his writing at the office, unlike some journalists who labored on feature stories at home. But home to Bob was a one-bedroom apartment on the Upper West Side that he'd been in for more than twenty years. It was as unkempt as bachelor apartments often are, with newspapers and magazines strewn in untidy piles, the detritus of someone who saved things, like clippings, and promptly dismissed them. He had a top-notch computer there, but the apartment was his burrow, his place to relax, listen to jazz, and read. It was not a place to work.

The phone rang, and Bob, who was writing a straightforward story about a bank merger in the Southeast, glanced at it quickly. He didn't recognize the number.

"Hello, this is Bob Mandell."

"Hello, Mr. Mandell. You don't know me. I've admired your work in the *Journal* over the years, and I thought you'd be the person in the press I should reach out to."

"Well, thank you for the compliment. What can I do for you?" Bob's curiosity was aroused.

"First of all, this has to be on background. I don't want to give you my name for publication. I really just want to point you in the right direction, and since you've been covering banking for so long, you seem like the logical contact."

"Okay, then we're off the record." Curiouser and curiouser.

"Well, I'm a senior finance person at Star Enterprises, which publishes the *Star*."

"I'm familiar with the *Star*," Bob said quickly. "Mr. Crumm has been in the news lately."

"This isn't about him." The caller paused. "The company has been struggling, and a working capital loan we had from Whitehall Banking Group was called a couple of months ago. We're in a pretty deep financial hole."

"It's a tough time in the newspaper business," Bob said, trying to inject a note of sympathy.

"It truly is." The man had a light tenor voice, unaccented. "Well, lo and behold, we had a major windfall come in last week, a $10 million investment."

"That sounds wonderful."

"Oh, it is, but—the source is a mystery of sorts. It came via a wire transfer from an entity based in Guernsey, you know, the British tax haven. We have the name of the company, but we can find nothing about them. They're not listed anywhere."

Bob stroked his chin. "Interesting. What's their name?"

"Tyne Investments, *t-y-n-e*."

"That's not a name I've ever heard of either." He scratched his knee. "What is it you think I could do?"

"I'm hoping you could run down the company and see who's behind it. Guernsey is one of those Wild West places where almost anyone could register, Saudis, Israelis, Russians, whatever. I suspect Tyne is a shell company since it doesn't seem to officially exist. While the money is by all appearances legitimate, and there are no strings attached that we know of, this could be a power play by some foreign entity."

"Uh-huh." Bob's mind worked. "Remind me, are you a public company?"

"No, entirely private. Crumm and his family essentially control it."

"So, this investor isn't interested in voting shares. Do—do you think Crumm was approached by someone from Tyne or whoever they are?"

"Anything's possible at this point. He claims not to know about it and to be pleasantly surprised." He sighed audibly. "It was a handshake deal between Crumm and the Whitehall chairman in London a few years ago that garnered that original loan. But then that man, Sir Reginald Downing, had a stroke a couple of months ago. He's since died, and the bank decided to call the loan."

"I do remember reading about his death. And there were no other banks willing to step in?"

He snorted lightly. "Hardly. I'm almost ashamed to say it, but Star is as popular with lenders as a skunk at a ladies' social."

Bob blew out a breath. "This is sounding more and more interesting. You know how to reach me, obviously. How can I contact you?"

Two seconds of silence. "My first name is Tom; that's all I'm prepared to provide right now. Here's my office number," he said, giving Bob the numbers.

"Well, Tom, I'll try not to disappoint you. I'll let you know what I find out. Is there—is there any chance you might want to go on the record at some point?" News stories were always more authoritative if the sources agreed to be identified.

"I guess it's possible, depending on how things go," Tom said slowly. "But not for now."

"Agreed. Thanks for the call, Tom. This has definitely gotten my attention."

Bob opened a new document on his computer and labeled it "Tyne Investments," and wrote in Tom's contact information and a couple of sentences summarizing their conversation. Then he clicked on the icon for "contacts" and scrolled down to Theodos Markopolos.

He picked up the phone and dialed the number in Queens. On the fourth ring, a familiar voice came on.

"Bob, how are you?" The voice was thick with a slurry that Bob knew was Greek.

"Good, Theo. It's been a while, but I have a job for you."

"Ahh. Well, I'm not too busy. What is it?"

"I've been approached by a senior finance guy at Star Enterprises, which runs the *Star*, the tabloid. It seems that an unknown entity has just invested $10 million in them, and they want to see who this unknown investor is. They think it may be a foreign entity since it originated in Guernsey."

"Hmmm, Guernsey. Well, that is always an interesting place to set up. Lots of secrets, lots of shell companies."

"Exactly. This guy does indeed think this is a shell company. There is no record of it that they could find."

"I see. So, what is the name?

"Tyne Investments," Bob said and spelled it out.

"Okay, I have it." Bob heard music playing softly in the background. He knew Theo worked from home, but that's all he knew, apart from the fact that Theo was the best person he knew for ferreting out corporate information, especially involving little-known entities such as shell companies. He'd been indispensable to Bob on several stories Bob had done at the *Journal*, using an array of computers and special programs to decipher information that companies tried to keep from prying eyes.

"I realize this could take a little while," Bob said.

"Yes," Theo said. "Guernsey can be a hard nut to crack open. But I have a database on companies there." There was a pause. "I do have a project I'm working on this morning, but I should be able to start this afternoon."

"Great. Please keep me posted. Oh, and I'll make sure the *FT* pays you your standard rate."

"Very good. I will be in touch."

About eleven the next morning, Bob was in his office, killing time waiting for an interview by looking at the *New York Times* website. His phone rang, and he saw it was Theo.

"Theo, hello. Have you found something?"

"Yes, but it wasn't easy. I had to dig through several layers of companies to find Tyne. It seems it has made investments in the UK and Australia but none in the US before this."

"Uh-huh. Kind of like a Russian doll, where you pull off one doll and find another and another, right?"

Theo coughed. "Interesting you should say that. Tyne is controlled by Rubicon Investments, which is a well-known operation. It's run by a Russian oligarch, Maxim Ripovsky."

Bob sat forward in his chair. "An oligarch?"

"Yes. He's been actively investing around the world for at least ten years, tech, real estate, more. He's based in London, as a lot of those Russians are."

Bob was barely able to contain his excitement. "Can you spell his name for me?" Theo did so.

"Ripovsky?" Bob chuckled. "That's almost too rich."

"Yes, it's a funny name."

"Can you send me a list of the Tyne investments?"

"Yes. I will put them in an email—wait, I don't have your new email."

Bob gave it to him, then said, "Thanks a million, Theo. Send me a bill and I'll put it through for payment."

"Good, good. And, there is something that occurred to me when I was going through their activities." Theo paused, almost for effect. "If you rearrange the letters in Tyne, you get *nyet*, as you know, the Russian word for 'no.'"

"My God, you're right," Bob replied softly. "That didn't occur to me. I know Tyne is a place name in Britain, but this is wild. It probably isn't a coincidence, is it?"

"Probably not. These Russians are very clever, and they

like playing jokes on the West."

"Uh-huh. Well, you've been a great resource as usual, Theo. I'll get back to you if there's anything else. Thanks much."

"Very good, Bob. Happy to help. Look for my bill soon. Bye."

Bob sat back and tugged at one ear. He decided he would call Tom, the Star source, and let him know what he'd found and see if Tom had any more information for him. This was getting very interesting.

CHAPTER 23

Back in London and once again at the Savoy, Corbin stood at the sink, shirtless, and reached into the toilet kit for his razor and shaving cream. He wasn't thrilled by the idea of having to make another quickie trip across the pond, but he had felt compelled to attend Sir Reginald's memorial. The morning service would be followed by a meeting with Robertson, the new chairman, and Ransom. He peered at his eyes, rimmed with red, and frowned at what seemed like pouches that had sprung up under them. Red-eye flights, he thought, were often precisely that.

Dressed in a dark suit and somber blue tie, he made his way down to the lobby and out the revolving doors, carrying a slim briefcase. The driver was new to him, tall, with a military bearing and brown hair cut very closely around the neck and ears. It was ten-thirty, and the service was to begin at eleven.

The drive along Fleet Street, the historic home of Britain's press, was very short, but the congestion in the City made it seem longer. Pulling up outside the enormous St. Paul's Cathedral, the driver announced, "Here we are, sir," before opening the door for Corbin. It was a cool day, breezy, with spit in the air, and Corbin was reminded that he hadn't brought the "brolly" that Londoners carry religiously. *Damn fickle weather*, he thought to himself. At least in New York, rain usually announced itself and lingered; you could prepare for it.

He looked up and admired the imposing façade of St. Paul's with its Greek columns and classical sculptures. From the ground, he could barely make out the grand dome and the golden spire above it. Walking up the steps, he found people gathered in small knots; formally dressed, they were chatting with each other quietly.

Corbin took a program from an usher, an older man in a suit with a bright yellow boutonniere, and walked over the checkered tile floor of the cathedral, a feature that surprised him. He had expected smooth marble. He followed others to the area where the service was being held and elected to sit toward the rear; let those who knew him sit closer, he thought. An older couple, very British in their ruddiness, were seated along the aisle, and he smiled as he moved past them.

The service began promptly at eleven, with the cathedral's massive organ blasting out Elgar's "Pomp and Circumstance March No. 1," that most British of tunes. An Anglican priest officiated, resplendent in a white robe with a red sash on his shoulders. Corbin stood with the rest of the crowd and did his best to sing along with the hymns, most notably "Eternal Father, Strong to Save," the Royal Navy Hymn. He had no inkling of Sir Reginald's history with the British Navy.

Two men stepped forward separately to give eulogies. One was Robertson, in his official capacity as chairman of the bank, and the other was a white-haired fellow, slightly stooped, whom Corbin learned had been Sir Reginald's childhood friend. In the front row, which Corbin could barely make out, was the family. He saw an older woman in a lavender suit bring a handkerchief to her eyes at intervals, and he wondered if it was Sir Reginald's wife.

The service closed with a string trio—violin, viola, and cello—playing Albinoni's haunting Adagio in G minor. Corbin was touched by the ineffable sadness of the music, which almost seemed to spiral upward in melodic waves toward the interior of the dome. When the last, languid note sounded, the trio sat with their instruments while the priest gave a blessing and ended the ceremony. Corbin smiled at the couple in his pew, but they were swaddled in sadness. He waited for them to leave, then followed them out, mingling with the other mourners in the slow procession to the front doors.

Outside, his eyes caught Robertson and Ransom, who seemed to be waiting for him on the steps. He waved and walked over to them.

"Beautiful service," Corbin said with a nod.

"Yes; yes, it was," said Robertson. "Especially moving to those of us who worked with him." He was a slim man of average height, his sandy hair combed in a careful part; everything about him seemed neat and trim.

"Yes, I'm sure." Corbin didn't know what else to say.

Ransom looked at his watch. "Why don't we plan to meet at the bank in a half-hour? There will be some lunch set up, and we can talk as we eat. What time does your plane leave?"

"Four-forty," Corbin replied.

"Very good. There should be ample time. There is one important item we need to discuss."

The lunch echoed the last one Corbin had attended: finger sandwiches, a salad, some biscuits. *British companies are so unimaginative about cuisine*, he thought to himself. Back in New York, every lunch would be different, a chance for the corporate chef to show off his talents.

They removed their jackets, set them on the back of the chairs, and dug in. A brief discussion ensued about the general state of the bank, both in the UK and the US, with Corbin describing the lending climate in the US, which had been strong, in large part because of low interest rates.

Ransom leaned forward and looked hard at Corbin. "There is something important that has just come up that we need to discuss."

"Of course. What is it?" Corbin was genuinely curious.

"Well"—he looked at Robertson, then back at Corbin—"we've been approached by a major investor who has bought 2 percent of the bank's stock on the open market. As you can surmise, that's an awful lot of money. Now, he's told us he wants his company to have a seat on the board and have a say as to our strategic direction." Ransom's black eyebrows seemed to knit together for a moment.

"Wow." Corbin shook his head slowly, trying to do some math in his head. With the bank's market capitalization of close to $100 billion, this meant the investor was ponying up something on the order of $2 billion to buy the stock. "That's what you'd call a major investment. Who is this guy?"

"A Russian named Maxim Ripovsky. He lives in London, and the UK is his home base," Robertson said. "So at least it isn't coming from the Kremlin. But—but we are given to understand that he is an oligarch with significant ties to the government there."

Corbin sat back and blew out a breath. "My God, really? I don't think we want any part of an oligarch coming in the door, do we?"

"Certainly not," Ransom said firmly. "He already has the shares, but we have no obligation to honor that purchase with a board seat, especially given who he is."

"Have you told him that?"

"No, not yet." Robertson leaned back and sipped his soda. "We wanted to get your thoughts first. The US has had a lot more experience dealing with unruly investors. Did you ever experience anything like this in your previous companies?"

"No, but there certainly is a history of these things being

done in banking, starting in the eighties. Some worked, some didn't." He paused and looked at them in turn. "What more do you know about this guy and his investments?"

Ransom said, "We had our people look into Ripovsky. It seems he's made enormous sums in the past ten years through a series of companies, mostly investing in real estate and software, largely here in the UK and Australia. We understand he has done other deals recently in New York." Ransom paused to wipe his lips. "Of course, his company is private, so we have no numbers, only informed speculation."

Corbin bit his lip softly. "What is our policy on board seats? I agree that we're not obligated to give him one, but can't he petition to have his name or whomever he designates put up for election at the annual meeting?"

"Yes, he could do that. That's something we could well face," Robertson said. "But we've never had a contested election, and we would rather not start. Yet—and yet—he would be within his rights to seek the seat if we didn't accede to his request to add him more or less immediately. That's what he wants."

"And the annual meeting is in the spring, right?"

"Yes, late April."

"It's now October, so that gives him a lot of time to organize if he wants to seek an elected seat."

"It does," Ransom said. "And we certainly can't take him lightly. He's very rich, and we have to assume he's used to getting his way."

"Well, huh." Corbin folded his hands. "I'm certainly in agreement that you should give him a firm no on the seat. Thank him for his investment, of course, and let him lay out what kind of strategic thoughts he might have. Certainly couldn't hurt to see what's on his mind."

Robertson nodded. "That seems to be good advice, and I think we'll move forward along those lines."

"Okay." Corbin leaned back in the chair. "And you say he's

making investments in New York?"

"That's what we've heard."

"Well, I'll put some people on it and try to find out more. What—what's the company name he's using for these investments?"

"Rubicon Investments," Ransom said.

Corbin smiled. "It would be something red, right?"

CHAPTER 24

Crossing the marble floor toward the elevator, Winston took stock of the lobby. It was sleek and gray and white, with Scandinavian-style furniture, so different from the lobby in his building with its Oriental rugs and plush armchairs. Inside the elevator, he pushed the button for the penthouse, marked "P." The ride up was quick and silent.

The elevator opened on another marble lobby, white with deep veins of gray. Winston saw himself reflected in a huge mirror with an ornate carved wooden frame. As he was taking in his reflection, a stocky man dressed in a navy jacket and dark slacks approached him unsmilingly. "Mee-ster Chrom?" The accent was thick, and his head was shaved so drastically that only a patina of stubble remained. If there was a picture in the dictionary accompanying the word *thug*, he'd be a good candidate, Winston thought quickly.

"Yes?" Winston said simply.

"Follow me."

They walked into a large room with floor-to-ceiling windows opening onto the Gotham skyline. There was thick carpeting underfoot and several modern sofas and chairs of fabric and steel in gray tones. Winston saw a wet bar to his right, a glass and metal affair with several stools in front. A door farther to his right seemed to lead into a kitchen.

Ripovsky came through that door moments later. "Winston, thank you for coming." His smile had all the warmth of a Siberian winter. "Please sit down," he said, motioning to one of the upholstered chairs. He had a different look, a brown jacket over a cream-colored turtleneck, but his black hair was once again carefully slicked back.

Winston's eyes darted about as he sat down. The stocky man, whom Winston took to be a bodyguard, was standing behind the sofa where Ripovsky now sat. This sudden request for an in-person meeting was a bit unnerving, but Winston knew how much money was at stake.

"I'm a little disappointed, Winston," Ripovsky said with his hand on his chin. "The advertising we spoke about has not materialized, and what is worse, after my agency sent over the materials, they received an invoice. We had agreed that this would be free."

Winston spread his hands. "These things aren't that easy, Max. Sometimes there is confusion." He realized he had forgotten to alert the ad department to expect full-page ads from Rubicon Investments that weren't to be invoiced.

"Some confusion is understandable, yes, but you are running the company, are you not?"

"Yes, yes." Winston desperately wanted strangers to think he had his hand on the rudder; even though Ripovsky clearly knew better, he thought a bit of flattery would help—sugar with the vinegar.

"Then you need to get this done. It was one of my conditions. It would be bad to put that additional ten million in jeopardy."

"I will ... I will see to it even if I have to pay for it myself," Winston heard himself saying.

"Would you do that?"

Winston thought hard for a moment. "Yes. I—I could route

the payment through my attorney's office. I would pay him, and he could pay the paper. That way, it isn't coming directly from me."

Ripovsky shifted in his seat. "That should work, I would imagine," he said slowly. "How soon could this be done?"

"Oh, very soon. In a matter of days." He'd have to call Mitch and explain the situation as carefully as he could without raising any red flags.

"Very well. I will have the invoice sent to your attorney." He turned over his shoulder. "Sergei, please get some paper and a pen for Mr. Crumm to write this down, or"—he turned back to Winston—"do you have a business card for him?"

"I'm pretty sure I do," Winston said, reaching back to his hip pocket for his wallet. He opened it and thumbed through one of the compartments, then pulled out a card. "Here it is. Please give me enough time to call him and explain the situation before you send over that invoice."

"Certainly. We will fax it tomorrow and assume he will know what to do with it."

"Alright," said Winston, visibly relieved. He was proud of himself for coming up with a plan B on the spur of the moment, and it emboldened him. "Say, where is Natasha? She makes quite an impression."

A trace of a smile spread slowly over Ripovsky's face. "Yes, she does. She is back in London, on an assignment." He glanced over his shoulder again. "Sergei, please show Mr. Crumm out," Ripovsky said, then added something in Russian.

Sergei merely nodded and stepped around the sofa. Winston said a soft "thank you" to Ripovsky and followed Sergei to the elevator, where the Russian pushed the button for the lobby. His hands were huge, Winston noticed, with fingers as thick as bratwurst, at least it seemed that way. Winston stepped into the car and congratulated himself on his escape.

Four hours later, a lanky young boy rode up the elevator alone. His jeans were so tight that they seemed to be a second skin, and he wore a gray fisherman's sweater that sagged around his waist. His eyes were red-rimmed from the drugs he had just ingested an hour earlier, and a tattoo of a crescent moon was visible at the nape of his neck, just below a ragged hank of blonde hair.

Sergei greeted him wordlessly and led him back to the bedroom, where Ripovsky was sitting in a chair, dressed in a pale-blue bathrobe with the letter *R* in gold on the right breast. He motioned to the boy to come in, and they sat together on the bed. Ripovsky put his arm around the boy and nuzzled his neck, but the boy barely reacted. It was as if he was in another world.

Sergei closed the door and took a seat outside, where he picked up the remote and turned on the small Sony TV on the nearby stand. He found the channel for the soccer game and settled in. From past experience, he knew it would be some time before the door would open again.

CHAPTER 25

Adrienne stroked her chin. Was it really her job to arrange a function at the Cosmopolitan Club? Winston could have foisted that job on his secretary, she mused, but then she realized that he was asking for her buy-in, making her a partner in the event. He did that now and then, and in a way, she welcomed it; it made their bond stronger. She looked at the phone on her desk, then turned away. She'd deal with the call later.

She realized that most of the biggest possessions in their lives—the penthouse, the *Northern Star*, the house in Florida—were entirely his choices, and she didn't begrudge him that. He was a wealthy man with a weak man's insistence on appearances. Not for him a log house in the Catskills or a beach house on Cape Cod. He needed more grandeur. There were times when she would have liked more informality, an opportunity to let her hair down, in a way. But she hadn't challenged him on these things, and by this point, any undoing was nigh impossible.

She had no idea how much longer he would be working. While major corporations had a retirement age of sixty-five for chief executives that was practically chiseled in stone, for private firms such as Star, there were no rules. He could keep going past seventy, probably, but she was sure he'd want to stop well short of that. He was sixty-one now, and his decision, she felt, would hinge in part on the potential challenge for the chairmanship. If he lost that, certainly, he wouldn't stay on for years longer.

That brought to mind her own coda, her design career and how it might end. Adrienne saw the line continuing under someone else but with her brand intact, the way it often worked in the design world. That departure was far from imminent; she saw herself working for at least five more years, perhaps ten. She was fifty-five and felt as energetic as someone twenty years younger. But if Winston retired, her own plans could change.

Indeed, what would he do in retirement? He was no intellect, but he took an outsized pride in the *Star* and his place in it, and it was hard for her to picture days when he wouldn't be ferried to the office. He didn't have outside interests or hobbies that could keep him happy in the city, so that meant he'd almost certainly insist on moving to Florida and spending more time on the yacht.

She blew out a breath. There were things about his behavior that annoyed her, like grains of sand rubbing inside a bathing suit. First and foremost was his aversion to responsibility. If something went wrong, he'd usually look for a scapegoat; he seemed constitutionally incapable of admitting that certain problems were his fault. She thought it was a habit he'd picked up in his childhood that he'd never outgrown, that had been allowed to go unchecked like a garden gone to seed. If anything, Adrienne believed, it had just gotten worse in recent years.

And then there were the challenges to his position and status, a perfect example being the suit brought by the downstairs tenant over the massive water leak. Winston had taken it as an affront and a threat to his reputation, but she knew it would have been an easy matter to settle with the board and make the problem disappear with no publicity. Instead, it had metastasized into tabloid fodder.

Yet, Adrienne knew he was a good father who practically doted on Amanda. Perhaps it was the sorry situation with his own children, who, it was clear, wanted little to do with him. She didn't know what mistakes he had made with them, but he seemed intent on staying close to Amanda, figuratively holding hands whenever he could. Now that she was away, Adrienne sensed that he too missed her.

She looked down at the legal pad she had brought out to jot down the numbers for the reception, and her mind started working through the logistics: how many guests, the need for a cash bar, who to handle the catering. There were lots of variables, and she started writing them down. She wouldn't bother Winston until everything was sewed up.

CHAPTER 26

Drumming his fingers on his desk, Bob debated how much information to share with Tom, the Star executive. He really didn't want to give away Ripovsky's name yet—that was his hole card. But he decided he would tell him that the source was Russian and that he was trying to find out more. Meanwhile, he hoped he could ferret out more information about the Whitehall loan.

He dialed the cell number he'd been given, and it was answered on the third ring.

"Is this Bob Mandell?"

"Hi, Tom. I have found out a little more about the investment by Tyne."

"Yes?" He sensed a note of excitement in Tom's voice.

"It definitely seems to be Russian. I'm trying to dig further to find an identity—"

"Russian? Well, I wouldn't call that a good thing, not in this day and age."

"Yeah, probably not," Bob replied. "As you probably know, most of the big money players in Russia these days are oligarchs, many tied to the government. They're rich, and their reputation precedes them; they can be pretty ruthless."

He heard Tom sigh. "Great, just great."

"I'm still gathering background information," Bob said. "Would you tell me something about the Whitehall loan"?

"Ummmm." The line was silent for several seconds. "I guess I can give you some details, still off the record. It was a fairly conventional working capital loan, arranged by the merchant banking group they have in London. Since Sir Reginald had facilitated it, the bank certainly attached a good deal of importance to it."

"And it was for $20 million?"

"Yes."

"And it recently became nonperforming?"

"That's right. We've had a lot of issues in the past year or two. I don't think I could give you an accurate list, but certainly, the revenue side was the main issue. I don't need to tell you what's been happening to the newspaper industry."

"No, you don't."

"It got to the point that they warned us that if they didn't see enough improvement, they would call the loan. And then they did."

"Well, Crumm had brought in the loan. Did he try to get the bank back in?"

"He did, but Sir Reginald had suffered a stroke and was replaced, and Crumm had no leverage there. He called the bank's CEO in New York but got nothing but a polite brush-off."

"Who is that CEO, do you know?" Bob knew the big New York banks very well, but Whitehall, with its British parentage, was a different animal.

"Van Sloot, Corbin van Sloot."

Bob snorted lightly. "Shades of the old Dutch aristocracy in New York?"

"I guess."

"Tell me, will the source of this investment change the paper's approach to it?"

"Are we still off the record?"

"Yeah, sure," Bob said breezily.

"It might. The Russian origin is troubling. We'll need to talk it through a bit more. But at this point, there have been no conditions that I'm aware of. And we really need the money."

"I'm sure." Bob paused, almost for effect. "I'll let you know if I can pin down an identity," he said, lying gracefully.

"Thanks. That would be great," Tom said. "If you don't reach me, just leave a message and I'll get back to you."

"Very good. Will be in touch. Bye."

Bob grabbed his coffee mug and headed for the kitchen. He wanted to dig further into the other shell entities whose names Theo had given him. What was Ripovsky up to? Very likely no good.

He looked again at the email from Theo with the names of the two other shell companies linked to Ripovsky: Crimson Opportunities and Greenway Ltd. Other than being the names of colors, they signified little to him.

A Google search of Crimson Opportunities turned up nothing, but he did get a hit with Greenway Ltd. There was a link to an article from the *Wall Street Journal* from the previous year; he read through the short item, which involved the purchase of a thirty-story residential tower on Fifth Avenue that the company had bought from the Drapkin family for an undisclosed price. It mentioned that Greenway was a subsidiary of Rubicon Investments out of London, but offered nothing about Ripovsky.

Bob smiled to himself. Here, at least, was a US investment—and a real estate one at that—that could be tied to Ripovsky. But Crimson was a cipher. He decided to lean on Theo again to see if he could dig anything more up.

"Hi, Theo?"

"Hello, Bob. Was that information useful to you?"

"It was, it was. But I'd like to see if you could find out anything more about one of those shells in particular. I did find an investment from one of them listed in the *Journal*."

"Okay, but I'm swamped right now on a big project. I'm afraid it may be a couple of days."

Bob sighed inaudibly. "Well, that's alright. The one I'm interested in is called Crimson Opportunities."

"Right," he said, drawing the word out. "I'll see what I can find. But like I say, it may be a few days."

"That's fine, as I say. I know you'll do your best when you have the time. Give—um—give me a call if you run something down."

"Will do. Bye."

Bob hung up and thought hard. Rubicon Investments, the parent, was a recognized corporate entity in the UK. Certainly, there could be worthwhile information to glean from looking at any news articles about it, as well as from a computerized database on British corporations that the *Financial Times* had in the main newsroom. Information on Rubicon, being a privately held entity, would be limited, but he had to look.

He'd already read a good profile of Ripovsky in the *London Times*. It was five years old, but the Russian had opened up about his background and his investment philosophies—and he'd clearly charmed the interviewer, a woman, into fashioning quite a flattering piece. He'd come off like a dashing foreign potentate deigning to invest in the Old Empire.

But Ripovsky would be the last piece in the puzzle. Bob would ask for an interview only when he had the story mostly done; he didn't know what to expect. If Ripovsky was as secretive and clever as he surmised, a refusal was more than possible. It was likely.

CHAPTER 27

Larissa really did like New York, more so than London with its eternal showers and constant emphasis on tradition and propriety. New York had an edgier vibe that made it more exciting, more vibrant, even if money was the coin of the realm and Manhattan's streets were often dirty and chaotic and the sun so often hid in its stately canyons. The winter with its ice and snow and frosty mornings reminded her of Moscow, but it certainly wasn't as cold. The summer heat, however, enervated her.

But London had been her principal home for four years, ever since Maxim had recruited her from her post as a business analyst in Moscow. He had installed her in a luxurious flat and had arranged for her boyfriend, a former Russian hockey player, to live with her. While she did a useful analysis of business trends and potential buying opportunities for Rubicon Investments, she also was periodically called to New York, where she could do the same kind of work.

It was early November, and she was getting ready to vacate the apartment. Her Louis Vuitton bags were packed and sitting by the door; her flight back to London was leaving that night. She took an Uber to Ripovsky's building, turning up her coat collar against the chilly breeze as she crossed the gray slab of sidewalk. He was expecting her.

"Elena!" he exclaimed when she walked into his penthouse apartment. "You've done very well. The videotapes are very convincing, very powerful. We have the *kompromat* we need."

"I'm glad," she said with a faint smile. The recorder had been remotely controlled, and she hadn't known when it was on, which gave her something of the creeps. One of Ripovsky's sullen lieutenants had removed the video bug from its hiding place two days earlier, saying very little; she stayed in the living room reading, and he was in and out within five minutes.

"Come, sit for a minute," Maxim said expansively, motioning to the sofa. "This assignment was not so bad, was it?"

She sat, crossed her legs, and sighed. "I really did like Corbin, and he was a good lover. So, yes, not bad at all. I have to say I'm sorry for him—"

He cut her off quickly, surgically. "Business is business, as you know. Personal feelings are fine up to a point. But we can never let them get in the way of the goal."

"Of course."

He smiled. "I have had the £50,000 wired into your London account, and with that, of course, my gratitude."

"Yes, thank you, Maxim." She looked at Sergei, who stood stoically, his hands folded. She tried to ignore his presence, but there was something sinister about it—almost like a looming shadow—that was hard to ignore.

"So, you are off tonight?"

"Yes," she replied.

"And you have the keys to the apartment?"

"In my purse, yes."

"You can give them to Anatoly when he takes you to the airport. And what time should he pick you up?"

"About seven, I think. My flight is at ten-forty-five."

"Wonderful." He beamed. "I will see you in London in a

few weeks. Please give my regards to Mikhail." Mikhail Urinov was her boyfriend in London.

She smiled reflexively and stood up. "I will. Thank you, Maxim, for everything. It's an honor to work for you."

"And it's a pleasure to have you in our little family. Have a good trip, Elena."

As she waited in the spartan lobby for the Uber that would take her back to her apartment, Elena reflected on the hold that Ripovsky had over her, something she often doubted she could ever shake. Her father, a minor city official in Moscow, had been dipping into a pooled department expense account and had siphoned off hundreds of thousands of rubles over a period of about five years. He was clever, and it was more of a slow and intermittent bleed than a hemorrhage.

When Ripovsky was recruiting her, he had several people assigned to digging into her background, which included her family. It was then that the embezzlement was uncovered by a sharp-eyed forensic accountant who had been charged with looking into her father's monetary affairs. Tunneling like a mole into her father's departmental expenses, he found the evidence, clear as day.

In his final interview with her, Ripovsky presented the evidence. She was shocked beyond words.

"Elena," he had said, "I want to hire you and pay you handsomely. This would mean moving to London. I would pay for your boyfriend to move as well if you wish. I do hope you say yes. If you don't, I will be forced to expose your father. It wouldn't come directly from me but from reliable sources. I don't need to explain to you what could happen to him."

Her heart had been in her throat. "I need to talk to him," she said finally. "If this is true, I will come to work for you."

She'd waited in the family's drab apartment for hours before her father returned from work. A portly man in his late fifties, he came in whistling and beamed when he saw his daughter. But the smile drained from his face when he saw her expression. He knew something was wrong. At her urging, they walked into her bedroom and closed the door.

Five minutes later, Uri Mesinov was wringing his hands and fighting off tears. "I did it for the family," he told her. "It wasn't a lot of money, but it helped us get by. You know how corrupt things are in Moscow. Who was going to miss a few rubles here and there?"

She told him that Ripovsky was holding this crime over her, and it would go away only if she agreed to work for him. "He's a very rich and powerful man, and in many ways, this would be a job of my dreams," she said. "But this is a cruel trap, and he is obviously used to exerting pressure to get his way. Now, I need to do this. I can't risk having you exposed."

He had sighed and folded his hands, almost as if in prayer. "I'm sorry to put you in this position, Elena. Truly. I will stop skimming. If someone found out, others could as well."

"Poppa, I'm so very disappointed," she had said, her voice quavering. "I may be leaving for London in a few weeks, and if that happens, I will miss you."

He had stood and reached for her for a consoling embrace, but she held up her hand, and he stopped.

"No, Poppa. Not now. I need time." And she had abruptly walked out of the room, leaving him stock still, as lost as a man who had just awakened from a bad dream.

At the airport, she walked up to the TSA agent, a heavyset man with wire-rimmed glasses, and handed him her red passport, which he opened and peered at closely, comparing the photo to the woman in front of him. He read the name, Elena Mesinova, written in Cyrillic and English, and checked the date of birth, 18/3/92, which used the European practice of listing the day first. Seeing nothing amiss, he handed back her passport, smiled, and said, "Enjoy your flight."

Ten minutes later, seated in the British Airways area, she

pulled out her cell phone and looked at her messages. There was one from Corbin: *"Hope to see you tomorrow. Pls confirm."*

She pursed her lips. He was smart and handsome, and he treated her wonderfully. But her life was not her own. Larissa Thibault was the second alias she'd been asked to assume but probably not the last.

To her, Corbin was like a lot of powerful men who mixed sophistication and sex like a potent cocktail. They saw beautiful younger women as both a challenge and a kind of entitlement. She, on the other hand, saw herself as something of an actress, a Meryl Streep who could immerse herself in a part and become someone else. She had played her part skillfully, seducing Corbin and providing Maxim with precisely what he'd asked for.

And yet, something unspoken hung in the air. It troubled her. Corbin's anger would curdle into hatred—that was almost certain. He would realize he'd been duped, and the *kompromat* would be irrefutable. Blackmail was never pretty, but it certainly could be profitable.

CHAPTER 28

"How do I look, honey?" Winston adjusted his bowtie and checked the cummerbund, which strained around his belly like a ladies' girdle. Black tie was never his favorite mode of dress.

"Just fine, dear. You look the part of a host." Adrienne smiled and opened her black evening clutch to check the contents. She had on a long emerald gown with thin shoulder straps and a boatneck, one of her designs, with black patent low-heeled shoes.

"Well, we're off, then," he said breezily. They both took raincoats from the front hall closet and put them on before walking to the door. Winston checked to make sure he had his house keys.

George was waiting in the Town Car at the curb, and Winston held the back door open for his wife before walking around the back and sliding in next to her. They rode mostly in silence to the Cosmopolitan Club, a short hop away on East Sixty-Sixth Street. The evening was cool but not cold, a typical night on the cusp of Thanksgiving; any view of the sky was more or less blocked by the tall buildings in the heart of Manhattan as surely as if they were deep in a forest.

Once inside, they left their coats at the coat check and were directed to the large, tastefully decorated room where the function was to be held. They signed in and moved slowly into the crowd. Two middle-aged women who had been sipping drinks and talking saw Adrienne and came over to her.

"Adrienne, this looks like such a nice event," one said. She was an elegant blonde, tall and slim, who looked as if she could have been a model in her younger years.

"Thank you, Katherine. So good of you to make it," Adrienne replied. She motioned to Winston, who was standing at her side impassively. "I'm not sure you've met my husband, Winston." She half-turned to him.

"I don't think I have, though I certainly know who he is," Katherine replied with what seemed like a practiced smile. She extended her hand, and Winston took it. "I'm Katherine Moore."

"Well, it's very nice to meet you," Winston replied with a tight smile.

"Hi, I'm Carol Cavendish," said the other woman, extending her hand to each of them in turn. Shorter and plainer than Katherine, she was well turned out in a red wrap dress and a thick string of pearls around her neck.

"Is the guest of honor here?" Carol asked.

Winston craned his head. "I'm not sure. I'll have to go look." He turned back to them. "While I do that, I think Adrienne and I need to find the bar."

"It's over there," Katherine said, pointing. Not surprisingly, it was the most crowded spot in the room, where couples bunched together like fish at a feeding station. Braving one of these events without a little alcohol was hard to comprehend in this town, but Winston knew there was a fine line. Drunkenness was just not permissible.

Ripovsky was easy to find. He was in one corner, with Natasha by his side. He was the tallest man in the room, and Natasha was only a few inches shorter. They were talking to a couple whom neither Winston nor Adrienne recognized.

With their drinks in hand, a scotch and soda for Winston and white wine for Adrienne, they walked over and stood a few feet away, waiting for Ripovsky to see them and turn away from the other couple. That happened after a few moments.

"Hello, Winston. This is a beautiful event." Ripovsky, in a tuxedo with a bright red bowtie, smiled expansively. "And is this your wife?" he asked, looking at Adrienne.

"Yes. Max, I'd like to introduce my wife, Adrienne Rogers." Adrienne smiled up at Ripovsky, seemingly transfixed by his height.

"Nice to meet you, Adrienne," he said softly, extending his arm for a handshake. "This is my associate, Natasha."

He gestured at Natasha, who bowed her head briefly and said, "Halo, nize to mit you." There was the same tight, toothless smile Winston had seen at the lunch. He marveled again at her height and posture—ramrod straight, as if she had been punished as a child for slouching. Winston wondered how conversant she was with English.

"It's so good of you to be so generous to this charity, Mr. Ripovsky," Adrienne said, holding her drink at her side. "The food bank is always looking for help, even in the best of times."

"Please, call me Max," he said, turning on the charm like the dimmer on a light switch being pushed up. "And I'm happy to be associated with a good cause."

Adrienne had pulled from Winston a brief biography of Ripovsky, as much as Ripovsky had shared at the lunch, and had been told he was relatively new to the Big Apple. "I understand you're making some investments here," she said. "Are they primarily in real estate?"

"Yes, real estate principally," he said, his eyes flickering. "But, of course, I plan to help the arts as much as I can. I am still learning. Of course, being Russian, I would like to help the ballet and the symphony." Not a word about his investment in the *Star*.

Adrienne spoke for a minute about the American Ballet Theatre and the New York Symphony, both of which she knew well, as she had been on the Ballet Theatre board a number of years earlier. Just then, a young hostess making the rounds told them they could take their seats for the dinner.

"After you," Winston said cheerfully to Ripovsky, motioning toward the head table. "It's over there."

Not surprisingly, Adrienne, as the organizer, was seated next to Ripovsky, the charity sponsor. They were soon deep in small talk while Winston, seated next to one of Adrienne's friends he had barely met, tried hard to find something to say. She was talking to her husband, another stranger. The heady swirl of good drink and good company, of evenings spent rubbing shoulders with the city's elite, was something he'd never appreciated. Small talk to him, more often than not, was just small, too small for him.

He soon folded his arms and stared ahead, though his eyes were drawn to Natasha, seated beside Ripovsky. She too looked bored. Winston marveled at her broad shoulders and long neck. She wore a black sleeveless dress with little jewelry, only a pearl bracelet and pearl earrings. Her hair shone like spun gold. He sighed and reached for the rolls and butter; this could be a long evening.

CHAPTER 29

The long Thanksgiving weekend had been the usual cornu-
copia of good things for the van Sloots. Patricia's brother, his
family, Corbin's younger brother, and his family gathered in
New Canaan for the customary feast. The fine china came out
and then the silver service, with the goblets and the gravy
boat. Corbin was getting a little old for touch football and he
knew it, but he was out there on a relatively balmy morning
with a touch of mist in the air, with Corbin's long-legged
nephews and Justin running around the broad lawn, shouting
and laughing.

Now it was Monday, and the usual routine stretched
before him. He was daydreaming about that game when
Angela knocked on his door. "This just came for you, Mr. van
Sloot," she said, holding up a manila envelope and carrying it
to him.

This was odd. "Thanks," he said a bit distractedly, looking
at the envelope. There was no return address, and it was
marked "Priority Mail," addressed to him with his CEO title at
the headquarters address. He hefted it—it was very light, but
there was a bulge at the bottom.

Corbin undid the metal clasp and pulled out the contents:

a typed sheet of paper and a red flash drive. This was very strange. He turned over the paper and read it with a growing sense of consternation.

Dear Mr. van Sloot:

I think you'll find the video on this flash drive particularly interesting. I could have sent the video to you as an email, but I've done you a service by not putting it onto your corporate servers.

I'm sure you'll recognize the principals. This is an edited version—I have much more video of a similar nature.

In light of this material, I would like you, as CEO of Whitehall, to reconsider my well-meaning offer to obtain a board seat. I understand this was discussed between you and the company executives in London. As I am now the largest shareholder, I think I'm in a position to ask for this favor.

Should you choose not to act on this request within 48 hours, I will be forced to deliver a copy of this flash drive to your wife in Connecticut. I'm quite sure that is not something you would welcome.

I assure you this is not a hoax, and I await your response. You can reach me at 212-566-6000. Any attempts to involve the authorities will result in this video being shared on social media.

Sincerely,

Maxim Ripovsky, Chairman

Rubicon Investments

What the hell? A gnawing sensation coursed through his stomach. He took the flash drive, which looked innocuous enough, and inserted it into the USB port, then opened his document folder and scrolled down to where he saw the E drive listed, then clicked it. There was just one document, with an icon for a video labeled "Whitehall."

He clicked to open it and sat back, then bolted forward. His eyes bulged. The video was very sharp, and it showed him and Larissa vigorously making love on her bed. He watched, transfixed. It went on for several minutes, complete with sound, the murmurings that often take place during sex. His face was shown clearly at several intervals; the evidence was unmistakable.

His mind reeled, groping like a drowning man gasping for air. Blackmail. Was Larissa aware of this? It was hard to believe she was involved, he thought quickly; she was too genuine. The alternative was almost unimaginable: that she wasn't this lovely companion and lover—she was a spy working for Ripovsky. If that was the case, she could have targeted him as far back as their first meeting in the art gallery—was that possible? Could she really be that cold-blooded?

He had no doubt that Ripovsky meant exactly what he said. The idea of Patricia seeing what was on that video was beyond frightening. His carefully ordered world would disintegrate like a glass pitcher falling on the floor and dissolving into shards. Divorce and disgrace, it would be a tableau of horrors, stretching as far as his mind could imagine. Corbin knew he had to call Robertson in London, lay out his infidelity, and hope he could persuade Robertson to reconsider Ripovsky's offer. The alternative was unthinkable.

Corbin checked his watch; it was just after ten. London was five hours ahead. He needed time to think, but this really couldn't wait. He'd call Robertson at eleven and hope to catch him then. Corbin would be unctuous, apologetic, vulnerable; there was no point in trying to make any demands. He'd screwed up big-time, and he'd have to throw himself on the chairman's mercy. First, he needed to think it through and come up with a script. He pulled out a legal pad and frowned, then punched the intercom.

"Angela, please hold all my calls. When I'm free, I'll let you know."

The phone in London rang three times before a woman's voice came on. "Mr. Robertson's office."

"Hello, this is Corbin van Sloot in New York. I need to speak to Mr. Robertson—it's urgent."

"I'm sorry, Mr. van Sloot, but he's in a meeting. I will have him call you when he gets out." Her voice was perfectly measured, polite, reassuring.

"How long do you think that might be?"

"No more than a half-hour, I believe."

"Alright, thank you. I'll hope to speak with him then."

Alone in the office, the sun dancing in and out of cloud cover outside, Corbin rehearsed his pitch. He wasn't sure what the right tone would be, but then he thought, *The hell with the tone.* This was a cry for help.

The minutes crawled by. Thirty-five minutes after his initial call, Angela buzzed him. "I have Mr. Robertson from London on the line."

"Thanks. Put him through."

"Corbin, what can I do for you?"

"I'm afraid I'm in a bit of a predicament, David. Please hear me out."

"Of course." There was a note of concern in his voice.

"Well, I took up with a beautiful young woman a number of months ago. We've been meeting at her apartment in Manhattan." He paused. "Say what you will about middle-aged angst or whatever; of course, I should have known better. But it happened. It certainly wasn't planned."

"I see, but what—"

"David, the worst thing that could have happened did. I was very careful about our meetings, but it seems that a number of our encounters—sexual encounters—were videotaped. I—I just received a flash drive this morning with some of that video. It's very damning."

"My goodness."

"So, you're probably wondering why this would involve you and Whitehall. Well, there was a note that came with the drive. It was from Maxim Ripovsky."

"What?" Robertson exclaimed.

"Yes. He mentioned the fact that you had formally rejected his request for a board seat. But now he intends to blackmail me to try to change that. He's saying that he will send a copy of the video to my wife if I can't persuade you and perhaps Thomas to change your minds and agree to seat him."

"My God," Robertson said softly. "Ripovsky. He certainly plays a mean game."

"David, my wife cannot see that video—my life would unravel; I know it. I'm asking if you would reconsider seating him. He's given me forty-eight hours to get back to him with a decision."

There was a long silence. "Corbin, this is very serious. I wouldn't presume to lecture you about morals, but this is clearly a major breach. I think I need to talk to Thomas and get his thoughts. This is not an easy decision. We certainly have no interest, none, in giving Ripovsky any more say about Whitehall."

"I certainly understand that. But I think you must know the position I'm in. I'm appealing to you directly for—for some kind of compassion, I suppose. I certainly don't want to prostrate myself, but that's what I seem to be doing. I don't think I have any choice. And as one director among many, including myself, how much influence could he have?"

"Perhaps not that much," Robertson said slowly. "I will talk to Thomas and perhaps one or two others here. We will keep this in the strictest confidence. But I understand the need to act quickly. I plan to call you at 9:00 a.m. New York time tomorrow. Will that work for you?"

"Yes, absolutely."

"Corbin, were there any other demands from Ripovsky?"

"No, no, just the board seat issue."

"Very well. Good night, Corbin—or as good as it could be under the circumstances."

"Good night to you, David, and thank you. We'll talk in the morning."

Almost reflexively, Corbin got up and started pacing around his office, as nervously as an addict needing a fix. This was a hell of a mess, and if they held out against Ripovsky, he wasn't sure what he could do. He was like a condemned prisoner, waiting on tenterhooks to see if there was a last-minute reprieve from the governor; in the movies, that could go either way. It was going to be a long day and a longer night.

CHAPTER 30

As Bob had suspected, the information on Rubicon Investments in the *FT* database was scant. It listed the company, its year of founding: 2011, the headquarters address in London, and Ripovsky's name as the chairman. Under company description, he found "private" and "investment manager." There was little more than an address and a phone number, but it did have a conspicuous logo, a red star.

His real interest, however, was in Tyne Investments and the two other shells whose names he had gotten from Theo. He checked the database for both Crimson Opportunities and Greenway Ltd. and found nothing. While he had the *Journal's* short item about Greenway, it would be good to find out if there were more transactions.

Staring at the wall in his cubicle, Bob realized there was another source he hadn't tapped, the *Financial Times* reporter in London who covered investment managers. He'd met the reporter briefly during her visit to New York in the summer, and he searched his memory for a name. Maura, wasn't it? He couldn't bring up a surname, so he called up the employee database and looked at the London employees. There it was: Maura Gregson, with a phone number. Bob remembered her vaguely as middle-aged, quite tall and severe-looking. She was one of the first women at the *FT* to write on money management, and she had a strong reputation in London for her knowledge of the beat.

He dialed the number and waited for a connection. On the third ring, a voice answered, "Maura Gregson."

"Hi, Maura, this is Bob Mandell in the New York office."

"Oh, hello, Bob. We met at the lunch this summer, I recall."

"Yes." Bob ran his hand through what was left of his hair. "I'm calling you to see if you can help me run down some information about a London investment firm."

"I'll certainly try," Gregson said. "Which one?" Her voice was husky with a sandpaper edge, a smoker's voice.

"Well, Rubicon Investments, but I'm really trying to learn more about some shell companies it operates."

"Hmmm. Well, that's Maxim Ripovsky's operation, as you probably know. He's very rich and very secretive, in that order." She paused. "I imagine he has a number of shell companies headquartered offshore somewhere."

"Guernsey, apparently."

"Ah. No surprise there. Ripping good place to hide things."

"I'm looking into an investment through something called Tyne Investments," Bob said, spelling the name out for Gregson. "But there are two other shells that I've found that I'm curious about, and I wonder if you've heard of either."

"Okay, which ones?"

"Crimson Opportunities and Greenway Limited. I've discovered a US investment by Greenway."

"Huh." There was a long pause. "The name Crimson Opportunities rings a bell. Very unusual name, you know. I believe I wrote something a couple of years ago about a transaction they did. I'll have to look it up."

"Would you?"

"Certainly. Are you on a deadline?"

"No, not at all," Bob replied.

"Very good. I'll try to get back to you tomorrow—I'm on a deadline right now here. Give me your direct line."

Bob did so, and they said their goodbyes. This was promising, he thought to himself, one of those happy instances where one journalist helped another, which wasn't always the case. He'd certainly been guilty himself of being less than cooperative, which was easier to get away with as one climbed the career ladder and figuratively kicked the rungs out for those below.

"Hello, Bob? This is Maura Gregson in London."

"Yes, Maura. Thanks for getting back to me so quickly."

"Not a problem. I found something from about two years ago. Crimson Opportunities was listed as the principal creditor for Phoenix Technologies, which had just gone under."

"I remember that company," Bob replied. "They were big into cybersecurity, and I know they had an office here in New York."

"And in London. Apparently, Phoenix declared bankruptcy and was later reborn as Fortress Technologies. It's privately held, and there's not much information on it. If Ripovsky is behind it, there's no suggestion of that. There's a British-sounding name listed as the CEO."

"Uh-huh. Well, cybersecurity is an interesting field, especially for the Russians."

"I would say so," Maura replied.

"And Fortress is headquartered in London?"

"It is. From what I remember, the UK office was quite small, but when the larger Phoenix operation in New York folded, the London office became the principal one." He heard her cough.

"Cybersecurity," Bob mused. "Makes me wonder if someone like Ripovsky, who may well be working with the Russian government, could be using Fortress to build troll farms or some other dirty work that helps Mother Russia."

"Well, we can speculate, but it would be very hard to prove," Maura said. "Bloody damned difficult, I imagine."

"Maura, have you ever met Ripovsky?"

"No, never any real reason to, and he generally steers clear of the press."

"I did read a very flattering piece on him, written over there a few years ago."

"I do remember that," Maura said. "More or less introduced him, though he'd been here for years. It did make him out to be quite a man about town, involved in good causes, the arts, all that, as well."

"I plan to interview him when I've done more reporting," Bob announced. "You know, see if I can get behind the veil."

He heard Maura chuckle. "Good luck with that one. I believe that veil is rather thick."

Bob realized that he really needed to ferret out more about why the Whitehall loan had been withdrawn, and that meant talking to someone senior at the bank. He had no contacts there and only one name without resorting to a directory—Corbin van Sloot. He wasn't sure how far he could get, but he would start at the top.

Sucking on his pen, Bob dialed the main number and asked for Van Sloot's office. He heard a click and then a woman's voice. "Mr. van Sloot's office."

Bob introduced himself and said he had a few quick questions in connection with a story he was working on.

"Can I tell him what this is about?" He'd heard the question so many times from well-trained intermediaries that he was expecting it.

"This is about a loan that the bank had made to a major New York newspaper."

"Just a moment. Let me see if he will talk to you." Another click.

A few moments later, Bob heard a smooth, urbane voice. "This is Corbin van Sloot."

"Thanks for taking my call, Mr. van Sloot," Bob said politely and repeated his credentials. "I'd like to ask about the loan that Whitehall had made to Star Enterprises that was recently withdrawn."

The phone was silent for several seconds. "Well, I can discuss some things about it if we are clearly off the record; call it background. You—you can call me a very senior Whitehall official or something like that. I like to think I can help the press. My father was an editor."

Half a loaf was better than none, Bob thought to himself; if van Sloot wouldn't go on the record, at least he would talk. "That would be fine."

"Very well. What did you want to know?"

"Well, what were the terms of the loan? And was it for $20 million?"

"Yes, that's the amount. It was a working capital loan that had been in force for a few years."

Good so far, Bob thought to himself. This corroborated what Tom at the *Star* had told him.

"And this had been more or less arranged by Sir Reginald Downing? That's what a source told me."

"Yes, although it was actually tendered by the merchant banking group in London."

"Can you say why the loan was pulled?"

Silence. "Well, you'd need to talk to the merchant banking group for a full explanation. The staff in New York really wasn't involved."

Bob pressed on. "But surely you can give me a general idea."

"Generally speaking, the loan was nonperforming. The company had apparently spent pretty heavily on some capital investments, and the newspaper business, as you know—and you probably know better than most of us—is in real trouble."

Bob thought hard. "Did anyone at the *Star* approach you about restoring the loan?"

"Ah—yes."

"Was it Winston Crumm?"

"No comment."

Bob stared at his computer. "Even though we're on background, no comment?"

"That's right."

"I'm tempted to read that as a 'yes.'"

"I wouldn't."

"Okay, but someone there approached you and asked to reinstate the loan."

"That's right."

"And Sir Reginald had passed away at that point?"

"Yes."

"What did you tell the people at Star?"

"What I just told you. The loan had been terminated by the people in London, and the decision was irreversible. I was in no position to override that decision."

"Really? You're the CEO."

"Yes, but I'm a big believer in the autonomy of our British partners, and I saw no reason to countermand them. The decision was clearly the right one at that."

Bob clicked his pen, a nervous habit. "Very good. I'll stand by the identification we agreed to at the outset, a very senior official at Whitehall."

"I'd appreciate that."

"Nice talking to you, and thanks for taking my call."

"You're welcome. And good luck with the story. Um—by the way, why such interest in a business loan being pulled? It happens every day."

"Well, a private investor has stepped in and given them the full amount of that loan. I'm trying to run that down."

"Really?" He heard Corbin's voice register surprise. "Can you tell me who that is?"

Bob chuckled. "This is where *I* have to say 'no comment.' Hopefully, you'll read it in a story in a short while. Once again, thank you. Goodbye."

CHAPTER 31

Two further texts to Larissa went unanswered Monday afternoon, and Corbin was beginning to suspect the worst, that she was indeed party to the video. He decided he had to break protocol and call her directly, but the call went to voicemail with no identification other than a computerized voice repeating her number and asking him to leave a message.

Work was impossible; his mind was racing in neutral, and concentration failed him. He decided he would go to her apartment and confront her, but he couldn't leave early—that would raise eyebrows. It would have to wait until five, still early but acceptable. He called Pieter and asked him to be outside then.

A cold snap had brought a few snow showers, and the sidewalks looked to have been sprinkled with sugar. He had Pieter drive up right outside her building; there was no point now in any subterfuge. Corbin asked him to see if he could find a parking space anywhere nearby—there was nothing on that side of the street—then got out and walked cautiously to the door. Since there was no doorman, he strode to the elevator and punched the "up" button. Once inside, he pushed the button for the third floor and folded his hands, his heart thumping in his chest.

Outside her apartment, he gathered himself for a few moments outside the cream-colored door and then reached for the buzzer. He heard it ring inside, the familiar sound he knew from his visits, but there were no other sounds. He pressed it again, but it echoed emptily. There was no point in knocking; anyone inside could clearly hear the buzzer. After a third try, he walked away, disconsolate.

Alone with his thoughts, Corbin dimly recognized the demons of arrogance. He'd been captivated by Larissa but blind to the notion that anything that happened between them might be on *her* terms. She had been like another perk, something luxurious and seductive, something he didn't have to ask for. The nightmarish video was a thunderclap that had shocked him to his core.

Outside the front door and back on the sidewalk, he looked up and down the block and didn't see the Mercedes. It was getting dark, but the streetlights had come on, and he could see well enough. Light snow was falling again and was outlined against the lights like a procession of shooting stars. It was a lovely sight, but Corbin's mind was elsewhere. He reached into his pocket for his phone and dialed Pieter, who appeared a few minutes later.

"Home, Pieter. This snow won't help, I'm sure of that."

"No, boss. And I've seen there is a crash on the FDR that is blocking the northbound lanes at Ninetieth Street. I need to go further north before we get on."

"Very good. Do whatever you have to do."

Corbin sat back and sighed. He turned on the backseat light and settled in with the *Journal*, but he had a hard time reading; his mind, like his world, was on the verge of implosion.

Promptly at nine the next morning, Corbin, still trying to recover from a terrible night of sleep enveloped in dread, heard Angela buzz him. "Mr. van Sloot, I have Mr. Robertson on the line from London."

"Put him through." Corbin's heart was in his throat.

"Hello, Corbin."

"Good morning, or at least it is here," Corbin said, trying his best to sound light-hearted.

"Well, Thomas and I have given it quite a talking through," he said. "We—um—we realize what a difficult and unfortunate situation this is for you. Very unfortunate, I must say."

"It certainly is." *Where is this going?* Corbin wondered.

"And we realize what a fearsome adversary Ripovsky is. That he would go to such lengths to blackmail you is incredible." He paused. "That said, it is our consensus that we can't give in to this scheme. If he wants a board seat, he will have to earn it."

Corbin was crestfallen. He knew this was a possible outcome, but he could only have hoped otherwise. "So, David—where does this leave me? This means he can go ahead and release that video, and the devil take the hindmost."

Robertson cleared his throat. "We discussed that at some length, Corbin. The simple fact is you've put us in an untenable situation. Your affair was, quite frankly, a poor decision, and the blackmail, which you certainly never could have anticipated, has compounded the problem immensely."

Corbin's mind swam. This was bad: no sympathy, no life raft bobbing toward him.

"So, what do we do?" Robertson went on. "The release of the video affects you and your family, not us in London. If he does indeed release it, it becomes a matter between you and your wife. If your marriage is strong, it may survive this."

Corbin stewed silently, a mix of anger and resentment boiling in his brain. He wasn't used to being lectured, much less by a Brit he didn't think was his intellectual equal.

"But there is another course of action," Robertson went on. "What we would like is for you to tender your resignation.

If the stain of this comes back to us, it will seem we acted in due course."

Corbin felt his face flush. "You're serious? Resign?"

"I'm afraid so. We will give you a generous, very generous, severance package. You've done a lot of great work for the bank, and we're not unappreciative. We will say that you left to pursue other opportunities rather than over some kind of disagreement. That might not withstand some scrutiny, but that's for you to handle."

"You know that the video could be the end of my career," Corbin said heatedly.

Robertson seemed unruffled. "That could well be. We hope not for your sake, but that's why we're willing to give you a parachute that could tide you over for some time to come."

"How much are we talking about?" Corbin asked, somewhat mollified.

"We're still trying to work out a number," Robertson said, "but it should be at least $25 million over time."

Relief washed over Corbin. "I appreciate the gesture, David." He'd made $16 million the year before, but $12 million of that was in stock options, and many of those hadn't yet vested and couldn't be cashed in—so $25 million was a nice number indeed.

"We will work up a press release and send it over to you later today for your approval," Robertson said smoothly. "We'd like to be able to announce this tomorrow. If it's any consolation, this would come out before Ripovsky said he would release his video, which might help your wife understand your decision. And—it's always possible—if Ripovsky realizes we've called his bluff, he may decide it's not worth putting that video out. He has leverage on you, but if you're gone ..."

"I can only hope," Corbin said. "I can't count on that. But thank you, David. I will look for that release."

They hung up, and Corbin sat deep in thought. Then he

reached for his computer. He needed to call his college buddy Sandy Campbell, who was a major compensation consultant in the city. Sandy could help him navigate these turbid waters; he just didn't need to know about the blackmail.

CHAPTER 32

Thanksgiving at the Crumm household had been, well, unexciting. Amanda and Adrienne did some baking. Adrienne had taught herself how to make a pumpkin pie, and the two of them collaborated on it as lunchtime approached, pouring the amber-colored filling into the prefabricated crust before loading it into the oven. They'd sat together earlier and watched the Macy's Thanksgiving Day parade, the TV extravaganza with its armada of floats and cartoon character balloons, an annual event whose permanence seemed to suggest that all was right with the world, at least for a day. Non-New Yorkers, on the other hand, might think inflated figures were fully appropriate for the city.

Winston was lost in another pro football game, the annual battle between the same teams, only one of which was likely to have any playoff aspirations. No matter; to look at him, he was as intent as if viewing it were part of a ransom demand.

Adrienne's sister and her husband would be coming over in the late afternoon for the big event, the roast turkey with all the trimmings. Carmelita would soon be busy preparing the turkey, a twelve-pound tom, which would be a beautifully cooked specimen, fit for a magazine spread, before Winston invariably mutilated it with his attempts at carving.

First, however, was lunch: grilled cheese sandwiches and a salad, nothing too heavy. Adrienne had a small glass of sherry, and Winston had a can of beer; Amanda sipped vitamin water. They sat around the table in the kitchen alcove, a wooden oval that could seat six, as sunlight streamed in through the tall windows and lit the table almost like a movie set.

"Mom, you didn't tell me about the charity event," Amanda said, dipping her fork into her salad. She had on ripped jeans and a green-and-white-checked shirt that smacked of Orvis or L.L. Bean. She'd pinned her hair up for the baking.

"Oh, it was very nice, honey. We raised a lot of money for the food bank."

"And this Russian guy was the big donor?"

"That's right." Adrienne smiled, and her brown eyes were warm.

"What was his name?"

"Ripovsky, Maxim Ripovsky. Your father had met him a few weeks earlier."

Amanda turned her gaze to Winston. "How did you meet him?"

He was chewing his sandwich with his mouth half-open, and he needed a few moments to swallow. Winston held up his hand briefly before replying. "Well, it was a business connection. He was interested in advertising in the *Star*. He's a very rich guy who has bought a few apartment buildings here."

Amanda asked, "Is he one of those scary-looking Russians, the ones with tattoos and no hair?"

"No, not at all." Adrienne chuckled lightly. "He's extremely tall and quite good-looking, very cosmopolitan. And his girl-friend—"

"Natasha," Winston chipped in.

"Right, Natasha. She's almost as tall as he is. Really. Quite an Amazon. I'd have to say they're one of the most striking couples I've ever seen."

"Sounds very interesting," Amanda said, taking a bite of her sandwich. "But, you know, with all the cyber warfare and everything that the Russians have been doing—just look at the last couple of elections—I'd be suspicious of almost anything they did. You know, like there is always some ulterior motive."

"I certainly hope not," Adrienne said. "He seemed very eager to please and polite. And very generous." She paused. "But I know what you mean. As a rule, I don't think the Russians are our friends."

"Definitely not. Don't you agree, Daddy-o?" That was her term for Winston; she called her real father simply "Dad."

"Yeah, they don't seem to be working on the level very much," Winston said offhandedly. He stood up. "I guess I'll get back to the game. Let me know if you need me for anything."

"We will," Adrienne said brightly, and the family tableau gently broke up.

Amanda had grown up reading the *Times*, since Adrienne made it part of her daily routine for many years. The daughter was fond of the Arts & Leisure section, which fitted her proclivities as a literature major, and that's what she was reading when she saw a small box headlined "Russian Donates 'Lost' Painting to MOMA." As she read it, Maxim Ripovsky had given the Museum of Modern Art a painting by Wassily Kandinsky, a Russian artist from the twentieth century, called *Red Trees*.

The article went on to say that the painting had been in private hands for over a century and had been considered lost by the art world. One curator said that, if authenticated, it could be worth $25 million.

"Wow," Amanda exclaimed and jumped up with the paper to bring it over to Adrienne, who was reading a magazine on the living room sofa. "It seems that Mr. Ripovsky has just donated a priceless painting to MOMA." She handed the paper to Adrienne, who spent a couple of minutes looking at it after Amanda plopped herself down in an armchair.

"My goodness," Adrienne said, handing the paper back to her daughter. "He is really making a name for himself in New York."

They heard shouting from the other room. "Stuff 'em! Hit 'em!" was followed by a groan.

They both rolled their eyes. Winston's enthusiasm for teams he didn't care about could only be construed as a way of staying entertained in the face of yawning boredom.

"I wonder if your father knows about this painting," Adrienne said, referring to her first husband, Philip Rogers, a professor of art history at New York University. "Sounds like it could be in the era he specializes in."

"You're right. Why don't I call him?" Amanda exclaimed. If history was any guide, Rogers, a Scrooge about holidays like this, would probably be reading in his well-appointed bachelor apartment before going out for a sumptuous dinner.

Rogers answered on the third ring. "Hi, honey. How is the holiday *chez* Crumms?"

"Just fine, Dad. The usual. Say, did you see that item in the *Times* about this supposedly lost painting being donated to MOMA?"

"I did. Very interesting. I've done a certain amount of research on Kandinsky over the years, and this would indeed be quite a find. I remember seeing a photo of it many years ago. It would be from his early period, over a century ago."

"Could it really be worth that much?"

He sighed. "It could if it was authenticated. There are so many forgeries that crop up. And, let's face it, for it to turn up unannounced, having supposedly been acquired from some private estate—these things definitely get the antennae up."

"Uh-huh." She bit the nail on her index finger. "And if it

were a forgery—?"

"Well, it would be worthless, certainly a black mark on Mr. Ripovsky, though I'm sure he would claim that he was told it was genuine. And it would be hard to prove he knew it was a fake. In the high-profile art world, you have nothing to gain by trying to pass off a bogus masterpiece."

"That's what I thought," she said. "How—how long could it take to authenticate it?"

"Good question; a few weeks, probably. I don't know the person in charge of that area, but I'm sure he or she is plenty competent."

"Did you know this Ripovsky guy was a huge donor for a charity function that Mom threw a few weeks ago?"

"Huh. No, I didn't. Well, the Russians have a lot of money, the oligarchs, that is. I assume that describes Ripovsky."

"I think it probably does. Well, thanks, Dad. Enjoy your dinner. We're having the usual."

"You enjoy too. I'm happy I'm not there. Thanks for the call. Bye."

Not far away, Maxim Ripovsky sat in his favorite chair, grinning. The piece from the *New York Times* had been pointed out to him by his public relations manager. It was validation, beyond a doubt to anyone reading it, that his campaign to widen his footprint in the city was working.

CHAPTER 33

Rain lashed at the windows in Corbin's office, a chilly December rain that did nothing to lift anyone's spirits and certainly not his. He looked at a few notes he had scribbled down as well as Ripovsky's number. When it was nine-thirty, he lifted the receiver and dialed the number.

"Rubicon Investments." The woman's voice was foreign, inflected.

"Good morning, this is Corbin van Sloot, CEO of Whitehall Banking Group, calling for Mr. Ripovsky."

"Just a meenit, pliss. I weel connect you." The line seemed to go dead for a moment, then he heard a faint click.

"Hello, Mr. van Sloot. What news do you have for me?

"Probably not what you were hoping for, Mr. Ripovsky. The chairman in London has made it very clear he is not ready to seat you. He's very aware of the video, but he has chastised me and says it won't affect his decision."

"I see." There was a pause. "You made it very clear to him the impact this could have on you and your family?"

"I did. I have to say, Mr. Ripovsky, that this blackmail is unworthy of someone seeking to be on the board of a major bank, and the chairman essentially said that. But he feels that

I've brought this on myself, and that I need to resign."

"What?" Ripovsky exclaimed.

"That's right. My resignation will be announced this morning. With that, you will no longer have any leverage on me." He paused to let that sink in. "Of course, I would hope this changes the situation with the video. Releasing it hurts me, but it doesn't impact any campaign to join the board, which you can still do, of course, through the proper channels."

A long pause ensued. "Well, this is surprising, I must say. It's unfortunate for you that I have already ordered some of the videotape to be sent to your wife. It should be on its way by now."

Corbin snorted; he couldn't control himself. "You're a cold bastard, Ripovsky. I think that you'll find blackmail isn't a way to conduct business in the West. It will come back to haunt you. There are already a lot of suspicions surrounding rich Russians like you—this kind of thing simply confirms those."

"Well, you are entitled to your opinions. We'll see how things develop in the years ahead."

"By the way, was Larissa working for you?"

"Who is Larissa?"

"The woman I'm seen with on the video."

"Oh yes, Larissa," he said softly. "She is certainly a beautiful woman. Very sexy."

"So, she was working for you?"

"She does work for me from time to time. She's a wonderful business analyst, and"—Corbin could almost picture him grinning—"she has other attributes as well."

"She certainly does. She is very good bait for a trap."

"Ah, yes, well ... I will say goodbye, Mr. van Sloot. I think you should be more careful in the future about the young women you associate with." He paused. "It would be odd for me to wish you good things, but I don't consider you an enemy."

"Wish I could say the same. If I could prosecute you, I would. Goodbye to you."

Corbin set down the phone and stared outside, past where the rain was still beading in long drops on the window. He took a deep breath. How could he intercept the video? His future was riding on it, and he didn't have much time to spare.

CHAPTER 34

Elena had agreed to meet Natasha at a lovely old pub on Bond Street, long one of London's most fashionable districts, with a raft of high-end stores: Burberry, Louis Vuitton, Asprey, Cartier, Hermes, Dolce & Gabbana, and many more. Being a few minutes early, she stopped in briefly at the Hermes store to look at scarves but recoiled at the prices, some of which would be a month's rent in Moscow.

The two women knew each other only superficially; Natasha's role as a companion to Maxim intrigued Elena, as did Natasha's physical stature. Elena worked on a separate floor, and on most working days when they were both in the office, they rarely encountered each other.

It was Elena who had reached out. Natasha had also lived in Moscow until a few years earlier, and Elena knew they had that in common. She also wanted to see if she could ferret out some details about what Natasha did, which supposedly involved marketing. But what kind? She knew Natasha spoke little English, and after all, they were in London.

She walked into the pub, a symphony in dark wood highlighted by a long bar with a mirror behind it, as well as shelves stocked high with liquor bottles that gleamed from the light overhead. She asked the barman for a menu and took a table for two against the wall. There were a number of other customers, mostly men, at other tables. One she noticed, a middle-aged man with a goatee and wire-rimmed glasses, seemed to look her up and down approvingly.

Elena wasn't a big fan of British cuisine, but she liked pub food, simple and comforting, unpretentious, much like what she'd had growing up in Moscow. Shepherd's pie was a particular favorite.

A server approached and asked if he could take her order. She took him to be a Slav; tall, thin, and angular, his dark hair lank, he spoke with a pronounced accent. There were a lot of Slavs in London, many of them Croatians.

"Not yet. I'm waiting for a friend," she said, smiling. "But I will take a Samuel Smith brown ale." She'd developed a taste for some of the bitter British ales, so unlike anything she'd had in Russia. He nodded and glided away, as light on his feet as a ballroom dancer.

The beer arrived a minute later, accompanied by a tall, frosted glass. He poured it for her stoically. He was just setting it in front of her when Natasha walked up. When the server saw her, his eyes widened almost theatrically—she was one of the tallest women he'd ever seen. He sidled away.

"*Preevyet kak pazhivayesh?*" Natasha said in Russian.

"*Spasseba preekrasna,*" Elena replied.

Natasha apologized for being a few minutes late; she had been stuck on a phone call, she said. Slipping off her raincoat, she revealed a light-blue dress shirt with a bow at the neck and dark slacks. Elena sensed that all eyes in the pub were fixed on the blonde Valkyrie in front of her as if she were an exotic animal at a zoo.

"*Neechevo, pazhaloosta.*" Elena smiled reassuringly.

The conversation continued in Russian. Elena picked up on something of a provincial accent that she couldn't quite place. She wanted the shepherd's pie, and Natasha took bangers and mash; Elena did the ordering.

Elena probed gently, trying to draw Natasha out, nodding amicably at her answers. Natasha told her she had been working as a physical trainer at a high-end club in Moscow when Maxim had spotted her and asked her to help him set up a training regimen. A few months later, he told her who he was and asked her to come to London at five-times her Moscow salary. How could she refuse?

She found him brilliant and somewhat mysterious. He was often away from the office, in New York or elsewhere, and there were long stretches when she wouldn't see him. And then he would summon her to come with him, sometimes on his Gulfstream jet, to meet with people. Since most of these meetings were in English, she was essentially a presence at his side, smiling at the right moments but mostly silent.

He had set her up in a luxurious one-bedroom flat, and she had an expense account that allowed her to buy almost anything she wanted. But she had grown up middle class, she said—her father was a railway engineer, and her mother taught school—and with three siblings, there was little opportunity to buy luxuries. So, she felt conflicted about spending.

"I've heard that your job involves marketing," Elena said to Natasha. "Do you work to sell clients on Maxim's properties?"

Natasha tossed her head back and smiled. "*Nyet.*" Since her command of English was so poor, Maxim had her trolling through major property listings in Russia to see if something might catch his interest. She used a Russian database that was, she said, notoriously balky and often outdated, but it did periodically turn up things of interest. Maxim's instructions to her were to focus only on properties listed for 400 million rubles or more, somewhere just north of four million British pounds. Often, she would be on the phone with property managers in Russia, trying to gauge their level of interest in selling, any offers, that kind of thing.

"And then he just calls you if he needs you with him?" Elena asked.

"*Da.*" Sometimes he called and gave her very little time, perhaps as little as two hours' notice, she said. She didn't mind, she added; he was an amazing man, so smart, and everything was always first class.

Leaning forward conspiratorially, Elena asked what he was like as a lover.

"Maxim?"

"*Da.*"

Natasha stared at her as if she had two heads, then leaned back and smiled, one of her lips twisting slightly upward. "Maxim and I are not lovers," she said. "He is what the British call a 'pouf.' He likes boys."

Elena recoiled in shock, then slowly smiled. This had to be a joke. "You're a funny one, Natasha. Seriously, what is he like?"

Natasha shook her head slightly. "No, this is true," she said. "He has never touched me. He is always courteous, and he likes me to stand next to him; we look like quite a couple. It makes an impression on people."

"Do you have any proof that he is gay?" Elena asked.

"I've never seen him in bed or anything," she said, "but I've seen boys and young men go into his hotel rooms late at night. Sergei opens the door for them. And I've never seen him with a woman."

"My goodness." Elena tried to conceal the shock she was feeling, then decided to change the subject. "Do you have a boyfriend, then?"

"*Da*, Ivan Sarapov. He is in the export business, mostly electronics." She threw her head back slightly and reached for her drink.

"I don't want to pry, but do you live with him?" Elena asked, leaning forward.

"Not all the time. He spends a lot of weekends with me,

and we've traveled some together."

"And if Maxim asks for you when you're with Ivan?"

Natasha smiled ruefully. "I have to do whatever Maxim wants me to," she said. "He's the boss."

The rest of the lunch passed in a blur. Elena paid the bill, but Natasha contributed a tip. They exchanged air kisses at the door and went their separate ways. For Elena, the walk back to the office was very different from the norm; lost in her thoughts, she was practically oblivious to the other pedestrians, even the men who ogled her.

Maxim? She was shocked, confused. But there was another emotion that surged into her brain; it was very much like disgust.

For Elena, homosexuality shouldn't have been such an issue. She was a modern woman, educated and smart, and the zeitgeist almost everywhere in the developed world had moved very far in recent years. Marriage between two men and between two women was increasingly common in Western countries, something unthinkable years earlier. She knew in her heart that many gay people were in committed, loving relationships, just like heterosexual couples, even though those relationships in many cases were hidden for years.

But she couldn't get her head around the idea of Maxim, who almost seemed superhumanly manly, satisfying his urges with male prostitutes. The idea was almost incomprehensible. The use of prostitutes was common among many well-heeled Russian men, but they frequented women. Elena realized that, as long as she had worked for Maxim, their interactions were always strictly business. His private life was an enigma.

She stewed on these thoughts during the afternoon, and when she got back to the flat, she rushed over to Mikhail to get his thoughts. Mikhail, a salesman for an import firm, was cooking pasta in the kitchen. As a product of the Russian hockey system, he came from a world of men dominated by men. Surely, he would find this detestable, she thought to herself.

"I have to tell you something I learned today from Natasha," she said in Russian after giving him a perfunctory kiss.

"What's that?" he asked, half turning to face her.

"She says Maxim is gay, and he hires male prostitutes."

His blue eyes widened, and he turned to her. "Really?" he asked, his voice rising a half octave in surprise. "That's certainly not the image he projects."

"I know, I know," she said. "I have a hard time believing it."

"Let me practice English," he said. "This doesn't change your work with him, does it?"

"No."

"Then you must accept it for what it is. Men, just like women, can deceive." He bent over to turn down the flame beneath the pot on the stove.

"I suppose. So, you don't find it truly surprising?"

"Surprising, yes. But I think this is just something you must try to ignore."

"I know," she said. "I'm just having a hard time with it."

The next morning, with the chilly fog transforming the streetlamps outside to mere silhouettes, her emotions were still churning, a bilious mix that had worked its way down to her gut. She'd done Max's bidding with the *kompromat*, seducing a very nice man, but that sexual escapade was something Max would never do with a woman. That didn't seem right, not at all.

Elena felt a renewed surge of sympathy for Corbin; he knew how to be with a woman. She had ignored a few days of his texts, and he had stopped texting. She thought she knew why: Maxim had delivered the kompromat. Corbin would despise her, think her wicked, a seductress working to get blackmail material. It gnawed at her.

That morning, running a scenario for a business acquisition, she decided she would reach out to Corbin. It would be painful. He was a gentleman, but he had been deceived, blackmailed; anyone would be angry. But she felt she owed him something, not an apology exactly but a rationale. As a businessman, he would understand.

She checked her texts; the last one from him was on Monday. It was now Thursday. She went to his last text and hit "reply," then wrote, *"I think you must hate me—I hope not. I want to talk to you and explain some things. Will you call me? I am in London."*

It was probably forty minutes later that her phone rang. She saw it was a New York number but not his cell.

"Hello?"

"Larissa, I'm calling only because you said you wanted to explain some things," Corbin began. "I want to know how you could be involved in something like this. Did you know that Ripovsky blackmailed me with this video?"

"Yes, I knew he would."

"He's responsible for my resigning from the bank. That happened yesterday." She sensed the anger in his voice, a tone she'd never heard before.

"What? Oh, no."

"Yeah, well, my counterpart in London wasn't ready to give in to the blackmail, and I became the sacrificial lamb. I— I'm afraid that Ripovsky is sending my wife that video now."

"Oh, Corbin. I'm so sorry to hear this."

"Are you? You said you wanted to explain this, so start explaining."

She told him that Larissa was an alias, that the apartment, the backstory of her family in France, her consultant's job, everything, had been arranged by Ripovsky, and she had been working for him in London for four years. He had installed her in the apartment and tracked Corbin, then arranged for her to bump into him in the art gallery.

"I guess I should have realized it was all too good to be true," he said wistfully. "By the way, what is your real name?"

"Elena."

"Elena what?"

"I can't tell you that."

"Okay. What do you do for Ripovsky?"

"I'm a business analyst. I look at potential acquisitions."

"Well, you're smart and beautiful. He should be thankful he has someone like you."

"Yes, I think he is."

"I bet you got a bonus for delivering the video on me," he said sarcastically.

She said nothing, then, "I've learned something about Maxim that bothers me greatly. I think I know of a way that could help you negate—is that a word?—what he has done to you."

"Huh, what is that?"

"I learned yesterday that Maxim, despite all appearances, is gay. He has boys and young men brought to his room, and I'm sure he pays them."

"What? You're kidding."

"No, deadly serious. I've been thinking that if you had someone who could watch over his apartment building, they would see these boys coming and going. Photographs could be taken, and then you could turn the tables on Maxim. Threaten to expose him with these photos."

"Hmmm. Are you serious? These aren't the kinds of things I do. This would have to be something for a private detective."

"Yes, and when I was in New York, I collected a few names of people in that business. It was part of a project for Maxim. I can send you those names, and you can choose."

She heard him huff. "God, you are serious about this, aren't you?"

"I am."

"Couldn't this come back to you?"

"If all I do is send you some names by text, I don't think so. I will take that risk."

"I don't know, Elena, is it? This sounds a little far-fetched, but I would l love to put some heat on him for a change. Please send me those names. I need to think about this some more."

"Corbin, can you find another job?"

"Oh, I'm sure I can. It may take a while. Just remember, now, I owe my current predicament to you—entirely to you."

"I know, and I'm sorry."

"Don't try to snow me with your apologies. You're a good actress, and you did your job very well. Let's just leave it at that."

A lump formed in her throat. "I suppose so," she managed to say.

"So, we understand each other. When I think of you, I'll try to focus on the good times we had together. But it certainly wasn't a happy ending. Goodbye, Elena."

CHAPTER 35

Whistling to himself, Winston strolled through the French doors and out onto the vast flagstone terrace of his mansion in Boca Raton, admiring the wide swath of green lawn stretching toward the Intracoastal Waterway. He'd had a fortifying breakfast of ham and scrambled eggs, and now the sun was warming things up into the sixties.

Things were looking up. Ripovsky had come through with the second ten million, as he said he would, after Winston had cajoled Mitch into fronting him for the advertisements in the *Star*. Adrienne was still basking in the afterglow of the Cosmopolitan Club event, and the *Northern Star* was docked not far away. Winston thought they should consider a trip to Bimini sometime soon, provided the weather was good, a high-speed sprint across the Gulf Stream.

Clad in his customary khakis and polo shirt, Winston stretched out in the patio chair. It was great to be back in Florida, especially with the mid-December northerlies, those unheeding bullies, blasting through Manhattan. He and Adrienne had flown down two days earlier on a private jet— he didn't own one but had a fractional ownership that gave him the opportunity to use one more or less when he wanted.

They hadn't flown commercial in at least fifteen years, one more factor distancing Winston from normal people. Amanda would be coming down that afternoon, flying commercially but in first class.

He thought back to Ripovsky's financial rescue. Winston had finessed it, brought it home with no damage to himself or the brand. Ripovsky's conditions were met easily enough, and the Russian had never insisted on any favorable coverage for himself or his country—a good thing, since as a rule, Winston had no more say in the editorial side of things than anyone else on the board. The editors knew better, and deep down, Winston understood why.

The two weeks running just past New Year's had become an annual Florida retreat for the Crumms. Someone of Winston's stature might have jetted off to Europe or Aspen, but Winston was a creature of habit, something that seemed to annoy Adrienne from time to time, but she never harped on it. Winston would never acknowledge it, but he was like the sot at the end of the bar who came in every night and sat at the same stool. And they enjoyed occasional socializing with people at the yacht club, most of them rich northerners who also went south, much like migrating birds following an instinctive path.

Just then Adrienne walked out and took the seat next to him. She had on a bright green running suit, though she never ran or played tennis, just did some basic yoga most days. She set down her coffee cup on the small, tiled table and smiled at him. Her dark hair was pulled back from her face. Large, round Fendi sunglasses completed her look.

"Looks like a lovely day," she said.

"Yeah, doesn't it?" He pulled at a pant leg idly with one hand. "Hard to beat."

"What are your plans?"

"Well, I thought I'd go over and check things at the boat, talk to Dirk. I wanna make sure things are ready if we want to go over to Bimini."

She sipped her coffee. "That would be nice," she said with only a faint note of enthusiasm. "A day trip, right? And on a nice day? It can be rough out there." She remembered a trip a couple of years ago with the boat rocking and rolling like a carnival ride, sending both of them below decks to ride it out.

"Of course. We can do it on short notice."

"Good. And I'm sure Amanda would want to go along."

"Yeah, I'm sure she would."

Winston sauntered through the kitchen door into the garage, a three-car affair with a golf cart in one bay and two cars in the others: a Mercedes 250 SL, a swank little sports runabout for Adrienne, and the black BMW 750 that Winston piloted to the yacht club and other local haunts. The BMW was a corporate lease, another perk that Winston had taken advantage of. The license plate read "Star1."

He got in, started the engine, and backed out onto the driveway, the gravel crunching audibly. Winston loved the sound. When he reached the main road, he turned south at the light and headed for the yacht club. Traffic was reasonably light, and the palms overhead rustled in the breeze. He toggled the infoscreen to a favorite oldies station, featuring music from the seventies and early eighties, an era Winston remembered fondly, apart from disco. Whenever a disco hit came on—anything from the Bee Gees was a particular offender—he would change the channel.

Ten minutes later, he pulled into the parking lot at the yacht club and took a space near the entrance. His left knee had flared up, and he shuffled slightly as he went through the front door, said hello to the cheerful woman at the front desk, and walked through the spacious lobby and out the door to the slips. The *Northern Star* was moored at a long slip to his left, tied front and aft, and as immobile as Gulliver staked down by the Lilliputians. He smiled as the boat's navy-blue hull sparkled in the light reflected from the water below.

Climbing the short ladder and stepping onto the main deck, Winston said hello to a slim young guy cleaning the outside windows that surrounded the main salon, then went through and down the mahogany stairs. He made a beeline for the captain's quarters and rapped on the door.

"Yes?"

"Dirk, it's Winston. Can I come in?"

"Of course." The door opened, and Dirk nodded slightly. He was slightly under average height and his hair was starting to go gray, but he held himself very erect. His white uniform was spotless, and he had three gold bars on the black epaulets on his shoulders.

"I just wanted to see how things were going," Winston said amicably. "We're thinking about making a run over to Bimini one day soon, just a day trip."

"Okay." Dirk sounded hesitant. "I, uh, I was going to call you this morning. I've gotten another offer."

Winston looked puzzled. "An offer to do what?"

"To captain another yacht, in the British Virgins for the season. I would stay through the duration of your visit, of course."

"You're bailing out?" Winston was livid.

"Yes. You know, we had agreed long ago that either party was free to cancel this arrangement with notice." He had a hard time meeting Winston's eyes, but his voice was firm.

Winston pounded his fist on the door, a sharp sound. "I can't believe this. Who is making this great offer?"

"Simon Fairbank, the tech entrepreneur. We agreed to it yesterday."

Fairbank! Winston screwed up his face. Fair was fair—except Winston never recognized reciprocity if it wasn't on his terms. After all, he had purloined Wilson from Fairbank two years earlier.

"How much more is he paying you?"

"Forty percent more. It certainly was an offer I couldn't turn down. I imagine it's hard for you to understand—"

"Well, I always appreciate loyalty," Winston snarled. "You seem to value money more."

"Mr. Crumm, being a captain isn't exactly lucrative. We do it because we love it. So, if someone wants me and will offer me a higher rate, I can't ignore that."

"I see," Winston said coldly, though he clearly didn't. He couldn't counteroffer; he was already getting questions from the accounting department about the boat's expenses. "I should fire you right now, but we do want to make that trip to Bimini, and my family and I can't run the boat alone." He realized full well how little he knew about the equipment on the bridge, the captain's purview; a voyage without a captain was an invitation to misadventure and possibly disaster.

"I did say I would stay through your visit," Dirk said, "and I mean it. Let me know when you want to go, and we'll take care of it."

"Fine." Winston frowned, spun around, and quickly went back up the stairs. He almost tripped on the way up and blasted out the f-word so loudly that anyone on board could have heard him.

CHAPTER 36

Corbin had a hard time sleeping that night with his mind churning on just how he could keep the video from Patricia. She'd be curious, as anyone would, about a surprise package, presumably a small manila folder or a FedEx envelope. Actually, the more he thought about it, the more he sensed Ripovsky wouldn't trust regular mail, which would be slower. Perhaps the flash drive would be hand-delivered by one of his henchmen, dropped outside the door as surreptitiously as a gift basket from a neighbor.

Morning dawned cold and clear, and Corbin rose early, his head as fuzzy as if he were hung over. But he knew what he had to do. His resignation had been announced the day before, but Patricia knew nothing about it. It would be a minor story for the business pages, which she never read. He would break the news to her, but only after he made sure the video was safely in his hands.

So, he would stay home—that was entirely in keeping with his resignation—but he'd have to devise an excuse for not treating it like an ordinary workday. He padded around the den in his gray bathrobe and slippers, thinking hard. He couldn't say the office was closed for the day; that would make no sense. If she asked why, he couldn't come up with a reasonable explanation.

That meant it had to be a personal day for him. But for what? He tossed a few ideas around, going through each like a collector comparing items in an auction lot. He eventually hit on something that sounded a bit far-fetched, perhaps, but logical: sprinklers in the executive suites had inadvertently gone off, soaking the rooms. He had been alerted to that in a text earlier in the morning, and the company was advising all senior executives not to go to work until the damage was evaluated and cleanup begun.

Corbin walked back into the master suite and saw the bed was empty. He went to the bathroom, where Patricia was seated, brushing her hair in front of the mirror on her side of the expansive vanity. She had just come from a shower and smelled of soap. He bent over and kissed the top of her head.

"Honey, it's weird, but there's been an incident at the office," he said, straightening up. "The sprinklers in the executive suites went off somehow, and the rooms are soaked. I just got a text about it."

She glanced up at him. "That's odd. Has this ever happened before?"

"Not since I've been there. All of us on that floor were advised to stay home today while they clean it up."

She turned back to the mirror, where she could see his reflection. "Is there anything in your office that would be damaged?"

He paused to consider her question. "I don't think there's anything vital. It wouldn't be good for the upholstery, and some papers were on top of the desk. But other than that, I don't think it should be too bad."

"That's good." She turned and looked at him again, her face smooth and lovely in the soft light. "What will you do here today, then?"

"Oh, I'm sure I can find something. I really should review

some of our latest financial statements and talk to Rich. I may ask him to sell some things and reinvest." That sounded entirely plausible, especially since she left all the investment matters to him.

"Okay. Well, I'll be going to the shelter this morning." Patricia had been volunteering at a women's shelter in Norwalk for a number of years. She'd said many times how much satisfaction she got out of listening to and trying to help women from abusive households, and often their children as well. She didn't have a background in counseling, but she was poised and straightforward yet empathetic, and she always had someone with more experience to turn to if the situation warranted.

"Sounds good," he said cheerfully.

"Would you go check on the kids?" she asked with a smile. "Still a school day for them."

He smiled back. "On it," he said, and spun on his heels and walked out.

Patricia had come back from the shelter, and they had just finished lunch. Corbin's anxiety level had bumped up a few notches—he was much more comfortable with the notion of intercepting the package when she wasn't home. But here she was, as oblivious to his crisis as if she were watching TV in another room. He'd checked outside the door every half-hour or so. Nothing.

She'd asked him if he had moved on any of their investments, and he lied, said he had without much further explanation. The talk turned to the winter holiday. They had rented a property in Vail for a week, starting on the twelfth of February. It would be their second trip there, after a visit to Steamboat Springs a year earlier.

"You know, the Comptons will be out there part of that time. We should get together with them," she said. The

Comptons were friends who had two kids roughly the same age as theirs.

"Sure. Have you talked to Anne about it?" He tried hard to keep his mind on the conversation.

"Yeah, but only casually. I need to get their dates from her."

"Sounds good. It would be nice for the kids to all get together."

"It would. And it would be good for us adults to have a little social time of our own." She smiled.

"Amen. It's hard to keep kids entertained all the time, even with all their gadgets." He drummed his fingers on the table. "Anything on your agenda for the afternoon?"

"I'm playing paddle with the girls at two," she announced. *Paddle* meant platform tennis, a cold-weather game played outdoors and scored the same way as tennis. Patricia wasn't a keen tennis player, but she seemed happy running around in the cold weather, chasing a yellow rubber ball, laughing with her friends, and savoring a glass of sherry afterward. He was delighted by her interest, and he played on some weekends himself.

"Great. I think I'm just going to read for a while." He went to the silent living room and sat in one of the armchairs and pulled at his lower lip. Would the doorbell ring? If it were FedEx, that would be possible. He'd have to beat her to the door.

Corbin was relieved when she left at one-forty-five, calling out a cheery "I'm off." He tried to concentrate on the *National Geographic* in his lap, but his attention was fitful. It was an achingly clear winter day with the sun slanting through the tall windows, but he couldn't appreciate it. He didn't like lying to her; he always tried to be honest, sharing his career issues and their mutual interests with unflagging concern. But this was different—the stakes were too high.

It was just after two-thirty when he thought he heard the

crunch of gravel in the circular driveway out the front. He rose swiftly and practically jogged to the door. He could make out a black sedan hustling away from the house, and he opened the door. A plain manila envelope lay on the doormat, and he bent over to pick it up.

It was addressed to Patricia van Sloot and stamped "Urgent" in red letters. There was no return address and no postage; it had clearly just been dropped off. He saw a bulge in the envelope. This had to be it.

Walking back into the kitchen, he took a paring knife and opened the envelope. In it was a single sheet of paper and a red flash drive. He turned the paper over; the message was succinct:

> Dear Mrs. van Sloot:
>   I think you will be interested in the contents of this flash drive, which should tell you something about the man you married.

There was no name, no signature, just "An interested party."

Corbin strode into the garage and put the flash drive on the workbench. Then he reached for a claw hammer and smashed the drive into several pieces, which he tossed into the trash bin.

Walking back inside, he went to the office and bent over the shredder. He fed it the envelope first, then the paper sheet. He took a deep breath, and a wave of relief washed over him like a warm shower. Ripovsky, who surely assumed Corbin was in New York preparing for his departure, would never know the package had been intercepted. The nightmare was over.

CHAPTER 37

Reporters are often pulled away from longer-term projects for more immediate coverage, and that was true for Bob as well. He found himself being asked to deal with a couple of major stories for the *FT* shortly before mid-December, forcing the Ripovsky project onto the back burner. He chafed a bit, not only because that was his nature—patience wasn't encoded in his DNA—but because the upcoming Hanukkah season was a time he always took off, and that pushed the story back further.

This habit was odd, in a way. Bob was far from Orthodox, and even for observant Jews, Hanukkah was a relatively minor holiday. But it gave Bob a break before the Christmas crush, and he found it easy to work during Christmas week with a goodly portion of the office up and gone and with it the usual clamor. And he dedicated one day every year during Hanukkah to spend visiting his mother in her New Jersey nursing home.

Five days later, his holiday over, Bob walked over to Jeremy's office to update him on the Ripovsky story. He knocked on the door, and Jeremy, who had been reading through a sheaf of papers, looked up and gestured for Bob to take the seat in front of Jeremy's desk.

"So, where are we now, Bob?" To Bob, his tone was a trifle condescending, but that's how he always pictured Jeremy, who definitely dressed and presented himself in the British tradition, including wearing cuff links. To Bob, those were a vestige of the go-go 1980s, along with yellow ties and suspenders.

Bob proceeded to outline the basic thrust of his story. Ripovsky had made a second $10 million investment, still without any apparent quid pro quo, that effectively made up for the loss of the Whitehall loan. The use of the secretive shell company was an important feature of the story—it raised key questions. Bob was going to spotlight Ripovsky as an oligarch who was starting to make waves in New York through actions both overt and covert.

Jeremy leaned back and put his hands behind his head. "And you haven't interviewed him yet?"

"No, that's my last piece in the puzzle," Bob said, his glasses glinting in the light. "I expect him to deny most of this or at least decline to comment. But what I have is solid."

"Well and good. Was Maura in London helpful?"

"She was. She came up with the name of another shell company that made a tech investment, which I'll be including in the story."

Jeremy stroked his chin where Bob could make out the beginnings of stubble, like dead stalks in a snowfield. "How much color do you plan to include on Ripovsky, his background, the way he lives?"

"Um, not that much, really. He's very secretive. Those details are really hard to come by, and I feel this story shouldn't sit much longer."

"But you will be talking about how he grew up, got rich—you know, the juicy stuff."

Bob spread his hands. "Sure, I do have some of that. He came up through the Russian basketball system, for instance.

He's very tall."

"How tall?" Jeremy, who was about six foot four, sounded intrigued.

"Apparently about six foot seven."

"Aha. Well, how soon do you plan to interview him?"

"Hopefully in the next couple of days, assuming he will do an interview. I want to get everything done well before Christmas."

"Good. I'll be away on holiday starting next week, but I hope we can finalize the story and get it out before I leave."

"Great, thanks." Bob smiled and walked out briskly, but quickly felt some pangs of uncertainty. He hadn't worked with Jeremy on a big story before, and every editor had his or her own set of standards and criteria. Hell, he knew of horror stories where editors rewrote stories completely just to put their own stamp on it. He just hoped Jeremy would be as keen on the story as he was.

CHAPTER 38

If the two days after his resignation announcement were a precursor of things to come, Corbin sensed that hard times lay ahead. The first challenge was bringing Patricia around to the notion that this wasn't a disaster, that he would be paid handsomely and that their lifestyle shouldn't be crimped—and that his sudden departure wouldn't trigger whispered gossip among their friends, the words that couldn't be uttered in his presence.

When he first told her, it was after a normal family dinner in which they all talked about what had been going on that day. The kids had repaired to the family room to watch TV, and he had pulled her into the study, a secluded space with tall built-in shelves full of books, telling her he had something important to talk about. As his story spilled out, she was increasingly incredulous—how could he resign? Her gray eyes flashed; she folded her arms. Her first reaction was truculence, not sympathy.

Corbin couched the situation as a major difference of opinion, the kind of thing that crops up when a company is divided between two distinct cultures. The death of Sir Reginald, he said, had brought in new leadership with a new game plan, one that seemed likely to minimize the American arm. It all sounded so logical that even he was buying into it. He assured her that Whitehall's parting compensation would be generous indeed, and he mentioned the numbers. Her eyes widened in surprise.

"I'm going to see my old friend Sandy Campbell, a compensation expert, to go over all the details of the package," he said earnestly. "I want to make sure all the 'i's are dotted and the 't's crossed. This is too important not to be fully vetted."

"That sounds like a really good idea," Patricia replied, sounding somewhat mollified. She sat on the edge of her desk and brought both arms to her sides. "What about you, honey? This will be a drastic change. It's certainly a sudden shock. How are you processing this?" Her eyes went to his.

"I'll be fine," he said with the most reassurance he could muster. "Executives lose their jobs every day, and the circumstances can be pretty ugly. But they're treating me well financially."

"But—what do we tell the kids? If you're not leaving for the office every day, it's going to be pretty obvious this isn't a vacation."

"I know, I know," he said, nodding. "I want to keep working. I have a career history, and there is no noncompete clause involved in all this. I can work for another bank or do something else. We'll have a big financial cushion to support us." He looked imploringly at her. As much as he loved her, he loved the idea that he'd won her, that she was an enduring symbol of his success; he needed her to believe that his resignation wouldn't upend their lives.

"What else would you do?" she asked quizzically. He thought he detected worry lines in her otherwise smooth forehead.

"I don't know. I need to give this some thought, of course, and we have a head-hunting firm that works with the bank. I know some of those folks, and I really think they could be helpful."

She blew out a breath. "I think we need to sit down with the kids and let them know what's going on. It will be a lot worse if they find out some other way."

"You're right, honey. Let's do it now, tonight." He wrapped his arms around her and gave her a hug, but he didn't sense much warmth in her response. Her body was slack. It was as if a stink bomb had been released in the room and she was feeling its effects. Now the whole family would have to experience it.

It was Thursday, and Corbin had been given this day and Friday to wrap up his affairs and clear out his office. Angela had greeted him with moist eyes and genuine sorrow in her voice; everyone in the building knew what had happened—at least the official version, that Corbin and the Londoners had agreed to part ways. If they knew the real story, tongues would be hanging out the windows. Angela told him she was going to arrange a send-off on Friday afternoon in the main cafeteria.

The truth was, despite his lofty station, cleaning out the office wasn't really any more difficult for Corbin than any middling manager since the furniture, computer, and all the associated technology he used every day belonged to the bank, leaving his personal effects and memorabilia—photos, knick-knacks, a few books—to be packed up. He did insert a thumb drive and spent a half-hour scrolling through his files to save anything personal and delete the originals. There was precious little of any concern.

At about eleven, he pulled out his cell phone and clicked on the text that had come from Elena the day earlier. It listed three private investigators in Manhattan with their phone numbers: Reliable Investigations, the Newbold Agency, and Certified Professionals. He decided to simply take them in order.

Reliable Investigations proved to be very *unreliable.* An operator's voice said simply that the number was no longer in service. Corbin wasn't particularly surprised; he sensed that this industry skirted the bright line of legitimacy, and companies could come and go like ponds spawned by seasonal rains.

The second call to the Newbold Agency was much different. An efficient woman's voice asked him to hold and connected him in a matter of seconds. A man answered, "Hello, Fred Baines."

"Mr. Baines? Hello, my name is Corbin van Sloot. I'm calling to ask about engaging your company's services for some surveillance work. Is that kind of work within your area of expertise?"

"That depends." His voice was deep and smooth, neither friendly nor unfriendly. "Is this related to a divorce?"

"No, not at all. I—I'm sorry, but I have to ask about confidentiality first thing. I'm the CEO of a major bank in New York, and I've already been the target of a blackmail scheme." He paused. "CEO" sounded a lot better than "former CEO," and it would be hard to challenge. "I'd like to think folks in your business are very careful about shielding the client's name and identity."

"Well, we are. That's what we're paid to do. So"—Baines drew out the word—"can you tell me more about what you want done?"

Corbin told the story haltingly, backtracking now and then to fill in missing details. He described the incriminating video and the surprising suggestion by the woman involved that he turn the tables on the perpetrator, whom Corbin described simply as a "Russian financier." He gave the street address that Elena had sent him for the apartment. Monitoring the building, he'd been told, would undoubtedly show several boys or men coming alone for encounters with the Russian.

He heard a long breath on the other end of the line. "How

did you picture this surveillance being done?"

"I'm really not sure," Corbin said slowly, and he meant it. "You'd be the experts there. I guess one way would be to have someone stake out the building with a camera and focus on the likely suspects, if that's the word."

"We could do that," Baines said, "but that's very time-consuming, and if the Russian isn't in the building, it becomes a real waste of time and effort and very costly to you, I would add."

"Ah, I see your point."

"What's his name, by the way?"

Corbin thought for a moment. "I guess you do need to know that."

"It is important."

"It's Maxim Ripovsky," he said, spelling it out. "He's based in London but uses this apartment in New York a lot."

"Okay. The name means nothing, but I'm not exactly up on Russians," Baines said. "What makes a lot more sense is to monitor the security footage in the lobby, which I presume includes the elevator. I guess we need to have someone go in and check to see if the cameras are in place. That could be done easily enough without raising suspicion, and I have people who are very good at hacking into security cameras.

"Now, all this could take some time," he added, "especially given the fact that these sexual encounters probably aren't being done on any schedule and could be spaced widely apart. Are you prepared to be patient?"

"I am."

"Now—Mr. van Sloot, is it? Rich Russians tend to have a lot of security in place. Our most incriminating evidence would come if we could install a camera overlooking his door, but I think that's highly unlikely. Which floor is he on, by the way?"

"I've been told it's the penthouse," Corbin said.

"Yeah, not surprising." Corbin heard what sounded like a

tongue clicking. "When would you want us to start?"

"As soon as possible, I think."

"Okay. Well, here's what I propose. I can have someone examine the security cameras, probably tomorrow. Assuming that things check out, we can start monitoring on the weekend. Let's think in terms of a two-week contract that could be extended depending on what we turn up. If we're lucky, there may be a number of, er, providers coming and going."

"That sounds fine, I guess. What are we talking about—hourly fees, expenses, that kind of thing?" Corbin really had no clue how these people operated.

"I would do it as a flat fee that would include everything. Let's say $3,000 for two weeks, then see where we are. Give me an email and I will send over a contract. There's a lot of boilerplate, but you can't avoid that in this business. There's a feature where you can electronically sign it and then send it back."

"Alright. That figure sounds a little steep, but my contact assures me you're one of the top firms in the city for this kind of work." Corbin gave Baines his personal email address and thanked him.

"No problem, Mr. van Sloot. We work with a lot of well-to-do clients like yourself. We like to think we're thoroughly professional and deliver results. If you are fine with all this, one more thing: please give me your cell number. I promise your cell will be used primarily for messages, and any phone calls would be only for critical questions or important news."

"Very good," Corbin said, giving Baines his number. "I'll try to have the contract back to you by the end of the day. I—I've never done anything like this before, and it doesn't sit easily with me, but I want to move forward on it."

"I understand completely. We'll be in touch. We appreciate your business. Goodbye."

CHAPTER 39

Crimson Opportunities, Fortress, Tyne—Bob was assembling the pieces of his story, weaving them together like threads in a medieval French tapestry. Bob had researched Star Enterprises and saw that the controller was Thomas Burgee, so that was probably the Tom he had been talking to. Tom was still loath to go on record about Tyne, but even if he declined to be identified, it wasn't crucial.

Lots of difficult stories, financial and otherwise, relied on unnamed sources, Bob knew well—key voices to what investigative journalists often call "the road map." Critics of such stories often carped loudly that the information was tainted because the sources weren't named, but Bob dismissed all that. After all, Deep Throat wasn't exposed until decades after helping corroborate the details behind the Watergate scandal.

He knew he had to interview Crumm before he tackled Ripovsky. He suspected that Crumm and Ripovsky had come to some kind of handshake agreement, but he had no proof. If Crumm would admit to knowing Ripovsky, that would certainly help goose the story. But Bob had his doubts.

After setting up his computer to type in some notes, Bob dialed the main number for the *Star* and asked the operator to connect him to Crumm's office. After three rings, a woman answered, "Mr. Crumm's office."

"Hello. My name is Bob Mandell, and I'm a senior reporter with the *Financial Times*. I've been working on a story, and I'd like to get Mr. Crumm's comments."

Silence, then she said, "He's at his home in Florida for the rest of the year, I'm afraid."

"Well, this is important. Can you give me that number?" Bob gritted his teeth. The story really needed Crumm and his responses in it.

"Well, let me call down there and see if he's available. Please hold for a minute."

Some moments later, she was back on. "He'll speak with you now." He heard a click on the other end of the line.

"Hello, this is Winston Crumm."

Bob's heart was beating faster, and he plunged ahead. "Mr. Crumm, this is Bob Mandell. I'm a senior reporter with the *Financial Times* here in New York."

"Yes, what can I do for you?" Bob thought he detected a note of suspicion, even of hauteur; Crumm wasn't going to lie down for him.

"I've been told by a very reliable source at Star Enterprises that the company has been the recipient of $20 million coming from a Russian oligarch. Are you aware of this investment?"

The line was silent for a good five seconds. "I'm aware of a big investment, yes, but I don't know where it came from. My financial people have told me about it. We—we see it as a vote of confidence in our newspapers."

Bob suspected this was a lie, but he couldn't challenge Crumm on it. "Are you aware of any strings attached to this investment?"

"No, not that I know of," Winston said breezily.

"Does the name Maxim Ripovsky mean anything to you?"

"No, should it?"

"It's his company that is making this investment after the

working capital loan from Whitehall was called."

"Well, I do know about that loan being canceled. That was a problem for us, certainly. But this investment has helped us a lot, and you say it's Russian? Even if it is, their money is good, isn't it? They're making a lot of investments in New York these days."

"Yes, they are."

"By the way, you say this information about the investment came from someone at Star. Who?"

"I've told that person I won't use his name."

"I see. You reporters and your sources," he said, spitting out the last word like a watermelon seed.

"It's part of what we do, Mr. Crumm. People can be afraid of retribution, and sometimes they're only willing to talk anonymously."

"And you believe everything they say?" Winston sounded like he was in full battle mode.

"Not necessarily. Everything has to be checked out."

"Uh-huh. Well, I think we're done here."

"Of course. Thank you for taking my call."

"You bet. Goodbye."

A small gift dropped into Bob's lap shortly after the Crumm call. An item in the *Journal*, coming out of London, linked Fortress Technologies to a troll farm, presumably operating somewhere in Russia, that was spreading disinformation on social media, rumors and innuendo aimed at sowing discontent in the US and other Western democracies. This information had come from intelligence agencies and was, of course, indignantly denied by a spokesman for Fortress.

Bob cackled lightly when he read it. This was one more question for Ripovsky, though Bob assumed he would get a firm denial or at least an excuse that Ripovsky wasn't actually running the company. The reporter sipped on his coffee and checked his watch: three-fifteen. He would try Ripovsky's office in the morning.

Shortly after 9:00 a.m., Bob picked up the phone and dialed the number for Rubicon Investments. After he identified himself, the secretary put him on hold for what seemed like twenty seconds. Then a voice answered.

"This is Maxim Ripovsky."

"Mr. Ripovsky, my name is Bob Mandell. I'm a senior reporter with the *Financial Times* here in New York. I would very much like to interview you about your investment in Star Enterprises."

"What investment is this?" Bob sensed wariness in his tone.

"With the help of someone at Star who works in finance, I've been able to track $20 million coming into the company through a shell entity called Tyne Investments. I'd like to ask you a few questions about that." Bob literally held his breath.

There was a long pause. "I see. I feel uncomfortable discussing such matters over the phone."

"Could I come to your office and talk in person?" This could be good or bad, but meeting him in the flesh would allow Bob to add a little color to the story, describing Ripovsky, his office, etc.

"Ahhh—yes, certainly. Not tomorrow; I am busy, but perhaps the next morning?"

That would be a Thursday. "That would be great. What time?"

"Let me see." A pause. "How is ten o'clock?"

"That would be fine. I have the address."

"Yes. Please check in at the desk and you will be directed to my office."

"Thank you for accommodating me," Bob said, making every effort to sound genial.

"Mr. Mandell, was it? I will expect you then. Goodbye." Bob wondered if this was a parting word from the spider to the fly.

CHAPTER 40

Bob took a cab to Ripovsky's office, leaving plenty of time for the traffic, slowed to a crawl by icy rain. He wore a coat and tie, unusual for him, but he felt he needed to show professionalism. Khakis and a dress shirt wouldn't do, but Bob still wore the soft black Reebok shoes he sported every day. He carried a zippered leather briefcase under his right arm like a security blanket and wore a broad-brimmed canvas hat to ward off the rain.

Ripovsky's building, as he suspected, was modern, glass and steel, with extensive views onto Madison Avenue. Bob walked across the spacious tiled lobby to the white metal desk where two women were stationed. He approached the closest one, a beautiful young brunette wearing what looked to be a starched white blouse. She looked up as he approached and smiled, offering an array of perfect teeth.

"Whot ken we do for you, sir?" Her accent was noticeable but not thick.

"I have a meeting scheduled with Mr. Ripovsky at ten. Bob Mandell," Bob said.

She looked down for a moment. "Oh yehs. He ees expecting you. Please take the elee-vator to the feefth floor," she said, waving toward the elevator bay.

In the elevator, Bob felt a surge of adrenaline course through him. This was certain to be a challenging interview—he had no idea what to expect, no more than did a jittery job candidate meeting with a potential employer. He'd thought about taping the interview, but he had only a few questions, and many interview subjects, he knew from long experience, balked at being recorded, felt somehow that a recording created unwanted permanence. Others seemed to welcome a recorder, seeing it as certifying accuracy.

When the elevator opened, Bob saw a double glass door in front of him with incised letters: *Rubicon Investments*. He tried the handle on the right-hand door, but it was locked. He saw another young woman at a desk inside; she looked up at the sound and pointed. He followed her finger and saw there was a buzzer with a speaker. He pushed it firmly and leaned toward the speaker.

"I'm Bob Mandell of the *Financial Times* here to see Mr. Ripovsky."

She held up her hand and picked up the phone. He saw her bend over for a few moments with her head to the receiver. Then she buzzed him through.

This woman, a blonde with a short chic cut, said, "Please go down the hall to the door at the end. Mr. Ripovsky is expecting you." If there was any warmth in her voice, Bob didn't detect it.

He padded down the carpeted hall and knocked at the dark wooden door.

"Come in," a voice responded.

Bob walked in and was immediately taken aback by the size and grandeur of the office, with immense windows stretching to the ceiling and a huge wooden desk in front of him. Ripovsky got up from his chair and walked around to the front of the desk and extended his hand. "Mr. Mandell? Maxim Ripovsky." He had on a shirt with wide blue vertical stripes and a black tie with small red figures.

Intimidation jolted through Bob like a jigger of scotch on an empty stomach. Coming as Bob did from a family of short people, Ripovsky loomed over him like a comic book ogre; Bob's head reached only the Russian's chest. Bob gulped, extended his own hand, and forced a smile. "Nice to meet you. Thank you for seeing me."

Bob became aware of another man in the room, sitting in a chair to his right. Ripovsky motioned to him. "This is Trevor Richter. He's my personal publicity person, and I've asked him to sit in on this meeting."

Richter stood and extended his hand. Middle-aged and blonde, Richter had a sharp look and an air of superiority that had Bob thinking of one word: Nazi. Bob felt his discomfort rising; he'd have to try to assert his authority over this interview, drawing from his deep well of experience. A cub reporter faced with the same challenge might have lost his or her nerve, but he wouldn't.

"Please, sit down," Ripovsky said, motioning to a padded chair. He took a seat in another chair next to Richter and looked at Bob expectantly, albeit with a stare that could have pinned Bob to a corkboard like a prized insect.

Bob brought out his notebook and a pen, fumbling a bit as he did so. "As I mentioned over the phone, I've been looking into the infusion of $20 million in two installments into Star Enterprises." Bob wondered if his voice sounded squeakier than usual. "I know the vehicle is Tyne Investments, and with some help, I've been able to trace that entity to you."

"I see. Yes, I acknowledge that Tyne is one of my companies. I had hoped that my investment would remain anonymous, but clearly, that is no longer possible." Bob was impressed by Ripovsky's English, spoken carefully and precisely.

"What prompted you to make this investment?"

Ripovsky smiled and turned quickly to Richter, who nodded. "I am relatively new to New York, and I want to do good things here," Ripovsky said. "There would be no point in my giving money to the *New York Times*. I knew Star has been having difficulties, and I thought I could have more impact there."

"And there were no strings attached to this investment, no requests?"

"No, none."

Bob had his questions lined up. "Why twenty million?"

Ripovsky shrugged. "It seemed like a good number, one that could be immediately helpful to them."

"Were you aware that Star's bankers had recently called a loan to Star for twenty million?"

"No, I wasn't," Ripovsky lied.

"So, the fact that your investment and the loan were for the same amount is a coincidence."

"Apparently so, yes." Ripovsky looked down for a moment and tugged at his sleeve. Bob felt Richter's eyes boring into him.

"Do you know Winston Crumm, the CEO at Star?"

Ripovsky pursed his lips. "I have met him socially."

"And you didn't discuss this investment with him?"

"No. This was intended as an anonymous investment, made directly to the company's bank account."

"Okay. I've also been looking at another of your companies, Crimson Opportunities. It acquired Phoenix Technologies and turned it into Fortress Technologies, now headquartered in London."

Ripovsky gave him a tight-lipped smile. "You have done your homework, Mr. Mandell."

"Fortress was named in the *Wall Street Journal* recently as being involved in a troll farm operated by Russian agents to sow dissent in the West," Bob said. "Were you aware of that story?"

"It was pointed out to me, yes," he replied with a decided edge.

"Can you deny that Fortress is involved in these activities?"

Richter spoke up. "Mr. Ripovsky is an investor in Fortress, nothing more. He has no say in their daily activities and no knowledge of any troll farm." Ripovsky nodded.

"Well, those are my toughest questions," Bob said, forcing a smile. "Let me ask you about your future investment plans or other areas here in New York."

"Well, I have some things going on," Ripovsky said, appearing to relax somewhat. "I can have someone send you a list of my investments in real estate and the like. I also have given heavily to one of the local food banks and contributed a very valuable painting to the Museum of Modern Art."

"Oh, I wasn't aware of the painting," Bob said. "What is it?"

"A very old painting by the artist Wassily Kandinsky called *Red Trees*. I acquired it from a private collector in Russia."

"Very nice," Bob said, and he meant it. "Is there anything else you'd like to mention?"

Ripovsky looked briefly at Richter, then back at Bob. "Not at the moment, I think."

"If I can ask, what is your net worth?"

Ripovsky shook his head slowly. "That is private information."

"But am I safe in calling you a billionaire?"

"Oh yes, certainly." There was a hint of a smile, the corners of his mouth turning up slightly.

"Well, I don't think I need any more of your time," Bob said, closing his notebook. "Thank you again for agreeing to see me." He stood up and reached into his front pocket for his wallet, pulled out his business card, and handed it to Ripovsky. "Please have someone contact me if there are any other donations or other things you've done here that you'd like to add."

Ripovsky was still seated. "Tell me, Mr. Mandell, why such

interest in an investment in a local newspaper? They are certainly no threat to the *Financial Times.*"

"Well, I think it's noteworthy when a Russian financier makes a very large, secretive investment in a major New York newspaper—one that happens to replace an expired loan literally dollar for dollar." Bob stood his ground as if an invisible hand was supporting his back.

"I think I explained that to you. It is a coincidence." Ripovsky stood up, once again looming.

"Yes, I do have that answer. Well, I won't hold you any longer."

"Thank you, Mr. Mandell." He didn't offer his hand.

"And thank you." Bob nodded at him and at Richter, who had a scowl that made him look only slightly more sinister. "Goodbye." He turned and walked out the door, giving one last glance out the windows at the gray and damp slice of Gotham he'd be returning to.

At two-thirty in the morning, when Bob was soundly asleep at home, the middle-aged man with a bristly crew cut unzipped his gray janitor's uniform and stepped out of it. He'd been hiding in a coat closet for more than an hour as the cleaning crew finished up. Some overhead lights were still on, but the newsroom was dim and deathly quiet. He padded around, looking for the right cubicle; it took him ten minutes to find it, on the next floor above, which he reached by a stairwell. He carried a small black flashlight that he flicked on as he needed it.

Fortunately for him, all the cubicles were marked with names. "Robert Mandell," the tag said in block letters. He pulled out his surgical gloves and sat down in front of the computer, the chair squeaking a bit under his heft. He knew what to look for, he thought, but the challenge was first to find an operating password and get into Bob's files. However, he was an old hand at such tasks, having honed his skills in Moscow working for the GRU, Russia's military intelligence directorate.

His hands flew over the keyboard as he tried various tricks, but then he succeeded in logging in as the system administrator, and the rest was child's play. The logins for the staff were listed by name, and there was Bob's. The man grunted slightly in satisfaction.

Plugging in the passcode, the man saw a collection of files pop up on the screen. He was hoping to find something by name, and he quickly saw it, a folder labeled "Tyne." He clicked on it and saw a number of Word files; one was much longer than the others. No matter, his instructions weren't to locate one document; he was to erase the entire folder. He clicked back to the folder icon and highlighted it, then hit the "X" button on the task bar for "Delete." Then he went to the Windows home screen, clicked on "Recycle Bin," found the file, and deleted it there.

At that point, he nodded, stood up, and left the cubicle as silently as he had entered. It was only five floors down to the lobby. He collected his uniform from the closet, packed it in his small duffel, and started down the stairs. He would report his success to Maxim shortly by text. The boss would be pleased.

CHAPTER 41

Bob read through the Friday issue of the *Financial Times* and thumbed through the *Wall Street Journal*; he would take the weekend section home with him. He yawned and stretched, interlacing his fingers over his head. Then he turned on his computer and went to his files.

People in the cubicles nearby heard an explosion of f-bombs and wails, which erupted volcanically when Bob realized the Tyne file was nowhere to be seen. What the hell? How had it disappeared? He couldn't replicate everything he had done, and he was beside himself. He stood up and balled his fists. This couldn't be happening. No one came to check on him; they'd heard similar shrieks from Bob's area before.

Think, think, he told himself. He went to the main screen and clicked on his recycle bin—maybe it was there. But the only things in there were Word files, perhaps a dozen of them, and none recent.

Wait, wait—he remembered he'd been told in his first days at the *FT* that the servers had been built to recover deleted files, a fail-safe set up in case of inadvertent keystrokes. Journalists had been known to lose stories, and weeks of work, by hitting the wrong keys—a rare but serious problem that management realized needed a high-tech solution.

He sat back down and clicked on the icon for the company directory, which was broken down by department and alphabetized. There was a general number for IT, and he dialed it.

"IT, this is Christian."

Bob tried to keep the panic out of his voice, but the words came tumbling out like a freshet after a summer deluge. "Christian, this is Bob Mandell. I've lost a key folder in my computer—it's gone. It's critical that I get it back. It represents weeks of work."

"Okay, we'll see if we can recover it." He sounded unruffled. "Give me the details."

Bob proceeded to tell him the name of the file and added, "It was here when I left yesterday, and when I logged on this morning, it was gone."

"Uh-huh. That's strange. Well, we'll go to the backup server and see what we can find. Give me a little time. I'll give you a call."

Bob couldn't read, couldn't sit still. His mind couldn't process anything. He decided to go to the cafeteria and refill his coffee cup. He couldn't just sit there and wait for the phone to ring.

Fifteen minutes later, back at his desk, the phone rang. It was Christian.

"Good news, Bob. I found it, and I've sent it back to you in an email."

Bob let out a sound that was between a sigh and a cheer, a guttural, primordial emanation from deep in his chest. "Oh my God, what a relief. That's wonderful. I can't thank you enough."

"No problem. But if this is as important as you say, I suggest you save it to a thumb drive. Then you'll have it right there if any problem comes up."

"That's a good idea. Thanks for your help, Christian."

"Okay, happy to help. That's what we're here for."

Bob sat back and sighed again. Disaster averted. Computers can have a mind of their own, he told himself; he was sure he hadn't done anything stupid. Sabotage was the furthest thing from his mind.

CHAPTER 42

On his commute into the city, Corbin would have had time only to skim the *New York Times* and the *Journal*. Now, newly unemployed, he had all morning—or even longer—to spend with the newspapers and anything else he wanted to read. The day stretched ahead of him like a featureless ocean, and all the cozy comforts of home with and the absence of his family made the hours seem especially long.

He had on some heavy khakis and a turtleneck, typical wear for the week before Christmas. It was in the thirties, and out the living room window, he could see the wind tossing the maple branches around as if the Furies were riding them.

Patricia was at the women's shelter. The van Sloot kids were in day school and would be getting out Wednesday for the usual holiday vacation. He was due to go back into the city the next day to meet with Sandy Campbell and go over his retirement package, which had been FedExed to him from London a few days earlier.

There was a lot of legalese, as he'd expected. He had thumbed through it, and it seemed in order, but he wanted a professional to review it carefully. After all, this was the magic carpet that he hoped his family could ride for years to come, whether or not he found another job without a long hiatus.

Rufus, their Portuguese water dog, was curled at his feet, a casual pile of inky black fur. Corbin had just started reading the Arts & Leisure section of the *Times* when he heard his phone beep to signal a message. He reached over and picked it up from the lamp table and saw the envelope icon. He clicked on it.

"Mr. van Sloot—Fred Baines here. We seem to have captured a few images that strongly suggest the male prostitution you wanted us to look for. The security footage shows one of the subjects of interest. I'm enclosing these short videos, with time stamps. I'm going to set up a Zoom call for later to give you a chance to review this, and we can talk further."

Corbin inhaled and clicked on the first video. It was relatively sharp, not the grainy image he was expecting. The view was slightly from above and looking directly at the elevator. It showed a slim young man, his face half turned away from the camera, coming into the lobby, walking directly to the elevator, and pushing a button. The timestamp in the lower right corner said 22:12.

He reran the video, which was less than twenty seconds long. The man—or man-child, perhaps—appeared to be of average height, dressed in a blue running suit and dark running shoes; his dark hair was shaved at the temples and long at the top of his head, tumbling over his forehead. He sauntered into the elevator when the door opened and moved his arm to punch the button, but the camera couldn't capture a floor number; the body of the elevator shielded that from view.

The second video showed the same man exiting the elevator at 23:08. Once again, he was the only person in the lobby. He never looked toward the camera as he strolled out of the frame, presumably toward the front door.

Stroking his chin, Corbin thought hard: this was proof of nothing, certainly nothing that could be presented as evidence in a court of law. The timing of the visit and its duration were suspicious, but only that. Would this be enough to rattle Ripovsky? He knew that there were ten days left in the contract with Newbold, more time to produce something more definitive, perhaps. Corbin had breathed nothing to Patricia about any of this—how could he? Moreover, the charge for the Newbold Agency was on his credit card, and she never saw those bills; he was truly flying solo.

A few minutes later, he checked his email and saw the Zoom link, which was set for a half-hour later. He busied himself with a magazine until the time came, then clicked on the link and went through the protocols.

He saw a middle-aged African American man with a goatee looking out at him, and then the man spoke. "Hi, Mr. van Sloot. Fred Baines. Have you seen the videos?"

Corbin was momentarily taken aback. It just wasn't what he had pictured—a Mickey Spillane, someone out of the hard-bitten detective school, or Humphrey Bogart in *The Maltese Falcon*. Baines was definitely not that. With a jacket and what looked to be a starched blue shirt, he looked more professorial than anything.

"I have, and I'm not quite sure what to think," Corbin said. "If this is indeed a male prostitute, it would be hard to prove. The timestamps are suggestive, though; he came and went in an hour, and it was very late."

"My thoughts exactly." He sounded energized. "For your purposes, I'm not sure we need conclusive proof, and let's face it, we aren't going to get it without some trick of surveillance I'm unaware of. We'll keep monitoring the lobby to see what more we pick up. There was another video, not quite as good, that I didn't send you. It was another day, and earlier; that guy arrived about eight-thirty."

An idea popped unannounced into Corbin's head. "This

may be crazy, but is there anything that could be done with a drone? You know, fly it up to the window and have a camera going."

Corbin saw Baines smile broadly. "I wish. We have started to do some work with drones, but you're talking about something being done at night, when the curtains would presumably be drawn, and the camera would need some kind of flash that would probably bounce off the glass even if the curtains weren't pulled. I just don't think the logistics work."

"Yeah, I guess not."

"Good thought, though. Actually, there is one thing one of the guys suggested. There is a convex mirror mounted high in the elevator—lots of elevators have them. If we could get in there and adjust it slightly and aim it at the buttons, we might determine if these guys are indeed going to the penthouse. That's assuming we can blow up the footage and capture the image in the mirror. It's a long shot, but it could work. There would be a second or two when the door was still open and the button was being pushed."

"Hmmm, interesting." Corbin had watched TV shows such as *The FBI* in which video surveillance seemed to be taken to amazing heights; maybe this could be similar. "That would be something."

"Well, as I say, it's something of a long shot. Meanwhile, we will continue monitoring. I may message you but probably won't send any video unless it is really compelling."

"Good, Mr. Baines. Works for me." He said goodbye and looked at his watch: eleven-thirty. Patricia would be back in a half-hour. Then they'd have lunch, just the two of them. Strange. But it might just be this way for some time to come.

CHAPTER 43

This was a good, juicy story, and Bob had gone at the writing part eagerly, more eagerly than he'd written anything in some time. Thomas Burgee at Star had eventually begged off on going on the record, but Bob had thanked him for the lead and for all the information he'd supplied. The Fortress Technologies story added another layer of complexity and suspicion surrounding Ripovsky, despite his denials.

Bob was going through the story a second time, seeing if he could dream up a better lead, trying to punch up the language, when he had a thought. He hadn't checked the internet at all for Crumm, and Crumm was quoted in the story essentially issuing a series of denials on knowing about the money. He punched in "Winston Crumm" in his Google search bar and saw there were hundreds of resultsant links.

Scrolling down through them, his eye fixed on one that read, "Crumm Wife Hosts Dinner for Russian Investor." The source was some kind of website, presumably a gossip site, that he hadn't heard of. He clicked on the link and sat back in shocked surprise. There, in color, was a photo of two couples in a dining room grouped behind a table: Winston Crumm, a woman Bob presumed was Crumms' wife, and Ripovsky with a very tall blonde. They were in evening dress, and all were smiling.

Exhaling, Bob read the text below the photo, which mentioned a benefit dinner that Crumm's wife, the designer Adrienne Rogers, had hosted for Maxim Ripovsky at the Cosmopolitan Club. The date was shortly before Thanksgiving.

Bob shook his head. Obviously, Crumm was lying about not knowing Ripovsky, which made his denials of knowing about any link between the investment and Star Enterprises even more suspect. Bob immediately dismissed the idea of going back to Crumm and challenging him with this. He'd lied once, and he'd probably lie again; what's more, he was unpleasant and, in Bob's mind, deserved no chance for redemption. The story would mention the dinner and damn him by association.

Bob loved taking down big targets, and the story was even more powerful now. He smiled. Jeremy was in the office for a few more days, and Bob would be able to take the article to him and argue for it getting big play. First, he had to plug in this information about the dinner and attribute it to the website; he wanted to call them and give them a virtual hug.

The next morning, the story had been polished and tuned and was ready for editing—then another burst of serendipity flashed before him. The *Times* ran a story on the front of the Metro section: "Russian Billionaire's Painting Deemed a Forgery." Bob actually learned about the story from Jeremy, who emailed him with a link.

Bob read a few graphs:

A Russian billionaire's painting, a gift to the Metropolitan Museum of Art that was announced with much fanfare last month, has been deemed a forgery according to forensic specialists at the museum.

The painting, Red Trees by Vassily Kandinsky, had been given to the museum by Russian financier Maxim

Ripovsky after reportedly being in private hands for more than a century. One specialist in early-twentieth-century art had said the painting could be worth as much as $25 million.

One of the forensic specialists, Mona Ruprecht, said they had determined that there were traces of another painting on the canvas, adding that the oils used were much more recent than would have been available to Kandinsky. "It was a very good, very credible forgery that could have fooled almost anyone," she said.

Reached at his office in Manhattan, Mr. Ripovsky vehemently denied knowing the painting was a fake. He said he had acquired it from a family in Russia that had amassed an extensive collection of art in the years before the Russian Revolution.

"I had no reason to suspect that this was anything but genuine," Mr. Ripovsky said. "This painting was among a number they told me had been hidden in a cellar to keep them safe from the Bolsheviks and later the Stalinists ..."

Bob spread his arms briefly in triumph. The story was centering more and more on Ripovsky and the questionable things he was doing or trying to do. It was one more weight on the scale suggesting that rich Russians were basically untrustworthy, even ominous—black hats riding into Dodge City—as they moved more aggressively to make inroads in the West. It was a story very much in tune with his own political leanings and one he was almost salivating to get into print.

###

Reading through the story one last time before he printed it out, Bob did a spell-check. He wasn't the best speller in the world, he knew it, and it would be an embarrassment of sorts to hand the story to Jeremy and have a few typos marring the final product. It was Monday, shortly after noon, and Bob had promised Jeremy he'd give Jeremy the story to look through by early afternoon. Their agreement was that, if all was well, it would be published on Tuesday.

Bob didn't worry about a headline; the copy desk would determine that. In fact, once it left his hands, the final product was all but certain to be modified, hopefully only slightly, like a suit being altered by a practiced tailor: a tuck here, a new gusset there. He took the printed copy and walked it down the quiet hallway to Jeremy's office. Jeremy looked up from what he was doing, nodded, and said, "Good, well, let me give it a read. Be back to you soon." He took the pages from Bob's hand and set them on the corner of his desk. "Just let me quickly finish this."

Back in his office, Bob called up the *New York Times* site and scrolled through a few articles, but his mind was on the story. He felt pleased with it—very pleased—but Jeremy could put up the figurative pylons to block the road if he found issues he wanted to be resolved. Sipping water from a paper cup, the reporter waited for the phone to ring.

At two-forty-five, it did. "Bob, I like it a lot, but come over and let's talk," Jeremy said. Bob tried to read a strong note of approval in his voice, but he wasn't sure it was there.

"Well, I think it's a strong piece of work with a lot of good reporting," Jeremy said after Bob settled in the chair in front of him. "It's clear that Ripovsky is a pretty shady character, and the suggestion that Fortress is running a troll farm could stick to him despite his denials."

"That's what I'm hoping," Bob replied.

Jeremy stretched his arms behind his head and leaned back in the chair. "I wish we had a stronger link between Ripovsky and Crumm, but we do have Crumm's denial that he knows him, despite the photographs and Ripovsky's admission that he had met him socially. Do you have a sense that they colluded on this investment?"

"I think there's a strong likelihood," Bob said firmly, "but I couldn't prove it. Ripovsky insists he simply wanted to help the *Star*, and Crumm insists he doesn't know him despite the photographic evidence to the contrary. I think we can let the reader connect the dots." He grinned.

"Yes, I think we can do that." Jeremy was staring at him as if he were trying to read Bob's mind. "And I do like the fact that this fake painting has cropped up, which is just more damning for Ripovsky, even if there's no way of determining whether he knew it was a fake." He paused. "I don't like the Russians, particularly the oligarchs who have set up in London. They operate in the shadows, and I don't think their long-range goals are anything positive for our democracies."

"I think that's true, which makes it important for us in the press to shine a light on some of their activities."

"Yes, yes, it does." Jeremy sucked on a pen he had put to his lips. "I think the only thing I would change is your ending. I think it could use a little more vigor."

Bob felt a sudden dampness under his collar. "How do you mean?"

"Well, you suggest that Ripovsky's investments could be the tip of the iceberg for Russian inroads into the US. I think we could hit it a little harder—that they may be wolves at the door or something like that."

"Okay, okay, I think I could do that." Bob nodded slowly. He really didn't want to change it, but this would be a relatively easy trade-off, and it would ensure the story fully passed muster. Challenging Jeremy on this trifle would be pointless. "Are—are we just talking about the final graph?"

"I think so. Just noodle on something and shoot it over to me. Then we'll be ready to go," he said briskly, summoning a smile.

"Okay, I'll do that as fast as I can," Bob said. He got up from the chair and walked back to his cubicle with a mild sense of relief. It could have been a lot worse, and the light had definitely turned green.

CHAPTER 44

The meeting with Sandy Campbell went well; he assured Corbin that the language in the Whitehall contract was straightforward and enforceable. They met in Sandy's Midtown office in the late morning and then went to lunch, giving both a chance to catch up. Sandy had been a friend at Dartmouth and had attended Corbin's wedding; they got together for lunch from time to time, and Sandy had expressed his admiration for the arc of Corbin's career.

Sandy was of average height, still looking youthful, and, true to his nickname, had hair that had gone from very blonde to, well, sandy. He'd built a reputation as an expert at one of the country's top compensation specialists; he and his family lived in Rumson, New Jersey, a lovely, leafy town on the northern edge of the Jersey Shore and home to quite a few A-list corporate executives.

Lunch was mostly small talk, the kind engaged in by old friends who were at the periphery of their individual social circles, talking about their families, especially their kids, and what they each knew of old college friends. The focus was the portion of a Venn diagram where their circles intersected. It was relaxed, comfortable, and gratifying for both. Corbin had a couple of glasses of wine with his veal, something he wouldn't have done if he were still at Whitehall.

After parting outside the restaurant with a firm handshake and an agreement to stay in touch, Corbin hailed a taxi for Grand Central Station. It was within a reasonable walking distance, but it was a dank December day that would have made for a cold and dispiriting walk. Inside the station, he looked for signs to the Metro-North line that would take him into Connecticut; it was still well before rush hour, and the cavernous station was unbusy, a far cry from what it would be in a few hours when the working hordes amassed for the evening trains.

His train ran only hourly except during rush hours, which meant he had a long wait; he went to a newsstand and bought a magazine, then settled down on a bench. The Whitehall contract was in his briefcase. He would sign and date it, FedEx it back to London, and with that, feel confident that the golden parachute should keep him and the rest of the van Sloots aloft for many years to come.

He hadn't taken the train for years, not since they'd lived in Bronxville, but he knew the drill: he'd get off at Stamford and wait for the spur line that went north into New Canaan. Since he boarded in midafternoon, the train was less than half-full and offered a true demographic mix, a broad range of ages, skewing to retirees and young people, probably students having made a morning jaunt into the city and now returning home. Women outnumbered men; quite a few seemed to be in groups, chattering away among themselves.

Alighting in Stamford, one of the largest stations on the line, he pulled out his phone and called Patricia.

"How'd it go?" she asked brightly.

"It went well, very well," he replied. "It was good having lunch with Sandy, and he assured me everything in the contract in is order. I just need to sign it and send it back to them."

"Great. I'll see you soon."

"Yeah, well, the train from Stamford doesn't leave for a while. It is what it is. I certainly got spoiled by those years of having a driver."

"Yes, you did." She chuckled. "That was as good as it gets around here."

Corbin was nursing his morning coffee and reading through the *Times* when his phone rang. It was shortly after ten, and he saw the call was coming from Sid Richardson, one of the partners in the head-hunting firm he had met with the week before.

"Hi, Corbin. This a good time?"

"Sure is. I don't have a lot on my plate these days, you know." He chuckled.

"Yeah, I suppose not. Well, I have an interesting lead I wanted to run by you."

"Shoot."

"I know you want to stay local. The chairman of a big community bank in Ridgefield just retired, and they have contracted with us. Of course, you're way overqualified, but if you can train your sights down a bit, I think they could be a good fit." His voice had the perfect timbre of a radio announcer.

"Hmmm. What's the bank?" Corbin stared at his phone as if it might give him the answer.

"First Peoples. They have a little under $2 billion in assets, and they've been growing quickly."

"Okay, I've heard of them. And you say the chairman just retired?"

"Yes, David Anderson. He was with Citibank before he pulled the cord there and helped start First Peoples back in 2010."

"Alright, Sid, I'd certainly be willing to talk to them. What, a search committee?"

"That's right. I think there would be three of them." He coughed. "If you're willing, I think we could set up something early in the new year, maybe the first week."

"That's fine with me," Corbin replied.

"Great. Let me get back to them and see if we can set a date. You should hear back from me before Christmas, but if not, have a merry."

"You too, Sid. Many thanks."

Hanging up, Corbin strolled toward the kitchen, where he knew Patricia was baking Christmas cookies, a long family tradition. He'd tell her about the call and sound her out, but he was sure she'd be supportive. Having a househusband, an early retiree, was never something she'd imagined; he was certain neither of them had. He'd already climbed to the top of his profession and was parachuting slowly down, but he knew he needed to keep working. The notion of living an idler's existence, sucking on the nipple of the Whitehall windfall, was more than a little troubling.

It gnawed at him, however, that his ongoing dream of joining the MOMA board seemed to have gone up in smoke. He was no longer working in Manhattan, and while that might not have been the death knell for his hopes, he no longer had the cachet of the top Whitehall post to tout. Then, too, his potential mentor, Turner, was gravely ill and in no position to help him. Some things, he said to himself with an inward sigh, are just not meant to be.

CHAPTER 45

Bob was in his office, basking like a seal on a warm rock. The acclaim for his story had been pouring in from others in the newsroom, both in person and by email. It had indeed been given great play, running over three columns on the front page under the headline "Russian Oligarch Props Up Tabloid." The *Financial Times* didn't run a lot of photographs, but a headshot of Ripovsky appeared on the jump page.

CNBC had called to set up a quick interview, and the Reuters wire had picked up a truncated version and put it out. This was what Bob lived for: the thrill of the chase, the trophy mounted on the wall, and fulsome praise for a job done well. No team effort for him; this was a solo flight, and he would get all the credit. If Bob could have done a cartwheel, a scary notion for someone of his athletic inability, he would have.

He was pleased that the story had run virtually unchanged, apart from the altered ending he'd given Jeremy. The headline wasn't his, as headlines never are the writers' prerogative at major newspapers, but it captured the gist of the story in which Crumm's denials seemed to contradict the evidence from the benefit. Bob didn't regret for a moment not pulling any punches on Crumm, who struck him as a blowhard and a liar.

All had turned out well; he'd gotten the story published before the Christmas hiatus, into which too many stories went to die—or at least failed to get the attention they deserved. Jeremy had proven to be a good ally, pushing the piece through, and the story had been rescued from the jaws of disaster by the backup server. He never would learn that a Russian operative had stolen into the office and deleted the file in the dead of night. If that had come out, the story would have been a bombshell exploding well beyond the sometimes-stultifying content of the business pages.

In the meantime, Bob thought to himself that he'd just relax and have an easy Christmas week. He'd come in every day, but with Jeremy and much of the senior staff out, it would be a stroll in the park with no pressure. But first, he had to prepare for the CNBC interview, scheduled for two that afternoon. It had been several years since Bob had appeared on TV. He didn't much care for the way he had looked on television—nobody else did either—but this was publicity that he and the newspaper couldn't turn down.

He strolled to the cafeteria, walking on cloud nine. Inside the door, apparently making a cup of tea, was Tara Pearson, the office beauty, a Brit who had covered the fashion industry in London before moving to New York. She looked up and smiled.

"Hi, Bob, that was quite a story. Congratulations." Her smile was warm and genuine.

"Oh, thanks."

"How long were you working on it?" she asked, dunking the teabag. She looked especially fetching in tapered wool pants and a dark-blue shirt; her hair was as beguiling as he remembered it, a chic cut that framed her face like the settings of a gemstone.

"A few weeks. There were a few details that didn't come to light until I was almost finished."

"I know how that is," she said. "Sometimes you have to start right in again and rearrange things. Can be a real bother."

He shrugged and smiled. "Fortunately, it wasn't too bad. It didn't really change anything, just provided a little more support for the central arguments."

Tara nodded. "That's good. Well, congratulations again." She smiled again and walked by him and out the door, trailing a faint whiff of perfume. Bob's heart was beating a little faster, but then he sighed audibly. Some journalists have swagger, a wry smile, or a tilt of the head. Bob had none of those, so flirting with her was like Rumpelstiltskin courting Snow White. Politeness and a whiff of condescension were all he'd ever get from the Taras of the world.

CHAPTER 46

He'd told his assistant to hold all his calls. For a man with tremendous poise and no shortage of cunning, Maxim Ripovsky was working himself into a rage, a red, foam-on-the-lips anger. He didn't ordinarily see the *Financial Times,* but Trevor Richter had called him to tell him about the story and his far-from-flattering role in it.

How could this have happened? Hadn't Feodor deleted the file? There was no way Mandell could have resurrected everything that quickly unless, perhaps, he had stored it on a thumb drive. And since when did reporters do that?

Livid, he'd called Feodor and demanded an explanation. "What happened?" Ripovsky asked in Russian. "You told *me* you'd erased the file."

"*Da, da,*" Feodor said, adding that he had removed it from the recycle bin as well.

"Then how could he recover the story?" Maxim asked heatedly.

"Perhaps he had saved it on a thumb drive," Feodor said sheepishly. "Or it's possible the newspaper has a backup server. I've heard of such things. There is no way I could have accessed that even if I had thought of it."

"This is terrible," Maxim said. "The story makes me look like a fool, and a crooked one at that."

"I'm sorry, boss. This should have worked."

"Well, it didn't. Never mind. I will talk to you later." Maxim semi-slammed down the phone and dialed Richter, who answered on the second ring.

"Trevor, this story is bad. I think other reporters might start calling me and asking about Tyne. I need you to help me think up a strategy." He paused, his left hand balling into a fist. "I'm planning to leave for London the day after tomorrow, and that may make things easier, but in the meantime ..."

"I know things don't look good," Richter said smoothly, "but that's what you hired me for. Any reporter who calls asking for you should be directed to me."

"What are you going to say?"

"I think it's safe to say you meant to make the investment anonymously, and that's why it was made through the shell," Richter said slowly. "That's essentially true. The connection with Crumm is only by inference right now—no one except Crumm could know about you approaching him, assuming that he indeed didn't talk about it. According to the story, Mandell asked him about it, and Crumm said he didn't know you, which is a lie, of course, but it's Crumm's lie."

"What about the Whitehall loan angle and my request to go on the board?"

"Again, I think that's pretty safe from prying eyes. Yes, the loan amount is essentially the same, but unless van Sloot talks—and you have compromising material on him—or the brass in London decide to say something, attempts to tie you and Whitehall don't go anywhere. And I don't believe the directors in London have said anything about your trying to get on the board; hopefully, they won't."

Maxim thought hard. "So, you think I could, as you say here, ride this out?"

"I think so, especially if you're back in London for a while.

Things should die down. Then we need to start playing up your generosity here once more. It's too bad that painting was a forgery—"

"Yes, damn it on Stalin's grave. I thought I was doing something really good, and it came back to sting me." He sounded both angry and sorry for himself, a witch's tea of unhappiness.

"I know, I know," Richter said soothingly. "Maybe we should be thinking in terms of money and not something that could blow up in our faces."

"Ah, I think you're right. My money is good until I bounce a check—and that is never going to happen." Maxim gave a rueful chuckle, like the sound of someone who knows the number of zeroes in the bank account.

"So, when are you leaving, again? The day after tomorrow?"

"Yes, an early morning flight from Teterboro. I should be in London in time for dinner."

"Okay, well, have a wonderful holiday," Richter said cheerfully. "And again, don't talk to any reporters other than to say 'no comment.' Leave the rest to me. That's what you pay me for."

"Oh, right, I almost forgot," Maxim said. "I know you enjoy vodka. There should be a case coming to your office very shortly—my holiday present."

"Many thanks, Maxim. It's a pleasure working for you."

"Very good, Trevor. You may not hear from me before I leave, and probably not over this Christmas period. "

"I'll be away as well. We're off to the British Virgins, Tortola. Always a great escape from New York at this time of year."

"Wonderful. Thanks again, Trevor. We will speak soon."

As he hung up, Maxim thought again about Feodor and the failed file deletion. The man had done what he'd been asked to do, but the result had been as effective as an assassin firing blanks. Should he make him an object lesson for others in the company? Maxim could see both sides, but he was undecided, a man on a teeter-totter. He decided to sleep on it.

He picked up the phone and dialed Tatiana at the desk outside. "If any reporter asks for me, tell them to call Trevor Richter at this number." He listed it. "No exceptions."

"Very good, Mr. Ripovsky."

He liked Tatiana—she was a good girl, smart and loyal, and easy on the eyes. He'd hired her away from the Russian consulate for twice what she was making there. *Money,* he thought to himself, *really does make the world go round.*

CHAPTER 47

The text from Fred Baines was practically euphoric: *"Our mirror trick worked! We have clear images of two young guys pushing the elevator button for the penthouse. Please call me when you can."*

Corbin walked into the study—he wanted to keep this call as private as possible. The kids were home. Justin was playing video games, probably *Fortnite*, and the two girls were reading in the living room near the Christmas tree, a fragrant ten-foot freshly killed fir that was now as decorated as a patchwork quilt, its branches festooned with heirloom ornaments from his family and Patricia's.

"Fred Baines here," he announced after Corbin dialed the number.

"Hello, it's Corbin van Sloot. You texted me about the mirror trick."

"Well, it worked better than I thought it would, and I'm always an optimist on these, ah, experiments," Baines said, his voice brimming with enthusiasm. "As I said, we have two good screen captures that show the button for 'P' being pushed while the guy is in the elevator. It's a little grainy but clear enough."

"And you have two of them?"

"Yep. One is one of the subjects we've seen before. The other is someone new but the same basic MO. They go up and come back down within an hour."

Corbin clicked his tongue and stared at one of the family photos on the desk. "So, how do you think we should proceed?"

"I can print these out and send them to you as, oh, eight-by-ten-inch prints, and you can relay them on to Ripovsky with whatever you want to say. And I would tell him you have security camera footage as well—though, you don't have to be more specific. Let him guess about that."

"Okay." Corbin's reply was subdued. "I think I know what to say. How, um, how soon can you get these to me?"

"I can FedEx them to you today, and they'll be there tomorrow."

"Great. I guess there's a few more days running on our contract ..."

"Yes, and we can keep monitoring. You've paid for it. But I'm not sure there will be anything better than what we have."

"Well, that would seem to pretty much wrap it up, then, Mr. Baines."

"I guess so, unless, as I say, something juicier comes along."

"Well, my thanks again, and I'll text you to confirm receipt of the photos."

"Sounds good to me, Mr. van Sloot. It's been good working with you."

Several hours later, after a good lunch of canned chowder, crusty bread, and a salad with tuna and tomatoes that he and Patricia shared at the round French-style table in the kitchen, Corbin was deep into the current issue of *Vanity Fair*. Feeling a tad drowsy, he walked back into the kitchen and started brewing a cup of Constant Comment tea. While the water was heating, he reached into his pocket and pulled out his phone.

He saw the icon for a message and clicked on it, then recoiled in surprise. It was from Elena.

"Corbin—I hope a private detective was able to find something you can use on Maxim. Please let me know. I am back in dreary London for the holidays here. Maxim is here too."

He muttered under his breath—Ripovsky was in London, so anything sent to his New York office might languish for some time. Corbin felt he should thank Elena for the detective contacts and tell her he did have material he could use on Ripovsky. But he also wanted to get the Russian's address in London; not only would that speed the photo delivery, but it would also signal that Corbin had taken the initiative to find the location of Ripovsky's office.

He texted her back:

"Thanks again for those contacts—one of the agencies did produce some compromising photos for me. Now I need to send them to Ripovsky's London office since he is not in New York. Can you give me that address?"

It was more than an hour before he saw a reply. She listed the address under Rubicon Investments Ltd., then added:

"Corbin, I am so sorry about the way we parted, and I understand your anger. I did have a job to do, and I did it, but I truly enjoyed being with you. You are a terrific man, and you know just how to treat a woman.

"I will be back in New York in a few weeks. Is there any chance we can get together, maybe just for lunch?"

Corbin stared at the screen. He snorted and shook his head reflexively. Was she serious? How could he trust her—she still worked for Ripovsky, didn't she? This was *not* going to happen.

The teakettle whistled, and Corbin turned to the reason he'd come to the kitchen. He thought hard as he dunked the tea bag and decided he'd wait a bit to reply to her. One of the best pieces of advice he'd ever had in business, one he'd gotten from a senior banker over predinner drinks early in his career, an older sage dispensing wisdom to a protégé, was not to shoot off a reply in anger or triumph, but to let the moment pass and think through the ramifications. It would be easy to vent, to hurl some poison-tipped reply at her. God knows it would be justified. The diplomatic angel on one shoulder eventually won out.

An hour later, he texted her back:

"Elena—We can never get back together. You need to understand that what you did to me and my career was a shock that I am still recovering from. I will miss your company, but no apology, no rationale, will ever be enough to overcome what happened.

"Also, realize that I am not working in New York anymore and perhaps never will be again. That means that meeting there is, well, I would say impossible.

"It should be very hard for me to wish you well, but I do. You're beautiful and talented in many ways. I treasure my memories of our intimacy—you were the most exciting lover I've ever had. Maybe there is something in the water, as they say, in Russia. Goodbye."

He lingered over the message, rereading it multiple times before slowly pressing the "send" arrow. He thought quickly of Patricia and what she would do or say if she saw that message, a cheater's furtive adieu to a lover. It was a frightening thought, and he dismissed it almost immediately.

CHAPTER 48

The Gulfstream had touched down at Heathrow in the late afternoon, gliding smoothly onto the tarmac as the sinking sun burnished the clouds. The black Bentley was waiting there, and the driver, Gregor, jogged to the plane and carried Maxim's bag to the car. They rode mostly in silence, though Maxim asked Gregor a few questions about his family and the upcoming holiday; traffic was thick, and the big car had to brake suddenly a number of times as other cars or taxis ahead darted in front.

In the murky twilight, Maxim had to turn on the light in the back seat to read. He scrolled through a number of articles, mostly in Russian, on his MacBook, marking those he wanted to read further. It was approaching seven and nearly dark when Gregor swung the Bentley into the drive next to the house, which Maxim could see had only a few lights on.

Maxim had bought a sumptuous townhouse in Belgravia several years earlier: five bedrooms, five baths, and a veritable quarry's worth of marble. It being his primary home, he had decorated it in a mix of sparse, almost-Scandinavian simplicity and more-ornate Russian pieces that recalled his childhood. His decorator, one of Britain's most prominent, had argued with him that the styles didn't really complement each other, but Maxim didn't care. It was his home, and his was the only voice he listened to—there was no wife to weigh in on all the décor.

Raisa, his cook, had prepared a light dinner of roasted pork strips with blini for him. Maxim trusted her implicitly and rarely offered any specific instructions or suggestions. She was a stolid woman from the Caucasus, and her dark hair, which had begun to go silver in places, was usually at least half-hidden by a kerchief. She was childless, and her husband had been killed in an industrial accident years ago; Maxim had rescued her from the depths of despondency and installed her in his home seven years ago. She worshipped him.

He ate by himself in the kitchen at a large wooden table with carved figures, intricate and supine, running around the edge. Raisa busied herself with a list of items she would need in the coming days now that he was back. She asked him in Russian, "Would you like anything sweet? I have some marlenka."

"You do? That would be wonderful," Maxim said, beaming. He was especially fond of marlenka, a cake made with honey and condensed milk that was popular in many parts of Russia.

She bustled over to the refrigerator, pulled out the cake, and cut him a slice that she put on a glass plate. Then she sat back and watched him eat it.

"This is marvelous," he said. "You make the best marlenka I've ever had." He might have exaggerated somewhat, but he loved to see Raisa flush with his praise. Maxim could be short at times with most people who worked for him, but not her; she occupied a special place in his world. He truly appreciated skillful cooking, in part because that was an art his mother had never mastered. Thinking back now and then, he wondered how he had fared so well on so many meals of soggy, unseasoned meat or too-thin borscht, things he would never have to endure again.

An hour later in his study, he watched an old movie, *RocknRolla*, about a Russian mobster who does a crooked land deal that energizes a host of local gangsters in London. Ripovsky didn't practice violence himself, but he loved to watch it; in his own world, he delegated it to others who seemed to have more of an appetite for it. All the sharp bursts of automatic gunfire in the movie brought a smile to his face, particularly when the shooting was so cartoonish, mass slaughter to an amped-up soundtrack.

He yawned and checked his watch: nine-thirty. Plenty of time to finish the movie. Sergei had arrived and was checking all the doors and windows, as he always did every night even though the security cameras at the front and back of the house were state of the art and would have detected a mouse scurrying in the grass.

Maxim paused the movie and checked his phone—nothing of any importance. He was still smarting from the *Financial Times* piece and its implications that he was untrustworthy and probably dishonest. No hint of that stain had ever appeared in the other London newspapers, and his largesse, especially for the arts, had won him a lot of admirers. He thought he would follow Trevor's advice and lay low for a while in New York, let time pass and focus on cash donations. The painting snafu had been painful.

He resumed watching the movie just as Sergei stepped inside the door and told him everything was fine.

"*Spasiba*," Maxim said. "*Spokoynoy nochi.*"

"*Spokoynoy nochi*," Sergei replied, waved, and padded off.

It was Thursday, December 23, and London was enveloped in its common coat of winter fog. The air was far cleaner than it had been a century earlier, when coal fires darkened the sky and soot settled everywhere, but Maxim didn't know that. He found the fog oppressive. By mid-morning, the fog had lifted some, but visibility was still minimal; cars in the roadway were mere shapes, gray phantoms moving in and out of sight.

Tonight was the annual Christmas dinner for Rubicon Investments, a celebratory affair for employees and a few of Maxim's friends and acquaintances. Once again, it would be at Sevastopol, a highly regarded restaurant that was a favorite of London's Russian community. Maxim had picked the date to conform to British tradition. Christmas was celebrated in Russia on January 7, but that made no sense in London.

That afternoon, he checked in with Trevor Richter in New York. Richter told him he had fielded a handful of calls from local journalists, but he had stuck to the script they had agreed on, and there were no loose ends he was aware of. Richter reminded him that he was leaving the next day on vacation, and Maxim again wished him a happy holiday.

Promptly at six, Maxim strolled into Sevastopol. The owner, Leo—he had been named after Tolstoy, he'd confided in Maxim some time ago—greeted him effusively, taking both hands in his own and walking him to the bar. His black jacket barely reached across his massive chest. "This evening is yours, Maxim," he said in Russian. "We are here to serve you and your guests."

"*Spasiba*, Leo. I thank you again for making the restaurant available to us." He smiled and clapped Leo's shoulder. Dressed in a black suit and a tie as red as a holly berry, Maxim truly looked the part of the host.

By six-thirty, most of the guests had arrived. Close to two dozen were Rubicon employees, and there were several of Maxim's invitees, mostly people with major positions in the arts, including dance companies and symphony orchestras. Some single people were in their twenties; a few older couples were probably in their sixties. Brightly colored murals decked the restaurant walls, showing a stylized view of the city of Sevastopol and its frontage on the Black Sea. There were samovars in the corners and red damask curtains on the windows, the kind of décor Muscovites knew in their bones.

Natasha came alone, dressed in a black gown that revealed half of her back. Elena was there with Mikhail; they were chatting up several Rubicon employees. Servers in white shirts and black pants circulated, passing around trays with caviar and blini. Eventually, the group lined up to pick from a huge table laden with fragrant Russian holiday fare: roasted pig, goose with apples, hare in sour cream, lamb, aspic, even some venison, along with pierogies and a cooked vegetable salad, a staple of Russian winter meals. There was wine, beer, and, of course, vodka.

For Maxim, it was an evening to show people his generosity and to celebrate another year of success for Rubicon. There would be a smaller celebration in New York in a few weeks, a more subdued event. This dinner tonight included the singing of some traditional Russian songs, helped greatly by a balalaika player, a burly black-bearded fellow, who strolled between the tables as he strummed his instrument. Smiles and laughter erupted as the Russians tried to remember the words and find the rhythm of the songs.

It was an evening etched with bonhomie and good cheer, lacking only the whirling Cossack dancers that show up in American movie comedies like "A Shot in the Dark," and it went on until after ten, with marlenka, other desserts, and black coffee. Maxim presided at the head table with Natasha next to him, and only when he rose to leave did others do the same.

As they drifted off into the night in taxis and Ubers, the group offered their thanks and farewells in Russian and English. Maxim stood by the door, shaking hands and air-kissing as the occasion warranted. To the assembled guests, he had been a perfect host, suave and generous; few had ever seen his darker side, the yang that he felt he needed to rule his empire. He waved to Natasha and went back to the kitchen to thank Leo again before he and Sergei threw on their coats and walked to the car.

It was midmorning, and Maxim had just gotten off a long call with one of his property managers. The pale sun peeked through the windows like a shy visitor as the intercom beeped and Vera was on the line.

"There is an envelope that has arrived for you," she said in Russian. "I will bring it in."

She opened the door, walked across the room, and handed it to him with a crooked smile; the right side of her jaw had been reconfigured after an auto accident years earlier. It was a FedEx envelope, and he took it and hefted it—it was light. It was addressed personally to him; the return address was initials and a street in Norwalk, Connecticut. Odd.

He pulled the strip to open the envelope and reached in. There were two large photographs and a printed note. The photographs triggered a short intake of breath; they were similar yet slightly different, but there was no mistaking what he was looking at. He stared at the photos for some time before he looked at the typewritten note.

Dear Mr. Ripovsky:

These prints were taken by a surveillance camera in the lobby of your building—I think you will easily recognize them. As you can see, the young men are pushing the elevator button for the penthouse, your apartment.

You could argue otherwise in a court of law, but I think you and I both know what these men are there for. I have video with timestamps showing them coming and going late at night—they are certainly not houseguests.

You've told me that you are holding onto video

footage of me and Elena—I know her real name—for possible future use, whatever that means. I have copies of these prints, as well as video footage of these men coming and going. So, I think we have what Americans like to call a Mexican standoff: we each have incriminating evidence on each other. If you choose to use something on me, be assured I will reciprocate. Otherwise, these prints will remain hidden safely away.

There is no need to respond to this note—and certainly not to claim innocence. Clearly, two can play this game.

Sincerely,
Corbin van Sloot

Maxim leaned back and folded his hands in front of him. He shook his head slowly and let out a long sigh, and then he smiled slightly. Maybe he had underestimated van Sloot, who had even uncovered Elena's identity. This *kompromat* had clearly required some time and effort, and, more importantly, a sense of where Maxim would be vulnerable, his Achilles heel. A standoff it was.

He had no intention of trying to continue this game. Van Sloot was no longer at Whitehall, so the video had accomplished nothing except, he assumed, genuine trouble for van Sloot and his marriage. Moreover, the London group at Whitehall had rebuffed him. *What was that American expression?* he thought to himself. *Nothing ventured, nothing gained?* He was someone who had ventured, and he would again when the time was right.

CHAPTER 49

Winston often thought he slept better in Florida than in New York. There were no sirens, no strange noises or lights, nothing to wake him at odd hours and force him to peer at the digital clock. The master bedroom suite in Boca was huge, and the coffered ceilings were high, at least two feet higher than those in their city apartment.

The day had started well with the Crumms enjoying a wonderful breakfast turned out by Carmen, their Cuban-born cook in Florida: crepes with fried bananas for Adrienne and Amanda, ham and eggs with thick Cuban toast for Winston. It was a mild morning, with a light blanket of ground fog that would quickly burn off and little wind, which augured well for their run over to Bimini.

Meanwhile, he was still stewing about Dirk when the phone rang at home, next to his chair. He was watching the Golf Channel, where the pros were playing a father-child tournament during the holiday break. He answered, and it was Larry Ahearn at Star.

"Hi, Winston. How are things down in Florida?"

"Okay, I suppose, Larry. My boat captain just announced that he's leaving to take another job. Really pisses me off."

"Sorry to hear that, Winston. But I have some other news you may not really like."

Winston felt his throat tighten as if it were being squeezed gently by a vise. "What's that, Larry?" His voice had lost much of its customary bluster.

"The board did a conference call this morning. We're embarrassed by the story in the *Financial Times*. It seems you knew about the Ripovsky investment right from the get-go while we were still trying to track down the source."

"Well ..." Winston froze. He didn't know what to say.

"I take your lack of denial as an admission. Why didn't you let us know about it?"

"He swore me to secrecy." Winston paused. "He wanted to keep it anonymous."

"So, he approached you with this offer?"

"Um—yeah, he did."

"Were there any conditions?"

"Well, as I said, one was secrecy about his identity. And he wanted to get some free advertising for some of his properties in Manhattan. I agreed to that, and it was done." He rubbed his cheek. "Larry, I don't know what harm was done. Without the secrecy, he wouldn't have agreed to the investment."

"But didn't you think you had a duty to tell us after the full investment was made? We had to learn from Tom Burgee that the source was Russian, but we didn't know any more until the story came out." Larry seemed aggrieved. "And this Ripovsky character really isn't the sort we want to be beholden to."

Winston sighed. "I apologize, Larry. I just thought I had to go along with his conditions for the good of the company. God knows we need the money."

"Well, Winston, we agreed to meet the day after Christmas to hold a special vote. We're going to talk about whether you should stay on as chairman. I'm sorry, in a way, that it's come to this, but it has."

"You can't do that!" Winston practically screamed. "The Crumms own this company!"

"Yes, but the board runs it," Larry said firmly.

"And who would replace me?" Winston demanded.

"Well, it would probably be Rob Graves," Larry replied. "After all, he is in the family. And let's face it; even without this, he's younger and more engaged than you are. Of course, if this happens, you'll still be on the board."

"This is impossible," Winston muttered. "Can I call in and make my case to stay on?"

"No. I think we all know the arguments, pro and con. And you won't be voting, at any rate."

Winston stewed and balled his fists. "And this is when? Two days from now?" he asked belligerently.

"That's right," Larry said. "I'll call you and let you know our decision. I promise. We owe you that. Bye now."

Winston pursed his lips. He'd try to keep this news from spoiling their outing. He would confide in Adrienne sometime, maybe the next day, and prepare her for the worst, along with railing about the injustice of it all. She'd be sympathetic, he thought—at least he hoped so.

CHAPTER 50

A cold rain spattered on the roof. The forecast had it turning into ice at some point, the kind of freeze that eventually turns the landscape into a kind of gelid wonderland, sparkling like diamonds in the winter sun.

Corbin was lost in thought. He longed to share with Patricia his traumatic duel with Ripovsky, but he knew that could never happen. There would be no gloating, no proverbial spiking the football after a touchdown. It really wasn't a victory, anyway, he told himself; it was, as he had told Ripovsky, a standoff. He had averted disaster as cleanly as veering a sports car away from a cliff.

But he needed to share this with someone, and that was Elena. After all, she was the one who had provided him with the right ammunition. Sitting in his home office, he composed a text message:

"Elena—I want to thank you for your leads on the private detectives. The one I hired was able to capture some still shots of young men going up to Ripovsky's apartment, often late at night.

"I sent some of those photos to his office along with a note. I think we're basically even now. I doubt you'll ever hear

anything about this, so I wanted to make sure you knew.

"Thank you again, and I wish you well in Merrie Olde England.

He checked his messages. Soon, he thought, he would get one from Sid Richardson about the interview with the bank search committee. Corbin was mildly apprehensive about interviewing, being analyzed by a panel of strangers. It wasn't a matter of self-confidence but of finding the right tone. He didn't want to seem too eager, but not aloof either. It would be a balancing act, one that required a real strategy—yet he had to be flexible, riding with the flow of their questions. A conundrum.

An hour later, with the rain still pelting down, he had a reply from Elena:

"Dear Corbin—I'm so glad this worked out for you. You are right that Maxim will never speak about this, and I wonder if it will ever come out.

"I wish you well with whatever is next for you, whether that is a new job or a chance to do something relaxing like travel. I hope they are good things. You deserve that.

He smiled and folded his hands. This would indeed be a new chapter in his life, whether or not First Peoples hired him. Almost certainly, there would be no more daily rides to Manhattan, no more lavish perks, no trips to London. He'd reached the pinnacle and was admiring the view when the rug was abruptly pulled out from under him. He'd screwed and screwed up. It was a blow—one he was still adjusting to—but not a mortal one. His family was fine, and that was vital. Whichever way the path pointed, he would be ready.

CHAPTER 51

Elena looked over at her phone as it rang and saw on the caller ID that it was Maxim. She picked up.

"Yes, Maxim?"

"Elena, please come to my office. There's something we need to discuss."

She blanched slightly—this was unusual but hardly unprecedented. It was the day before Christmas, and the workload was light. The office would be buttoning up things for the holiday.

As she walked in, Maxim smiled and gestured for her to take the chair in front of his desk. "You look very nice today," he said casually and smiled again. She dipped her head slightly in acknowledgment of the compliment. Then her eyes went to the print on the wall above his right shoulder, a Mondrian lithograph with bright geometric shapes.

"Thank you," she said softly. This was puzzling. He rarely commented on her appearance, and her clothes were nothing special for her, a navy pantsuit over a white tuxedo-type shirt. But her hair was tied back; that was not her usual look.

"Elena, you've been naughty," he announced with a frown. Her blood froze—had he found about the text to Corbin with the detective agencies? What else could there be? She stammered, "What—what have I done?" She had devised an excuse for the text should it ever come to light, but she wasn't sure how well it would play.

Maxim chuckled. "I'm just teasing. But I did see you were busy with the caviar last night."

She blushed, as much in relief as in mild embarrassment. "I do like caviar, I confess. I never had it growing up."

"Nor did I," he replied. "I'm trying to make up for lost time."

"I suppose I am too. It was always something for the people in the Politburo, you know—the top of the ladder."

"Yes, I know."

She looked at him and thought how different he was from the old-line Russian power players, overweight and excitable, the way she thought of Khrushchev. Peasants elevated far above their station. Maxim, however, was at the top of the new generation: rich, suave, cosmopolitan.

He paused and looked at her hard. "I may have another honey trap job for you, but it wouldn't be for a while, I think."

She knew this was his term for seduction and videotaping. She kept her eyes level and said, "Of course. Whatever you need."

He leaned back in his chair. "This would be in Miami. I'm trying to do some deals there. It's really a busy marketplace."

Miami, she thought. Well, that would be different—a tropical climate, lots of new money, glass and glitter, fancy convertibles cruising the palm-lined boulevards. A vibrant night scene. She knew that much without ever having set foot there.

"I realize that I would be taking you away from Mikhail again," he said. "But this should not be as long, not whatsoever as long as the assignment with Corbin."

She nodded. "I see." *So, that's it,* she thought to herself. *I may be at his disposal for some time to come. Was this going*

to be the accepted Russian way of doing business, using bed-
sheets and not spreadsheets?

"Well, I just wanted to let you know what might be coming," he said, resting his arms on the desk and leaning forward. "Oh, and let me remind you that we will have a day off on January 5 to observe the Russian Christmas. That's on the seventh, of course, but this year it falls on a Sunday."

"Thank you. That will be welcome, of course."

Maxim cocked his head. "Elena, would you and Mikhail like a paid vacation back in Russia to see family? You have certainly earned it."

She smiled. "That would be wonderful. I can ask him, but I'm quite sure he would be delighted."

"Very well. I realize it is winter there—would you rather wait for spring?"

She chuckled, running her mind back to the Moscow winter and its bitter gray cold and the clouds of steam obscuring the streets, with people bundled vainly against the chill. "I think we would probably wait. The winter cold is so penetrating. Perhaps in spring, yes. We would like that."

CHAPTER 52

It was exactly eight-forty-five when the phone in the home office rang. Winston walked in to answer it and saw it was Larry Ahearn. His pulse suddenly started to race.

"Hi, Larry. I'd say Merry Christmas, but it's too late for that." He tried to sound jovial.

"Hello to you, Winston. Hope it was a good Christmas down there."

"Oh, it was. Nice day, too."

A pause. "Well, I'm sure you're wondering what the board decided to do."

"Of course."

"I'm afraid it isn't good news. We talked about it for over an hour, then had a vote. There was a unanimous decision to take the chairmanship from you and give it to Rob. And we had a second vote. I'd rather have this conversation in person, but we voted to remove you from the board entirely."

"What!" Winston shouted.

"That's right. The decision hinged in large part on the oligarch investment and your unwillingness to inform us," Ahearn said. "But it went further than that. We talked for a while about your recent contribution to running the company, and it has not been really meaningful—"

Winston barely heard that last sentence—he was consumed with rage. "I'll sue. This is bullshit," he screamed.

"It's in the by-laws, so it's fully legal," Larry said as if he were explaining something to a child. "We'll position it as an early retirement. You're a wealthy man, Winston. You don't need the money."

"It's not about the money! I mean, what will people think of me—"

"That you've earned retirement after heading up a major publisher for years. And we'll arrange an annual retirement payout, just as we would with any other employee, but it will be a lot less than what you're making now."

"How much less?"

"I don't know just now. We're asked the finance folks to come up with a number. But it will include all the costs associated with your yacht. Those won't be expensed anymore."

Winston's anger morphed into something more like dejection. He stared at his hands. "When would this change happen?" he asked.

"It's already happened. The actions were concurrent with the vote."

"What, no transition period?" Winston's voice rose sharply.

"No. Nothing will be announced until you get back; there's no rush. You can come in any time and clear out your office."

Winston's head swam. Yes, he could afford his lifestyle, but this would be like taking away a free backstage pass to huge rock concerts, those arena shows where getting a good ticket was practically like winning a lottery. Paying for the *Northern Star* was a perk he had luxuriated in for many years, and now they were going to give him some kind of pittance for it?

"Is there anything else, Larry? I mean anything worse?" His voice was soft with resignation.

"No, nothing else. I—I called you as soon as I could. You

need to know about the change."

Winston thought hard. "What about Ripovsky's investment? If you all are so pissed that I didn't tell you about it and you have some misgivings, was there talk about returning it?"

Ahearn sighed. "There was. The publicity has been troubling, but we all know how important this funding is to Star. With no lenders out there willing to listen to us, we have to suck it up and keep his money. Fortunately, there are no strings attached—at least not yet."

"Will there be press on this resignation? I mean, will there be an announcement about this change?" He dreaded having to answer to any reporters or read a biting item in one of Hargreaves's publications.

"There will be, but there's no rush. We'll do it after the holidays, and it will be sure to mention some of you and your family's accomplishments in growing the company. You're a pretty major figure in town, Winston. There should be plenty of positive things to say."

"I would hope so," Winston harrumphed. He felt a wave of relief. Maybe the world wouldn't have to learn right away about the loss of his crown, which had glittered so brightly for so long. But as the company went forward, sideways, or whatever, it would be clear he would no longer be perceived to be at the helm.

"Winston, I know it may sound hypocritical, but I wish you a Happy New Year. We'll see you back in the city whenever you get back."

"Thanks, Larry. Same to you. This is a new world, and I'm going to have to get used to it." He uttered the last sentence with a decided edge.

"Right. Well, goodbye."

"Bye."

Winston sat at the desk for a good twenty minutes, ruminating on what had happened in the past few months. Ripovsky, the company savior, had been shown in the *Financial*

Times piece to be an operator and one with some questionable activities and possibly ominous motives. An old adage shot through Winston's brain: *Be careful what you wish for.*

What would his legacy be? Winston had never really thought beyond what seemed logical: his riding off into the sunset, years hence, as the retiring chairman of Star Enterprises. He and Adrienne would settle permanently in Florida, where the sun, the weather, and the *Northern Star* would ferry them into a ripe old age. Now, instead of a celebratory send-off, it seemed to him it would be more of a case of slinking off after the door closed behind him.

He stared out the windows toward the yard. A cold front from the northwest was rushing through with wind that tossed all but the biggest branches and brought near-whitecaps in the waterway. It seemed fitting—a cold wind bringing unhappy change. The events of the past few weeks had chipped away at the shell of his ego, and this latest board vote hit him like a two-by-four to the side of the head. Still, it wasn't the end of the world, he told himself. His public image would be frayed, but his pocketbook, if diminished, was full enough not to damage their lifestyle.

But then a wave of anger pulsed through him. God damn them! He picked up the autographed baseball—the one with all the signatures from the Yankees' World Series win in 1998—from the desk and hurled it at the window. The glass splintered with a resounding *thwack*, and the ball fell to the floor. Winston winced at the pain that shot through his shoulder; he wasn't used to throwing anything.

"Winston, what's wrong?" he heard Adrienne shout from the living room. Then he heard her footsteps on the tile floor coming toward him.

He sat back in the chair, then sat up, and flung himself out the door of the study and past her, mumbling, "I have to go do something." And he strode to the garage, snatching his keys and wallet on the way, and got into the Beemer. He didn't hear

Adrienne behind him.

He barely waited long enough for the garage door to open before he slammed the car into reverse and backed out. He took off down the street and waited impatiently at the light behind two other cars. He gritted his teeth. The *Northern Star*, his refuge, was only ten minutes away.

It was at the third light on the main drag when it happened. Winston hit the gas the second the light turned green, and then he felt a massive impact that hurled him against the door. A pickup truck had gunned through the red light from the street to his right. The two vehicles collided violently in the intersection with a screech of twisted metal, and the Beemer was flung across and off the road. The swaying palms looked on indifferently.

Winston drifted in and out of consciousness, but he had a surge of lucidity twenty minutes after the accident. He realized he was on a gurney, flat on his back, and he felt the jolts from the ambulance ride course through his body. The pain was intense, and he grimaced.

Then he heard the voices. "He's pretty fortunate. His car squeezed by the palm tree by a few feet and crashed into the hedge. If it had hit that tree, he might be a goner." It was a man's voice, inflected with a slight drawl.

"You're right. We would have needed the jaws of life, and you know how hard it is to save someone at that point." This was a woman. "What's our ETA?"

"Ten minutes, give or take."

Winston tried to talk, but nothing came out. Pain surged through his back like the twisting of a dull knife. His head had been immobilized, and he could see only the white roof of the ambulance.

He heard the woman's voice again. "I've told the trauma team to be ready. I think he'll make it, but he's lucky to be alive."

Lucky to be alive. But he was alive, and they would be taking care of him. He tried to smile, but he couldn't. And then he blacked out again as the Palm Beach County ambulance, its sirens shrieking, snaked its way through the holiday traffic on a chilly winter morning. Winston Crumm was no longer the captain of his fate. That was now in other people's hands.

ABOUT ATMOSPHERE PRESS

Atmosphere Press is an independent, full-service publisher for excellent books in all genres and for all audiences. Learn more about what we do at atmospherepress.com.

We encourage you to check out some of Atmosphere's latest releases, which are available at Amazon.com and via order from your local bookstore:

Dancing with David, a novel by Siegfried Johnson

The Friendship Quilts, a novel by June Calender

My Significant Nobody, a novel by Stevie D. Parker

Nine Days, a novel by Judy Lannon

Shining New Testament: The Cloning of Jay Christ, a novel by Cliff Williamson

Shadows of Robyst, a novel by K. E. Maroudas

Home Within a Landscape, a novel by Alexey L. Kovalev

Motherhood, a novel by Siamak Vakili

Death, The Pharmacist, a novel by D. Ike Horst

Mystery of the Lost Years, a novel by Bobby J. Bixler

Bone Deep Bonds, a novel by B. G. Arnold

Terriers in the Jungle, a novel by Georja Umano

Into the Emerald Dream, a novel by Autumn Allen

His Name Was Ellis, a novel by Joseph Libonati

The Cup, a novel by D. P. Hardwick

The Empathy Academy, a novel by Dustin Grinnell

Tholocco's Wake, a novel by W. W. VanOverbeke

ABOUT THE AUTHOR

Jeffrey Marshall is a writer and former journalist and the author of five books, including three novels, of which *Squeeze Plays* is the latest. He spent most of his career as a business and financial writer and editor, much of that in New York, and was editor-in-chief of two national business magazines. As a freelance writer, his work has appeared in publications as varied as *The New York Times, High Country News, Nonprofit Times* and *Tail* fly-fishing magazine. Marshall has degrees from Princeton and Northwestern. He lives in Scottsdale, AZ, with his wife, Judy, and dogs Maggie and Blaze.

Find out more about Marshall and his books at
www.jmarshbks.com

Made in the USA
Middletown, DE
10 November 2022